SWITCHEROO

Also by E.J. Copperman

Fran and Ken Stein mysteries

UKULELE OF DEATH *
SAME DIFFERENCE *

Jersey Girl Legal mysteries

INHERIT THE SHOES *
JUDGMENT AT SANTA MONICA *
WITNESS FOR THE PERSECUTION *
AND JUSTICE FOR MALL *
MY COUSIN SKINNY *
GOOD LIEUTENANT *

Haunted Guesthouse mysteries

NIGHT OF THE LIVING DEED
AN UNINVITED GHOST
OLD HAUNTS
CHANCE OF A GHOST
THE THRILL OF THE HAUNT
INSPECTOR SPECTER
GHOST IN THE WIND
SPOUSE ON HAUNTED HILL
THE HOSTESS WITH THE GHOSTESS
BONES BEHIND THE WHEEL

Asperger's mysteries (with Jeff Cohen)

THE QUESTION OF THE MISSING HEAD
THE QUESTION OF THE UNFAMILIAR HUSBAND
THE QUESTION OF THE FELONIOUS FRIEND
THE QUESTION OF THE ABSENTEE FATHER
THE QUESTION OF THE DEAD MISTRESS

Agent to the Paws mysteries

DOG DISH OF DOOM
BIRD, BATH, AND BEYOND

* available from Severn House

SWITCHEROO

E.J. Copperman

SEVERN
HOUSE

First world edition published in Great Britain and the USA in 2025
by Severn House, an imprint of Canongate Books Ltd,
14 High Street, Edinburgh EH1 1TE.

severnhouse.com

Copyright © E.J. Copperman, 2025

Cover and jacket design by Piers Tilbury

All rights reserved including the right of reproduction in whole or in part in any form. The right of E.J. Copperman to be identified as the author of this work has been asserted in accordance with the Copyright, Designs & Patents Act 1988.

British Library Cataloguing-in-Publication Data
A CIP catalogue record for this title is available from the British Library.

ISBN-13: 978-1-4483-1519-2 (cased)
ISBN-13: 978-1-4483-1518-5 (e-book)

This is a work of fiction. Names, characters, places and incidents are either the product of the author's imagination or are used fictitiously. Except where actual historical events and characters are being described for the storyline of this novel, all situations in this publication are fictitious and any resemblance to actual persons, living or dead, business establishments, events or locales is purely coincidental.

No part of this book may be used or reproduced in any manner for the purpose of training artificial intelligence technologies or systems. This work is reserved from text and data mining (Article 4(3) Directive (EU) 2019/790).

All Severn House titles are printed on acid-free paper.

Typeset by Palimpsest Book Production Ltd.,
Falkirk, Stirlingshire, Scotland.
Printed and bound in Great Britain by
TJ Books, Padstow, Cornwall.

The manufacturer's authorised representative in the EU for product safety is Authorised Rep Compliance Ltd, 71 Lower Baggot Street, Dublin D02 P593 Ireland (arccompliance.com).

Praise for the Fran & Ken Stein mystery novels

"A hilarious quest"
Kirkus Reviews on *Same Difference*

"It's Fran's resilience, intelligence, and – most of all – her irrepressible, sassy, laugh-out-loud humor that make this book so entertaining"
Booklist on *Same Difference*

"A terrific read"
Dru's Book Musings on *Same Difference*

"A wonderful, complicated and funny mystery . . . an insanely entertaining mashup of classic and cutting-edge tropes . . . looking forward to more excellent instalments from E.J. Copperman"
Deadly Pleasures Mystery Magazine on *Same Difference*

"With unique, larger-than-life characters (literally), and an outlandish premise, this one may appeal to Janet Evanovich fans"
Booklist on *Ukulele of Death*

"Loads of fun . . . zips along at a fast and furious pace"
Publishers Weekly on *Ukulele of Death*

"With an enjoyable mix of sci-fi and mystery elements, Copperman's latest features an intriguing and likable pair of detectives"
Library Journal on *Ukulele of Death*

"Wacky premise . . . [Features Copperman's] most offbeat protagonist to date"
Kirkus Reviews on *Ukulele of Death*

"Twisty and bonkers and fun"
Multi award-winning author Catriona McPherson on *Ukulele of Death*

About the author

E.J. Copperman is the nom de plume for Jeff Cohen, writer of intentionally funny murder mysteries. As E.J., he is the author of the Haunted Guesthouse series, the Agent to the Paws series and the Jersey Girl Legal mysteries, as well as the Fran and Ken Stein mysteries. As Jeff, he is the author of the Double Feature and Aaron Tucker series; and he collaborates with himself on the Samuel Hoenig Asperger's mysteries.

A New Jersey native, E.J. worked as a newspaper reporter, teacher, magazine editor and screenwriter, before his first book was published to critical acclaim in 2002. In his spare time, Jeff is an extremely amateur guitar player, a fan of Major League Baseball, a couch potato and a crossword addict.

www.ejcopperman.com

ONE

'Look at me, Austin,' I said, and I immediately regretted it. That's something I say frequently to prospective clients for K&F Stein Investigations, and I'm still wondering why I let my brother Ken have his initial ahead of mine. Toward the end of the interview, I ask clients to look me in the eye so I can see whether they really want us to do what they say they want us to do. A large percentage of our cases involve people who were adopted trying to find their birth parents, and this was one of those. So I had fallen on my usual routine to interview Austin Cobb, but I should have left this part out.

Austin, who was thirty-two years old according to his intake form (and there was no reason to disbelieve it), had identified himself to me as an 'autistic man with social skills issues,' and one of those issues was that he didn't like to look people in the eye. Because I was running on autopilot, I had asked him to do something I knew he didn't want to do. It was a bad beginning.

He grimaced a little, raising his cheekbones and narrowing his eyes while he flattened his mouth, but did as I had asked. He made eye contact. And I debated whether I should apologize for asking him to do that.

I decided against. I would treat Austin as I would treat any client, and if he asked me to make certain exceptions, I would try to accommodate them, but he needed to say the words first. 'I need to know if you're sure you want me to find your biological parents,' I said.

'I have asked you to do that.' Austin looked away and I did nothing to discourage that. He preferred to focus on the window, which would have been understandable if we had a view of anything other than the equally anonymous building behind our own. 'Why would you think I didn't want that if I just asked you to do it?'

It was a perfectly logical question, coming from a perfectly logical medical researcher with a serious temperament. Austin had, he'd told me, been adopted at the age of two and had no independent memories of his birth parents. His adoptive parents, to whom he referred as 'my real parents,' Carla and Spencer Cobb, had known about his autism when they adopted him and 'raised me to be myself as much as society would admit.' Austin did a little online advocating for the autism community and didn't mind expressing the occasional opinion.

'I ask it because I want you to really think it through,' I told him now. 'You might be envisioning an idyllic reunion with your biological parents, and maybe that's what you'll get. But it's also possible you'll get a less happy result. I've seen it happen both ways. I want you to tell me' (I left out the part about 'look me in the eye' this time) 'that you understand we don't know how this is going to go, and then say whether you want it no matter what. Because you don't *have* to do it.' (I'm a good detective but sometimes a lousy businesswoman. It is the least of my unusual qualities, but I'll get to that.)

'I don't think I'm going to find my birth parents and replace my real parents,' Austin said, sounding a little offended. It was hard to tell. His left hand, lightly clenched in a fist, was moving back and forth at his side, sitting in the client chair in front of my desk.

'I didn't think you expected or wanted that,' I told him, and the movement eased a bit. 'I just want you to have realistic expectations. So what are your expectations?'

Austin's expression became one of thought. 'I am especially interested in any genetic and medical information I might need going forward,' he said. 'I've seen the redacted records of my adoption and the section about medical history for both my birth parents, without their names, is, at best, superficial.'

My brother Ken, sitting outside my office area on his own, could hear everything being said in our conversation. He looked serious, which is not his usual state. Ken and I can never know about any medical issues we might have inherited because there have never been people like us before. Being a trailblazer is exhilarating on occasion, and a drag the other seventy percent of the time.

Ken's thoughts were probably about Austin and his situation (or about Igavda, our receptionist, who Ken hired based not on her expert command of the English language), but Austin was what I was concentrating on at the moment. And there was something in his demeanor, which admittedly I'd only been able to observe for about twenty minutes now, that indicated he was being honest, but not comprehensive.

'But there's something else you want to find out by meeting your birth parents,' I said, thinking out loud but relatively sure I knew what I was talking about. 'I realize you do medical research, but you probably got most of what you need from those records. What else do you want, Austin?'

His head vibrated a little and he forced his lips out of a pursed position in an eventually successful effort to relax enough to answer me. He didn't like being challenged, I could tell, but he still wouldn't look me in the eyes. That's not unusual.

'I want to know if they put me up for adoption because I'm autistic,' he said.

I hadn't anticipated that, but it made sense for the time thirty years before, when the decision had been made. 'They might not want to talk to you,' I reminded him. 'And if they don't, there's nothing I can do to change that.'

'I know.' His voice betrayed nothing. 'I expect that they won't want to talk to me.'

'Do you still want us to find them for you?' I asked.

And Austin finally looked at me directly of his own volition. 'Yes,' he said.

I knew better than to hold out a hand to shake. 'Thank you for choosing K&F Stein Investigations,' I said.

After Austin left the office, Ken got up from his desk, grabbed a Red Bull from the mini fridge just to show how millennial he is, and walked into my office. I had the electric fan on my desk turned on because it was warm but not hot, and our landlord wouldn't spring for air conditioning even if it was 120 degrees out. Celsius.

My brother sat down in the client chair Austin had recently vacated, took a swig of his energy drink and thought about – but wisely decided against – putting his feet up on my desk. 'The kid is gonna get disappointed,' he said. I'd like to point out that I had not requested any comments or advice on Austin's case, which is Ken's favorite time to offer comments and advice.

'Maybe,' I said, pretending to read some paper that had appeared on my desk in the past three weeks. Probably a bill. But since I didn't want to get into it with Ken, I could feign rapt attention about anything. 'Maybe not. First I have to figure out where his birth parents might be.'

'There's nothing in the adoption records?' Ken chugged the last of his caffeine cocktail. In deference to me he did not crush the can and toss it into the wastebasket like he was LeBron James at the free throw line. But I knew he wanted to.

'No,' I told him. 'His adoptive parents, Carla and Spencer Cobb, signed a non-disclosure agreement in addition to the adoption papers at the time. The agency they went through to adopt Austin released no information about his birth parents. It makes me a little suspicious.'

Ken, employing the acting skills that have kept him out of the acting profession, raised his eyebrows dramatically. 'A *little*?' he said. 'These people are more secretive than *our* parents, and nobody is more secretive than our parents.' He had a point there. We had barely heard from our parents in more than six months, and before that there had been breaks that had lasted decades. But I'll get to all the stuff about Ken and me in a minute. Sit tight.

'I think it's obvious there's something everybody except Austin doesn't want us to know, and Austin probably doesn't even know it himself,' I told Ken. 'Why? Do you want in on this case?' I had figured I'd handle it alone, but if my brother wanted to lend his enormous self to the effort, I wouldn't object. Less work for me.

He put up his hands as if I'd demanded his money or his life. 'No, I'm just an innocent bystander. I just thought it was interesting. But I've got a couple of things I need to be working on myself.' He had on his desk, if my memory served, one birth father who wanted to interfere in his daughter's wedding by insisting he escort her down the aisle, something her adoptive father – the one she'd grown up with, whom she called 'Daddy' – understandably objected to. Ken's job was to find a way to get the biological dad to take a vacation to Disney

World the weekend of the wedding, which was going to be in Puerto Rico.

'OK, then,' I said. 'I'd better get to work on Austin Cobb.'

Ken stood up, which took longer than it does for most people. He has been mistaken in the street for a small boutique hotel, but the arms and legs prove otherwise. 'Just one thing,' he said, raising an index finger as if the issue he was about to broach hadn't been percolating in his head for at least a half hour. 'I heard from an old pal of ours. Malcolm X. Mitchell.'

Oh, man. Not *that* guy.

TWO

This is going to require a little backstory. Go get a drink, hot or cold, soft or alcoholic, whatever puts you in the mood to hear a tale. Because Ken and I have one for you.

We weren't exactly born; that's the first thing. Our parents – the people we call our parents – were two wildly brilliant scientists we know as Olivia Grey and Brandon Wilder, although it's highly unlikely those are their real names. They met while working in New Brunswick, New Jersey, but living in Manhattan, and soon became involved in every way possible. What's most relevant to us is that they 1. Fell in love and 2. Started working on a very special experiment. *Two* very special experiments. Ken and me.

Our mother was working on a method of accelerating the healing process in humans by a very impressive rate. When our father, who was a genius cosmetic surgeon with a background in human anatomy that rivaled any Nobel Prize winner in medicine for the past hundred years, thought about Olivia's work, his slightly mischievous brain noted that, despite having married (we think) and trying to conceive a child (we know), they were still childless, and he decided they should take matters into their own labs.

In short, they created ways to grow human organs from some DNA samples (no, I don't know whose DNA and I don't want to find out) and manipulated tissues in some other ways I don't understand because I was a criminal justice major, and over the process of a couple of years they had filled the void they felt for children with my brother (first) and then me. They named us Fran and Ken Stein because my father has an impish sense of humor.

They had left us in the care of a woman we call Aunt Margie, who is not our aunt. She's a local radio reporter in New York and had gotten wind of my mother's work in rapid healing, thinking it would be a great story. And it would have been, except that our parents wouldn't tell her anything and denied the whole enterprise. But over time they became very good friends and Aunt Margie had agreed to see to Ken and me when we were toddlers 'for a while.' Which had now been over thirty years. Aunt Margie is a gamer.

But word had gotten around about Mom's amazing healing technique (which I know nothing about, see: criminal justice major) and either governmental or even more insidious organizations wanted to know more. Whether or not word of Ken and me had gotten around is not clear, but there have been times when people have come looking for us. Mom and especially Dad considered themselves dangers to their children because they were being pursued, and high-tailed it to parts unknown. Very unknown, in fact, to the point that we hadn't heard from them in decades.

Well, that's not entirely true, either. I had started receiving emails from a secure account my mother was using about a year earlier. The information she gave me, other than that she and my father were fine physically, was scarce. No idea where they were or what they were doing. We'd heard from a long-ago colleague that there was some work on a universal cure for cancer that would have caused considerable disruption, and therefore some anxiety, among established pharmaceutical companies and hospitals, keeping the heat on my parents to this date.

I'd only recently let Ken in on the emails from Mom because I'd been concerned that he'd go ballistic about it. Ken's always been the lead investigator in finding Mom and Dad. He worries about their safety but is also just a little bit angry at them still over what he sees as our 'abandonment.' I don't entirely blame him, but both of us understand why our parents did what they did.

When I'd finally sat him down and told him I'd heard from Mom, his eyes bulged and his neck veins became prominent. But his voice was quiet and forced to be calm. 'Tell. Me. Everything.'

There wasn't much to tell, but my brother listened closely. He was a little run down at the time because he was in need of a charge.

Yeah. We have to plug ourselves into wall outlets (via USB ports under our left arms and charging cables) about once a week to keep our energy at the right level. Other than that, we're just like you.

Except we're both really tall and, by human standards, ridiculously strong. It's a gift and a curse.

'Is it OK if I email Mom?' Ken asked at the end of his briefing. We were sitting in my bedroom, me on the bed and Ken at the desk, plugged into a portable charger we'd only recently found could help in a pinch.

I told him it would be fine, having checked with our mother. She'd been a little skeptical about my letting Ken in on our correspondence because her last memory of him was as an impulsive five-year-old. And while I could say that little has changed, that wouldn't really be true. He's much larger now.

Ken doesn't volunteer much when he's not acting like a frat bro. But I believe he has emailed Mom once or twice. He only let me know about one response, and all he did was express his frustration that she hadn't told him where she and Dad were at that moment. Because obviously after being concerned about security for pretty much all our lives and then not telling me for the times I'd been writing to her, Mom would definitely just send their coordinates through the web like an order for AA batteries from Amazon.

Now that you're caught up, there's Malcolm X. Mitchell. Or the guy who calls himself that.

Ken was first contacted by MXM a few months previously. Our pal Malcolm, whose name was probably Craig or something (we had no idea what his real name was, but Mom's last email had told me to steer clear of him at all costs), was in his late twenties, a few years younger than Ken and me, and had tried to foist himself off as an employee of the World Health Organization, then followed me on the subway to tell me to look for my parents in Spain, where they weren't. He was trying to get some information from us about our parents, and either we didn't know or more likely would not want to tell him, since we had no clue for whom he was actually working or what his agenda might be.

So the news today that Ken had heard from MXM again was not welcome.

'What happened?' I said. Then I sat back because Ken doesn't tell short stories.

'Well, he's learned not to call the office, and he didn't even email me directly.' Ken was looking serious, but he loves attention and was clearly enjoying the moment. 'This time Mal decided to contact me through Instagram.'

I hadn't even known Ken was on Instagram. 'How'd he find you there?' I asked.

'He didn't find *me*; he found *us*. It's the company's account.'

Of course it was. I refrained from saying, 'We have an Instagram account?' and settled for, 'So what did he say this time?'

'You're going to love this.' Ken does smug so much better than most, evidenced by the fact that I wanted to punch him in the jaw but didn't. 'He says he needs to get in touch with Mom and Dad and wants to meet us.'

Uh-huh. 'And I want two weeks in the south of France and a villa next to George Clooney's,' I said. 'Why does he think for one second that we'd agree to meet with him or put him in touch with our parents? A liar like him, of all people? Mom already told me to stay away from the guy.'

Ken smugged it up a little longer to better prolong the moment. 'He says he's our long-lost brother,' he said.

THREE

Once a week, or maybe twice if she's feeling it, Aunt Margie cooks dinner at her apartment, which is one floor down from the one Ken and I live in. And we're invited. It's actually more of a summons.

This week, Aunt Margie had roasted a chicken because Aunt Margie always roasts a chicken when we're coming for dinner. That's largely because the only thing she knows how to do in a kitchen is roast a chicken. If vegetarians were coming for dinner, Aunt Margie would roast a chicken. And then order in some appropriate food for her guests. She does at least know to cut carrots, celery and potatoes and put them in the pan with the chicken to cook. Ken and I aren't completely human, but we're not barbarians.

She was placing the chicken, on a platter and looking like every other chicken she'd ever cooked (not as roasted as I prefer, but good enough), on the dining table in what she calls her dining room. It's a small room off the kitchen that was probably used as a pantry in the 1920s. Just the place when you're hosting your two larger-than-life charges. But don't get me wrong about Aunt Margie; she's a darling and I feel like she's our second mother. Maybe our first mother. Certainly the one we knew most growing up.

But tonight I was just a little annoyed with her, because she had also invited Detective Richard Mankiewicz of the New York Police Department for dinner. Mank and I had been friends, then dated for a bit, and after I'd taken an extremely deep breath and told him the truth about myself and my brother, he'd walked away for a number of weeks. We had since patched things up to the point that I wasn't livid with him anymore, but Aunt Margie's unexpected inclusion of Mank at dinner – an obvious attempt to get us to reconcile further – was irritating.

Huddled together in her tiny little dining room around a table that would have been crowded with just Ken sitting at it, we complimented Aunt Margie on the dinner, which was a roasted chicken that I believe I have described enough, and then conversation died down for a while as we ate and tried to think of things to say. Except Ken, who is oblivious to any socially awkward situation because he thinks everyone is entranced with him.

'So this Malcolm X. Mitchell,' he said, still chewing. Remember what I said about us not being barbarians? That was mostly me. 'Frannie says I shouldn't answer his Insta message. I think it's the only way to find out anything else. What do you think?' He didn't specify who 'you' was, but Mank was a cop and Aunt Margie read news on the radio and roasted chickens.

Mank looked at me first. That was correct; points for Mank. If I'd signaled him to stay off the subject, he would have done so, but I just shrugged. I did want to make my argument first, though, so I said, 'You know what I think. He's like an internet scam. You answer him and you're giving away more information than you're going to get, and he'll use it against us. I say don't answer him. Pretend he doesn't exist.'

Ken had not been looking in my direction when I spoke; he knew my side of the issue. He'd been watching Mank. But he would be thwarted again.

'Your parents were very clear on this,' Aunt Margie said, putting a miniscule amount of yogurt butter on a roll she'd bought at Trader Joe's on the way home from her radio shift. 'Never make contact with a possible threat, and from what you've told me, this Malcolm person is a clear threat. He's nosing around about Livvie and Brad, and you remember what happened the last time someone did that.' Yes. It had ended with someone jumping off our roof, but that's another story (*Ukulele of Death*). Spoiler alert. Sorry.

Ken wasn't about to allow any more distractions from what he'd clearly thought was a direct request for advice from a professional (forget that I am, in fact, a professional and Aunt Margie was a crime reporter and the closest link to our parents for more than two decades). He put down the thigh he should have been eating with a fork and nodded toward our cop guest. 'Rich,' he said. 'What do you think, and don't look at Frannie before you answer.' Mank had expressed interest in getting us to the dating stage again and I was hesitant. I liked Mank, but it hurts you when you bare your soul to a man and he gets up and leaves the restaurant. I needed time to heal. And think.

Mank chuckled at Ken's remark. 'OK, I won't look at Fran,' he said. 'But I still agree with her and Margie on this. Your parents have gone to great lengths to stay out of sight. Talking to a guy who clearly doesn't know where they are and wants to find out isn't going to do you any good and might do him some. Which is in all likelihood what you don't want.'

My brother seemed stunned that the other man in the room didn't have his back. 'But he says he's our brother,' he managed to say after a few stammers. 'That means Mom and Dad made another . . . person like us. Don't we have to investigate that possibility?'

'Why do you believe him?' Mank asked. 'Does he look like you and Fran?'

'I'm the only one who's seen him,' I said. 'And no, he's not big like us. He's actually kind of skinny and looks like he'd fall over if you exhaled too hard in his direction.'

'You're exaggerating,' Ken said, pouting into his carrots.

'Were you there?' I knew he hadn't been.

'Kenny,' Aunt Margie said. 'Please. Someone getting this close always makes me nervous. Don't get back in touch with this man.'

If there's one person who can reach Ken with an emotional appeal, it's Aunt Margie. 'OK,' he mumbled. 'But I don't like it.'

'Take your mind off Malcolm,' I suggested. 'Help me with my new case.'

Mank looked interested, so I regaled them all (including Ken, who had heard it before) with the story of Austin Cobb and his quest to meet his birth parents. It was, of course, pretty standard stuff given that Ken and I specialized in such affairs, but it had snags that were at least a little more than I usually had to confront. 'The lack of records from the adoption agency is kind of weird,' I said. I speared a cubed potato on my plate. 'There are some that don't want to give away names unless a court forces them to do it, but this is more secretive than you usually see.'

'In what way?' Aunt Margie's reportorial instincts were kicking in.

'Usually they'll tell you they don't want to mention names,' I answered. 'When I contacted them this afternoon, they refused to even discuss Austin with me. Once they looked up his name, I was persona non grata. The woman I was talking to, who had been pretty cordial up until then, practically hung up on me.'

Mank was looking very cop-like, eyes focused without staring, hand up to his chin without stroking. He was all attention and no judgment, except I knew the judgment was just being concealed. 'How far had you gotten?' he asked. 'Did you say why you wanted Austin's information?'

I shook my head. 'I said I was a private investigator and I had some questions about Austin Cobb. Then the second Ice Age descended upon my phone and suddenly I was talking to myself.'

'Well, Austin told you his birth parents didn't want to have any contact,' Ken reminded me.

'No, he said he *expected* that they didn't. He doesn't know who they are and, I think, has no sense at all of what kind of people they might be.'

Mank likes to look under the hood and understand how an investigation works. It's one of the reasons he's a very good detective, but don't tell him I said that. 'So what's your plan of action, Fran?' he asked.

Aunt Margie, knowing she'd be able to hear from the kitchen, which was maybe six feet away, started to clear plates and gestured to Ken that he should assist. My brother, not realizing Aunt Margie wanted Mank and me to be alone, balked facially, then nodded and started helping. I let them do it because that meant I wouldn't have to. There's an upside to everything.

'I think the first thing is to contact the Cobbs and talk to them,' I answered. 'They were certainly involved when Austin was being adopted, and even if they don't want to tell me everything I need to know, I'm willing to believe they know more about his birth parents than Austin has been told.'

Mank nodded with a thoughtful expression on his face. 'Logical plan,' he said. 'What are you going to do when it doesn't work?'

I put down my fork so Ken could take it into the kitchen. 'Why do you think it won't work?' I asked Mank.

'I'm not saying it won't. But I'm sure you know you always have to have a backup plan.'

Well, in *theory* I knew that, but who likes to think their best bet will go bust? 'I figure then I'll take myself to the adoption agency and confront them in person. But there's also the Adoption Information Registry from the state Department of Health. I've dealt with them a number of times and they know me well enough. I'll get something out of them.'

Mank pursed his lips just a little, looking like he was savoring something other than Aunt Margie's roasted chicken. 'Good to have resources,' he said. He was holding back.

'What?' I said.

He had the nerve to look surprised. 'What, what?'

'There's something you're not saying. Say it.' I sat back and put my feet up on Ken's chair. If he and Aunt Margie wanted to be cute by leaving us alone, I could take advantage of it.

Mank looked at me for a long time, trying not to look either challenging or angry. 'You want what I'm holding back, but you don't want me to talk like an experienced detective with the NYPD because you think I'm patronizing you, which I'm not. How's that for what I'm holding back?' His face never looked anything but friendly and very slightly amused.

'You're still not saying what you're holding back,' I said, keeping my voice neutral. I'm pretty sure.

Slowly Mank shook his head in disbelief of my . . . I'd call it persistence. Mank might have said bull-headedness. I'll let you decide. 'OK, fine,' he said. 'I think you're playing it safe. I think you're afraid your client will find out things that will cause him sadness or pain, and you don't want to do that. Your perfect scenario here is to say you've checked around but couldn't find a decent trail to his birth parents, leaving him no option but to give it up and live his life. How am I doing so far?'

It had stung; I'll admit it. 'I think you're wrong, but if you think that I'm being too timid, tell me: What *should* I be doing instead? What's bold and, I assume, more effective? What's the NYPD's great detective think I am trying to hide from doing for *my* client?'

'I don't want to tell you how to do your job,' Mank tried.

'Oh, you'd like nothing better and here I am, asking. So tell me what your plan would be.'

'I think you need to check into anyone who might have been treating people with autism thirty years ago in the area where Austin was living when he was adopted. You can bet you'll find a psychologist or neurologist who either met with Austin's parents or knew someone who did. Use the fact that he's autistic to get the information he wants. I'm sure Austin would approve.'

I wasn't certain he would, but more infuriatingly, Mank was giving me good suggestions I hadn't thought of on my own. Who needed *that*?

So I sat back in my chair and resisted the impulse to close my eyes. What had I ever seen in this guy, anyway? Except that he was reasonably good-looking, intelligent, funny, kind and a good kisser? Is that so much?

'You know,' Mank said finally, 'I kind of thought our talking again would go better than this.'

I exhaled. 'Strangely, so did I.'

FOUR

Carla and Spencer Cobb lived in a small house in Queens, no doubt in the same neighborhood that Archie Bunker lived in the 1970s. (Google it.) It was brick in the front, vinyl siding everywhere else. It wasn't fooling anyone.

But Spencer, upon hearing that the investigator Austin had hired was coming to talk, had baked scones. Seriously. And Carla, two years from a young retirement after thirty years working at JFK Airport (she told me), had just gotten off her shift as a customer service manager for American Airlines. She had not changed out of her work clothes, a royal blue blazer and skirt with a light blue button-down shirt. She looked tired.

'I don't see how we can help you,' she said before I could even mention my conversation with their son. 'We signed an agreement at the time that specified we wouldn't tell anyone the details of Austin's adoption. We keep our word.'

Of course I had anticipated this argument; Austin had told me his parents would say that. He had also declined to join us for this meeting because 'they might be more open if I'm not there.' So far, he was not proving to be prescient.

'I understand that, and I would never ask you to violate the terms of the adoption in any way.' Even though Austin was well past the age of majority, this was his family and I wanted nothing I did to threaten that. 'But I am wondering if you can fill me in on some of the details that your agreement didn't cover. For example, did his birth parents tell you why they had chosen to put Austin up for adoption?' I couldn't imagine a legal document would cover that issue.

'Our agreement specifically won't let us talk about that,' Carla said. She was a lovely Black woman in her early fifties, if I had to guess. Yes, she looked a little sleepy after a full day of work, but she still had a vivacious energy that was apparent as soon as you got near. Spencer, a little older but more relaxed, spoke with a slight accent from an island I would not dare to try and identify. I don't do well with accents. Best I can do is tell Staten Island from Northern New Jersey.

'Well, how did you first find out about Austin and start the process?' I asked, wondering if even something that completely bland could be considered sensitive material.

As it turned out, I was lucky, and it did not. 'We were working with an adoption agency because we wanted to find a child who was roughly the same race as us and wasn't an infant,' Spencer said. He had the aura of an old soul, someone who wasn't quite comfortable in the twenty-first century. 'They gave us a call in the old apartment, remember, Carly? Up on 123rd Street.' Carla nodded. 'They told us about Austin, but they said we couldn't go to visit them because they didn't want to give us an address. So we met at a Dunkin' Donuts in Rockefeller Center. His birth parents were there, and a representative of the adoption agency, and Austin and us.'

The scones were wonderful, and Spencer had made his own clotted cream, which I thought was going above and beyond the call. Carla smiled watching me take a bite because this was clearly not her first Spencer scone. I took a while to savor before I could speak again. I'd brought the coffee with me and it was coffee. 'It was the summer I quit taking fast food jobs and started with the airlines,' she said. 'I'd been commuting an hour and a half in each direction and was settled down enough to be a mom, I thought.'

'Didn't it strike you odd that the birth parents didn't want you to know where they lived?' I asked when it was socially acceptable for me to open my mouth in public again. 'Did you ask about that?'

They exchanged a glance. At first I thought I had offended them by asking, as if I were insinuating that they were bad adoptive parents. But the look they shared was different; it was more embarrassed than upset.

'We didn't ask at first,' Carla told me. 'They had Austin with them, and we fell in love with him right away. It didn't occur to us until later that they were acting a little strangely. I guess when they sent us the agreement with all the things we couldn't say.'

'What kind of things couldn't you say?' I said.

Carla smiled in as friendly a fashion as you can imagine. 'We can't say,' she said, and we all had a laugh.

'You can't blame a girl for trying,' I said. 'But can you tell me what kind of people they were? Just the kind of vibe you got from them? Austin was a toddler, just two years old. Did he understand that he was coming to live with you? Was he upset that he was leaving the parents he knew?'

'Austin doesn't remember anything about it now, of course,' Carla told me. 'But it was odd. He didn't seem at all upset that he'd be leaving his home and the parents he knew. He wanted to come and sit on Spencer's lap the whole time.'

'I was telling him a story about pirates,' Spencer explained.

'As for what kind of people his birth parents were,' Carla said, 'well, without stereotyping I'd have to say they were the kind of people you would expect would have a medical researcher for a son. They were very serious and all business. But,' she gave Spencer a look and went on, 'we disagree on this. I think they had some kind of tension between them and Spencer says no.'

'They seemed fine to me,' her husband said with the weary tone of the 500th version of this argument.

To her credit, Carla did not roll her eyes to show me how ridiculous her husband could be. 'They never looked at each other and they barely looked at Austin,' she said. To me. 'I think they were headed for divorce.'

'Divorce!' Spencer seemed to find his wife amusing. 'You can get that from a half-hour visit from two people thirty years ago? When we were mostly paying attention to Austin?' He chuckled, a deep-throated sound that tempered wood might have if it could laugh. 'You've decided, so that must be what it was, Carly.'

She waved an exasperated hand in his direction. She never broke eye contact with me. 'You trust me; that's what happened,' she said.

'Yes, ma'am,' I said. I didn't want to get on Carla's bad side because even though I could pick her up in one hand and fling her across the room, I thought that would just make her mad. 'Can you tell me anything else about Austin's first two years before you adopted him?'

Carla, in the middle of pouring a cup of tea for herself,

stopped and regarded me with a suspicious look. 'I don't think there was any abuse or anything like that,' she said. 'If that's what you're getting at.'

I held up my hands as if surrendering. 'No, Carla. I'm just trying to get any detail I can. Austin has asked me to find his birth parents for him, and I intend to do what my client has requested. I completely respect the agreement you made about keeping things confidential, so I'm trying to uncover any detail that might lead me in a direction. I have no preconceived notions in my head; I just want to know what two-year-old Austin had experienced by then.'

'Well, they knew he was autistic.' Spencer seemed to really want to help me but knew that disclosing any of the information he'd agreed to keep quiet would get him in trouble, mostly (at this point) with his wife. 'They'd had him evaluated and he was classified at eighteen months. High-functioning, they said, like that term ever meant anything.'

When Austin had been diagnosed with autism, his neurologist or psychologist had probably called it Asperger's syndrome, a diagnosis which is no longer recognized today. When I'd met him, it wasn't immediately obvious that he had behaviors on the autism spectrum, but they surfaced within the first five minutes of our conversation. Austin tended to lecture rather than engage in back-and-forth and again, he tried to avoid eye contact when he could, but forced himself to make it when he had to. He used phrases like, 'obviously' and 'upon deeper examination,' which easily could have been attributed to his line of work. Scientists tend to talk like scientists. It doesn't mean they're not autistic.

'Did his birth parents mention it when you met?'

'They had to,' Carla said. 'Nobody wanted us to adopt our son without knowing about him. But we didn't care. He was Austin and that was all that mattered.' Carla was proud of herself, and justifiably so, for raising a well-functioning young man who had grown up with a few obstacles in his way.

'Did you get the impression they'd rather not say anything about it?' I asked. Maybe that was a way in. The Cobbs, understandably reticent, *wanted* to tell me something but couldn't figure out how to do it. Maybe they thought the adoption agency had listening devices in their home thirty years after the event. Judging by their quick glances back and forth, I was beginning to think the theory might have some merit.

'I don't know. It was a long time ago.' Carla clearly had an opinion on the subject and couldn't bring herself to express it. I was starting to feel like the Cobbs were afraid of the people from whom they'd adopted their son.

'Can you at least tell me if they were living in the city at the time you met them?' I asked. New York holds over eight million people. I wasn't requesting a really big hint.

But Carla pulled her arms tight into her chest as if trying to warm herself from a cold breeze. 'I really can't say.'

I was about to give up and make noises about leaving, but Spencer had plans of his own. 'Oh, let's not be silly, Carly,' he said. 'I don't think Marc and Helen would mind if we answered *that* question.' Then, seeing the truly horrified expression on his wife's face, he put two fingers to his lips. 'Oops,' he said.

'Spencer!' Carla couldn't put the words back in his mouth, but she wanted to put *something* in there and I didn't want to be present to see it. (In truth, they were a lovely couple who liked to play at being cantankerous but didn't have the stamina to keep it up.)

'I'm sorry.' He didn't sound the least bit sorry. That was a deliberate ploy if ever I saw one.

The least I could do was try to bail him out. 'Did you say something wrong, Spencer?' I asked. 'I really didn't hear you very well.'

Both Spencer and Carla smiled secret smiles at that one. I don't think either one of them remotely believed me, but they could make their peace with what had happened. Probably neither of them wanted to deny Austin the right to know more about his birth parents, and this way the information would never be traced back to them, because *I* certainly wasn't going to tell anyone. And if you think I just told *you*, keep in mind that I always change people's names in the interest of privacy.

That's my story and I'm sticking to it, just as the Cobbs could now stick to theirs.

Marc and Helen. It wasn't a great deal, but it was something.

FIVE

Even when you're a private investigator, agencies like to keep you on hold.

Corporations, government agencies and, in this case, private adoption services always present the customer/client/constituent with the assurance that 'your call is very important to us,' and then go about demonstrating exactly how false that statement is by playing maddeningly repetitive, bland music for a period of anywhere from five to five thousand minutes with periodic reiterations of the message that nothing could be more on their minds than your call. I've picked up phone calls from insurance companies hoping to sell me something I don't need at *all* faster than companies pick up one from me when I have actual business to discuss.

I had called the Friendly Family adoption agency, still operating thirty years after it had arranged Austin Cobb's adoption, without high expectations of finding out anything close to what I needed to know, but hoping any tidbit of information might point me in a direction.

It had been a busy afternoon of trying to track down couples named Marc and Helen who might have put their son up for adoption in the Nineties, and I'm sure you'll be surprised, but even the internet needs more to go on than that. The best I'd done so far was to find a business in Lake George, New York, called Marc 'N' Helen's Tackle Shop. I'd given them a call and gotten Marc. He sounded slightly older than Austin. And he'd been living in Minneapolis at the time in question, struggling through the trials of first grade.

Meanwhile, Mank's suggestion that I look up professionals who would have been dealing with children who had autism thirty years before was sounding better. I hadn't done the research yet, because I didn't want to admit to Mank that I thought it was a good idea, but if Friendly Family ever stopped the music and picked up, that might be next on my agenda after this phone call.

There had been plenty of time to think about these things because I'd been holding (according to my phone) for twenty-three minutes and seventeen seconds. I had the phone on speaker and it was face-up on my desk, so at least I could look at a few emails while holding. I'd have been searching for autism experts of the Nineties if it were possible for me to concentrate on two things at the same time.

Ken was not in the office, which wasn't the least bit unusual. He came in when he was working diligently on a case he'd decided to take on himself, and that didn't happen very often. When his workload consisted mostly – but not exclusively – of parts of cases I'd assigned him, he was less enthusiastic and tended to work from home if he was working at all. I'd fire him, but he put up most of the seed money for the business, and besides, there was no one else like me on Earth.

Finally the music stopped in mid-boredom and a woman's voice said, 'Friendly Family Adoption. How may I help you?' There was the clamor of a number of other people doing the same job, customer service, for any number of other concerns in the same room as my new pal. But any break from the hold music was like a new lease of life, so I practically dived onto my phone and put it up to my ear.

'Hello,' I said, because I was being especially creative that day. 'I'm a private investigator.' Trust me, there was an 'and' about to happen in that sentence, but it was cruelly not to be heard.

I was about to add the exciting news that she could help me when she cut me off. 'I'm sorry, but I'm not allowed to give out any information on an adoption we might have helped to arrange.' They must have gotten these requests all the time. I could almost hear her reaching for the disconnect button.

'Don't hang up,' I blurted because I had no idea how close her finger was to the phone. 'I'm not asking you to give out privileged information. I just have a few questions about an adoption that took place thirty years ago.'

'I understand, but we are not allowed to disclose any information on adoptions.' Like all good customer service representatives, this woman was trained in the fine art of repeating herself until the customer was infuriated enough to hang up. But she was dealing with a superhuman being today (well, kind of) and we don't give up that easily.

'Why?' I said.

It has been my observation that the one thing customer service representatives at big companies (or even medium-sized adoption agencies) are not scripted to reply to is the question, 'Why?' This is largely because, not actually working for the entity in question but for a customer service 'farm,' they don't *know* why and that throws them off.

'Why what?' she asked. It was a stalling tactic. Probably gesturing to a supervisor as we spoke.

'Why can't you give out information on adoptions that took place thirty years ago?' I asked. 'Clearly the person being adopted is over the age of majority. There's nothing to disclose that they might have objections to. Why can't you tell me what my client, who is the adoptee, wants to know?'

There was a short pause (thankfully without Muzak) and then the woman – who you will recall was trained to *assist customers* – spoke once again. 'There are issues of privacy and some of our adoptions have confidentiality clauses that still pertain no matter how old the child is now.' They hadn't worked too hard on that part of the script.

'The *child* is thirty-two years old and wants to know about his birth parents' medical histories,' I said, simplifying Austin's goals just a bit. OK, a lot. 'I don't see why that would be confidential at this point.'

'Because of HIPAA.' The Health Insurance Portability and Accountability Act, signed into law in 1996, has solved some problems, but as with most legislation, it created new ones at the same time.

'So you're saying my client isn't allowed to know about possible health risks he might be facing because it would require him to know about his parents' health records?' Maybe an emotional approach might have some value.

Then again, maybe not. 'I am not authorized to reveal those records or any other information about an adoption without the consent of all the parties involved,' my customer assistance buddy said. I was seriously considering driving to her place of business and throwing a cubicle or two out the window for effect, but law enforcement tends to frown on such things, and besides, I had no idea where on the planet the office might be.

'You don't even know my client's name yet,' I reminded her. 'How do you know you don't have the consent of everyone involved?'

'I am not authorized to reveal any records about any adoption over the phone.' The rules kept changing with the purpose of keeping me from learning what I needed to know.

'Who is?' I asked.

There was a pause of profound stupefaction on her end. 'What?' she finally managed.

'Who is authorized to discuss an adoption if you're not? I have legitimate questions and you keep telling me you're not authorized to answer them. So who is?'

Another moment where I pictured this woman looking around the room for help and finding none. 'May I place you on a brief hold?' she said.

'Define "brief."'

She did not make any effort to do that and, without gaining my consent, hit the hold button and activated the smooth jazz no doubt designed to drive potential troublemakers like me away. But I was made of sterner stuff and hung in there for another four minutes, during which I actually started to like the sax track being played. Then there was a click and my pal was back. 'I'm going to transfer you to the next level,' she said. For a second I felt a rush of elation, as if I were being promoted to something, then I realized I would have to tell my story to someone new all over again. Life is full of ups and downs.

Another few clicks. 'May I help you?' An older woman, not old but middle-aged, probably, with an air of calm and control. This was someone I could deal with, despite the fact that she was probably not going to tell me anything, either.

'I hope so,' I said. 'I am a private investigator who has been hired by someone who was adopted through your agency. He'd like to make contact with his birth parents, or at least put in a request to do so, and I've been having trouble finding out who they are or how to contact them.' This was a classic example of stating the problem without asking for anything from the other person, which tends to lead them to feel responsibility and work harder to find an answer.

The new woman, I assumed a supervisor of some kind, sort of snorted, which I thought was either very rude or a sign of some respiratory disorder. But again, I was mistaken. 'Fran?' she said. 'Fran Stein?'

I *knew* I recognized that voice. 'Betty Rosen? Is that actually you?'

'Who else would want to be?' she answered. 'How've you been?'

'Since the last time we spoke, what, two years ago? I'm the same. Weren't you working for the city's adoption agency?'

Betty laughed again (I now recognized the snort as a sound of amusement). 'The city,' she said with a tone that indicated she was not a fan of New York's government. 'They paid lousy and then extended our hours for the same salary. The private sector, Fran, that's what it's all about.'

'So you're working for Friendly Family's customer service?' Betty had been a supervisor in charge of adoption records when I'd known her, and had been a valuable source of information on many a case just like Austin's.

'No, for a separate customer service agency,' she said. 'I don't answer phones most of the time. I work for the agency and I have regular hours and a few bucks left over at the end of the month.'

'Good for you.' I actually meant it.

'So what exactly are you calling about to get the poor girl who answered your call all flustered?' Betty asked.

'The usual,' I said. 'My client wants to find out about his birth parents, but it sounds like the agreement must contain the nuclear codes or something because nobody wants to talk about it.'

'Uh-huh.' Betty was already clacking away on her keyboard. 'What's your client's name?'

I told her about Austin but left out his autism. He hadn't actually told me it was OK to mention it, and if I didn't want to use it for sympathy (which Austin definitely didn't need), there was no use in bringing it up. 'I met his adoptive parents, and they're lovely, but they act like their house might blow up if they talk about his birth parents. Are they in the mafia or something?'

Betty was clearly reviewing the file because she didn't laugh at my hilarious joke. 'I'm looking . . . hang on . . .' I didn't really have an alternative, so I did as she suggested. 'Yeah. I can't tell you anything. Wow. I've never seen a file so redacted in my life.'

After all this, nothing? 'Come on, Betty. There has to be *something* I can tell Austin in my next progress report. Can you at least tell me where they were living thirty years ago?'

Betty's voice was reflective of what she was reading, which must have been a doozy. 'Not really,' she said. 'Fran, I'm serious. These people were not kidding about remaining anonymous.'

'But Friendly Family must have run a background check on them at the time. That's not owned by the birth parents; it's owned by your company. What can you tell me from that?'

'I can tell you they don't want you to find them. This file makes that really clear. I can't tell you their names, their address, their email addresses, nothing. It's easier to find Amelia Earhart than these two.'

I couldn't compromise the Cobbs by mentioning the names Helen and Marc or I might have tried that to jog Betty a little bit. Instead, I asked, 'Did they have a criminal record, either one of them? You must have researched that at the time.'

Betty snorted, not a laugh this time. 'You'll recall, I was not working for this agency at the time, Fran,' she said, a touch annoyed. 'But I do know that if anyone had a criminal record that went beyond a couple of speeding tickets, Friendly Family would not have involved itself in the adoption. Does that help you?'

I groaned a little. 'Not really.' It just came out.

'I can tell you this, and it's just because I googled them when you asked, so I'm not giving you anything out of the agency's records,' Betty said, her voice softening a little. She always had been one of the adoption agents I was fond of working with. 'They're not both still alive.'

That was news. It wasn't especially helpful news just yet, but it might become something. 'How long has that been true?'

I asked, forcing myself not to ask whether it was Marc or Helen who had passed on.

'About twenty-five years, from what I can tell. There's no obituary on file, but there are police reports.'

An alarm went off in my head. 'Police reports! Are we assuming this was not a death by natural causes?'

Betty sounded a little smug in the 'I-know-something-you-don't-know' style. 'The only news report I have from the time makes it sound vague, but the authorities were not ruling out foul play,' she said.

'And you're not going to tell me which one, or how?' I asked.

'Nope.'

'Woof,' I said.

SIX

I didn't have anything but Betty's word on the demise of one of Austin's parents, and I didn't have much on it even with Betty's word. So I bit the bullet and asked my brother, via text, to do some internet research on the case. He, being my brother, did not answer.

To be fair, I didn't call his number, either, because talking to Ken can be as trying as climbing up the outside of an apartment building. Don't ask me how I know.

I figured he was at home going through the fridge without worrying whether food costs money or at his girlfriend's place, whoever she was this week. My brother is, against all appearances, an intelligent, caring, thoughtful man. And he'd kill me if he knew I told you that.

There was just no escaping it now: I'd have to act on Mank's advice. The problem was that I couldn't contact local neurologists or psychologists from thirty years before if I had no idea where 'local' might be. Betty wasn't forthcoming with that information and neither was anyone else on this planet. I had no contacts on other planets, so that possibility was no use, either.

In the 1990s, autism was hardly an unheard-of condition (despite the popularity of *Rain Man*), which it might have been twenty or even ten years earlier. But it was not as well understood by the public as it might be today. Because of the wide spectrum of autistic behaviors, people were not regarded as autistic unless they fit what might be considered the 'classic' profile, often not speaking at all and having extreme reactions to any unfamiliar situations. But there were scientists already working on understanding it better and they were fairly well known within the communities of people – mostly parents – who needed to seek them out.

So I was doing my own online research when my phone buzzed and the Caller ID showed Ken was on the other end of the call. And yes, I gave a good deal of thought (in a few seconds) to not answering, but then I remembered I needed him to do some work, and accepted the call.

'About time,' I said.

My brother was, apparently, not in the mood for sharp wit. 'Frannie,' he said, 'I just met Malcolm X. Mitchell.'

Given that was precisely what I'd insisted he not do, and what he had promised he would not do, Ken's news was probably not what I'd hoped to be hearing today. When I spoke again, my voice sounded like I'd been gargling with Drano. 'You did what?'

'I know what I said, but it was going to eat at me, and if this guy has a line on where Mom and Dad are now, it's important we find out so we can warn them now that we're in touch.' Ken has a way of making stupid things sound strikingly plausible. It is a talent I would dearly like to cultivate, but I'm too sensible a person, something he need not worry about. There are times I wish our parents had created only one superbeing, and then I remember he's older than I am.

'Do you have *any* idea how dangerous what you just did is?' I rasped. I was off Drano now and up to what I hear whisky is like. I have never had an alcoholic drink because I'm afraid of losing control. Ken, as usual, doesn't let that bother him.

'Just listen. I wasn't taken in. I don't think Malcolm is a friend of ours. But I think he knows some stuff and we need to find out more about him.' Ken sounded like he was outside, walking on the street. Just the place to discuss private business about our parents out loud.

'Can we talk about this when you get here, so that all of the Upper West Side doesn't hear about it in real time?' I asked.

'I'll be there in ten minutes,' he said, negating the reason for his call to begin with. 'But he does say he's our brother, or stepbrother, or half-brother, or something.'

'Ten minutes,' I said, and hung up. That's the kind of mood I was in by now.

It took him twelve minutes to show up, for the record, during which time I had compiled an extremely tentative list of autism experts in the tri-state area circa 1995 or so. There were eight names on the list.

My brother ambled in looking like an enormous version of the Ray Bolger scarecrow in *The Wizard of Oz*. He walks in a sort of loose-limbed style, everything dangling but huge. I knew that if a dangerous situation had presented itself, those limbs would no longer be so loose, but it was hard to tell at this moment. Ken was carrying two iced coffees from the deli one flight down from our office.

'Did someone order a wimpy iced coffee?' That's Ken when he thinks he's being ingratiating. He likes to tease me about ordering decaf because, frankly, I don't need help being stimulated. I can get anxious without half trying, and I enjoy sleeping at night. But my brother sees everything as a competition and every possible macho stereotype as a challenge for him to outdo. If I didn't love him, I'd beat the living crap out of him three times a week. And don't let him fool you; I could do it.

'No. No one ordered that. But if you have a decaf, I'll take it.' I reached out my hand and he placed the plastic cup in it but knew better than to hand me a plastic straw. I took a metal one from the holder on our side table and put it into the drink. I might throw plastic cups in the recycling, but no dolphin is getting *my* straw stuck up its blowhole. If you know what I mean.

'You're welcome,' Ken said with a snarky tone. I figured I didn't have to thank him because I hadn't asked for the coffee. And besides, there was the matter of him putting our whole family in danger by meeting with a shadowy figure/wise-ass.

'So look me in the eye and tell me exactly how it could be a good idea to go out and meet, *alone*, with a guy our mother told us to avoid at all costs. I'm listening.' I put my feet up on a chair next to my desk and laced my fingers behind my head. 'I'm still listening.'

Ken slumped into his desk chair, which is close enough to mine that we don't have to raise our voices to be heard. He looked aggrieved, as if I had somehow insulted him by pointing out that he'd done something stupid. Men.

'I explained this already,' he wheezed. OK, he didn't wheeze. It just sounded so weak and pathetic I didn't have a better word for it. Breathed, I suppose. 'He has this weird story about being another one of Mom and Dad's . . . projects . . . and I didn't see how we could completely ignore that even if we know it's not true.'

I fixed my gaze on him and he knew what that meant. 'And how did this meeting get arranged? He didn't contact you directly, did he? You got in touch with him. This was *your* idea.'

Ken unfixed his gaze and suddenly decided to watch Igavda, something he does a little more than I find comfortable. I mentioned it to Igavda once, and she laughed, but then her grasp of English is . . . vastly better than mine of Bulgarian, so who am I to judge?

'I took initiative,' he began, thinking that would help, 'because I didn't want him lurking out there waiting to be a danger and planning whatever he was planning. Besides, you were the only one who'd ever seen him, so I didn't know who I was looking out for.'

I let out the breath I was holding because I'd hoped I could develop the ability to breathe fire. 'OK, it's done. You breached security on your own dime, put everybody at risk, just because you wanted to meet Malcolm X. Mitchell. Fine. Can't change that. What did you get out of this little exchange? Where was it, anyway?'

'Across from City Hall, of all places.' My brother seemed to find that amusing. 'He had the feeling we live downtown, which we do, and I think he wanted to get a sense of how far. So I didn't leave for twenty minutes after we set it up. He thinks I took that much time longer to get there.'

'Genius, Holmes,' I said. 'You sure he wasn't following you from our building?'

'Absolutely. For one thing, he was already on the bench when I got there. Wearing his W.H.O. t-shirt like the time you saw him. He said he wanted us to be sure it was really him, and there wasn't a bunch of Malcolm X. Mitchells running around just to cause havoc.'

'He has a pretty inflated sense of his own importance, doesn't he? But I've seen the guy, and he's skinny and average height. He doesn't look like us. He's not like us. What's his game? What did he say he wanted?'

That's when Ken's serious face took over. He's not exactly putting on a performance when he does that, but he's communicating that I should know he's not taking something lightly. Like he usually does.

'What he *said*, which I don't believe for a minute, is that he'd been in touch with Dad, specifically, and was worried because he hasn't heard back for a month. He wanted me to tell him where they were.'

'Like you know,' I said.

That seemed to wound my brother a bit. He winced slightly. It wasn't like *I* knew where our parents were hiding out these days. 'Yeah,' Ken said. 'And I told him that. But that's when it got weird.'

'It wasn't weird yet?' I'm not always the most sensitive person on the planet.

Ken is used to that face and ignored what I'd said. 'It's what happened after. He was wearing that t-shirt, and you probably remember he'd cut off the sleeves.'

'Amazing, Holmes! A sleeveless shirt! Clearly the sign of a deranged killer! By the way, are there completely normal killers?'

Again, my hilarious commentary was lost on my brother. He gave me what he thought was a significant look, which made him appear to be constipated. 'Just after I told him he was a fraud and a bad one, he pretended to be insulted and put his hands behind his head. And I saw it.'

He saw it? I wasn't sure I wanted to know, but I was obliged to ask anyway. 'You saw what?'

'I saw the USB port under his left arm.'

SEVEN

'Well, that doesn't make a lick of sense,' Aunt Margie said.

On all things that relate to our parents, Aunt Margie *must* be consulted. She was the one, after all, who knew Livvie and Brad (as she called them) longer than Ken or me. She was there when our parents decided they had to leave us to keep us safe and she was the one who had, for years, received packages of cash that could only have come from Mom and Dad. Aunt Margie was their closest friend for a time. We were just their . . . science projects. No, that's cruel. Mom has made it clear that she and Dad think of Ken and me as their children and feel awful about not being there for us as we grew up. But I didn't choose to help adoptees find their birth parents because I *didn't* feel just a little bit abandoned.

In any event, Ken and I had gone back to Aunt Margie's apartment, knowing it was a day she was not working a shift at the radio station, because she always had a sympathetic ear, sound advice and, most of all, cookies. All were being put into play right now at her kitchen table.

'Isn't it possible Mom and Dad built another one of us?' Ken asked. 'I mean, this Malcolm guy seems a little younger than Frannie and me. Maybe when we were babies? They had improvements they wanted to install?' Ken might feel a bit more than a little abandoned. He tends to get testy when talking about Mom and Dad in the abstract.

But Aunt Margie shook her head. 'Not a chance. I was around by then and I would have known something was up. They spent time in their labs, of course, but not enough to create someone like you two. They never said anything about it, and Livvie actually told me once they wouldn't have considered it. Parents will tell you having two toddlers in the house makes you busy enough.'

I'd been considering all the possibilities since Ken had told me about Malcolm X. Mitchell's . . . unusual installation, and had come up with very little that was practical and sensible. 'Could someone else have learned about our parents' work and tried to duplicate it?' I asked the room.

Neither of them responded immediately, which was odd. Ken is very quick to tell me I'm wrong on virtually any suggestion I ever make, so I'd expected to hear, 'No' within a second or two. Aunt Margie, a little more open to possibilities, might have taken time to think, but usually not this long. I looked at them and they both appeared to be a little frightened.

After what seemed like a couple of weeks, Aunt Margie said, 'I really hope not.'

My stomach took a couple of quick turns and ended up in Queens. That was not what I'd wanted to hear. I'd much preferred to have had my brother mock me for such an idiotic remark.

'Nah.' Even he didn't sound convinced. 'Mom and Dad were too careful. There's no way they'd let someone else see their work.'

'Malcolm knew about us,' I told him. 'He figured out how to find us. He knew what we are. It's fairly obvious that there is a leak *somewhere*. We've been found before. If we contacted our parents now, they'd tell us to pack up and leave the city, or to leave without packing up. If we don't want to do that, we have to operate under the assumption that our lives are going to be different, and we have to be even more cautious than we have been until now.' And even as I said those words, they hit me emotionally for what they meant. I shouldn't be in touch with friends. I shouldn't do anything 'super' where anyone could see me. I couldn't do anything out of the ordinary to help Austin or any of my other clients.

I couldn't get close to Mank. But that, I told myself, was the least of my problems.

'We're not leaving town,' Ken said with conviction. 'I know too many women here.' I didn't respond because I was finding some consolation that he hadn't said *girls*. You take your victories where you can get them.

'Are you sure?' Aunt Margie is the most careful among us, and somewhat paranoid about our security. 'I'm sure Brad would say it's necessary.'

'He hasn't spoken to us in close to thirty years,' Ken said. 'We're adults now and we get to make our own decisions. I'm not leaving.' He crossed his arms and sat back in his chair, which creaked. Aunt Margie has not fortified her furniture as strenuously as Ken and I have found necessary.

I looked at her. 'We've established a business here and it's starting to get some traction,' I said. 'I'm not closing up shop because of Malcolm X. Mitchell, whether he has a port under his arm or not. He keeps trying to get us to tell him where Mom and Dad are. Since we don't know, we have nothing to lose.'

Aunt Margie pondered that. 'I suppose not. But you two have to be more careful.' Like we hadn't known that already.

So the next day I had another in a series of locks installed on our apartment door and made three keys.

Once I'd distributed them I went to see Mank. Yeah, I know I just said that I couldn't get close to him, but this was strictly business. The police have access to records that the government greedily likes to keep to itself. It's so much more than Google. And it pays to have a friendly cop when you need one.

I entered the precinct and headed upstairs to the detective bureau where, alas, I was 'greeted,' if you want to call it that, by Sgt Emil Bendix, which is not the way one wants to start the working day. Bendix, who thought TV cops from the 1980s were role models, was as open to female investigators as he would have been to a half-caf cinnamon latte with oat milk and an image of Gloria Steinem in the foam. Which is to say, not much.

'What are you lookin' for, Gargantua?' That's Bendix in a jaunty mood. He likes to point out that I'm taller than virtually every other woman he's ever seen and thinks that it's somehow a disadvantage or a weakness from my point of view. Bendix and I don't talk a whole lot. That's why I haven't thrown him into a wall with one arm yet.

Careful, Fran. No public displays of . . . anything.

'A good man, a just world and a steady income, not necessarily in that order, Bendix,' I answered. 'Thanks for asking.'

I did my best to walk by him without exchanging any further

words, but Bendix's one asset as a detective is his persistence, and that's because he doesn't have any other assets. He's not bright, observant or analytical. But he doesn't quit. Especially when he should.

Case in point: 'Your boyfriend is in the can,' he said, gesturing toward the restroom in case I had missed his nuanced statement.

'I don't have a boyfriend,' I told him. I tried to push past Bendix again, but in true male idiot fashion, he placed himself in front of Mank's desk in a position it would be difficult to pass, unless of course I used that throwing-him-against-a-wall option, which I had sworn not to implement. 'What do you want, Bendix?' It came out as a sort of exasperated sigh. Almost unintentionally.

He actually looked embarrassed and watched his shoes as his feet sort of scuffed back and forth on the floor. He looked like a fourth grader who didn't want to tell his mom he'd gotten a D on his math test.

'See, it's this. My sister-in-law's cousin – that is, my brother's wife's cousin – is getting married.' Those were some fascinating shoes; he seemed transfixed.

'Mazel tov, Bendix. You want me to help you pick out a pair of candlesticks or something?' Whatever Mank was doing in that restroom was taking far too long from my point of view. Maybe I should leave and come back later. Like, tomorrow.

Bendix didn't raise his eyes to meet mine, possibly for fear of hurting his neck. 'There's no one who would go with me,' he said into his soup-stained tie. At nine in the morning.

I'll admit it; I didn't get what he was saying to begin with, largely because I wanted it to be anything else. I stared at him, which didn't matter because he wasn't looking at my face. 'You want me to fix you up with someone? I don't really have that many friends.' It was an attempt.

And not a very good one. 'No.' Bendix's voice was even more faint. Luckily, my hearing is a lot better than yours. 'I thought maybe you'd go with me.' OK, so maybe I'm not that lucky to have really sharp hearing.

I needed an excuse, and I'd just foolishly told Bendix I wasn't dating anyone. 'When is it?' I asked. Surely I could invent a conflicting event I had to attend.

'October the sixteenth.'

'That's six months from now,' I pointed out, in case Bendix didn't know how calendars worked, which was a possibility.

'I just got the save-the-date thing,' he said. He coughed and looked up at me. 'Are you busy that day?'

Yeah, I had a dentist appointment. Except I didn't. Neither Ken nor I had ever visited a doctor of any kind for fear of being discovered. That was even more the case now. But that's irrelevant. I wasn't going to the dentist. I didn't see how I could even plausibly lie to Bendix about going to the dentist.

'I don't know,' I said, which was technically true. Who knows what they're doing on a random date six months in the future? 'I'm gonna have to check.' I never say, 'gonna.' That's how flustered I was.

'OK. So we'll make it a maybe.' There were boys who asked me out in high school (mostly on bets) who were smoother than Bendix.

'Or you could ask some other woman you've ever met,' I said.

Maybe that was cruel. Bendix looked sad and opened his mouth twice without saying anything.

At that moment Mank finally emerged and walked to his desk, smiling in my direction like things were just great. Didn't he know I'd just been asked out by a Neanderthal who thought women were invented strictly to cook dinner? Well, and maybe one other thing, but I was certainly not thinking about *that* right now.

Mank sat down behind his desk and Bendix, mumbling something incomprehensible, shuffled off toward his own. 'What's going on?' Mank asked, probably spurred by the look on my face.

'Where were you when I needed you?' I said sharply.

'When did you need me?' He sounded oddly hopeful.

'About a minute and a half ago.'

Mank looked toward the restroom door. 'I was . . . uh . . .'

'I know. Look. I need to know something about a suspected murder.'

His eyes narrowed. 'Is the WiFi out at your office, or on your phone?'

'This goes way beyond Google, Mank. Come on. I'm not asking for anything the NYPD doesn't want you to tell me.' I sat down in the chair in front of his desk despite not having been invited. What the hell.

I never really know how Mank is going to react to anything I do or say. That is, I'll admit (under pressure), part of his charm. This time, he looked at me as if deciding whether to be grumpy or just give in and help me out like he almost always does. And thankfully for me, grumpy lost. He was always my least favorite dwarf anyway. Sleepy is more my speed.

Mank put on a show of being put out, but he couldn't sell it. He let out a long breath, opened the laptop on his desk and looked at me. 'What?' he asked.

'I'm trying to track down a suspected murder that took place about twenty-five years ago,' I said.

'OK. What's the victim's name?'

'I don't know.'

That got me a quick sharp look. 'Where in the city did it happen?'

'I don't know. It might not have been in the city.'

Mank put his hands down flat on the desk. 'OK. What *do* you know?' That was wise of him. What I didn't know would have taken hours to relate.

'All I know is that the victim was either a husband or wife who sometime before was involved in putting their toddler son up for adoption through an agency called Friendly Family. There are virtually no public records I can find and the agency's not talking. The son was eventually adopted by a couple in Queens named Carla and Spencer Cobb, and his name is Austin Cobb. But the Cobbs signed an NDA and won't discuss the adoption despite the fact that their son is now in his thirties and can't be whisked away if they violate their agreement. Everybody is being very tight-lipped about this whole thing, but it appears that either the birth father or mother turned up dead about seven years after the adoption, and there's some speculation that the death was in fact a homicide.'

That seemed like a lot of information, but to an investigator (or police detective) it was virtually nothing. Mank resisted the impulse to rub his eyes in frustration, took a series of short breaths and looked at me. 'That ain't much. Where do you suggest I should start looking?'

'If I knew that, I'd start looking myself,' I answered. 'Isn't there cop stuff you can do that I can't?'

'Yeah. I can give people tickets and arrest them for crimes, and you can't. But Fran, there's no crazy police database that has all the stuff about Area 51 and the JFK assassination. If I don't know at least who I'm talking about, or the general area and date the crime might have happened, I have no way of researching any reports that were filed. You know that.'

I did know that. I had been hoping that the Area 51 stuff would be distracting enough to keep me from focusing on Malcolm X. Mitchell and my total inability to find out anything about Austin Cobb's birth parents. 'OK,' I said. 'Can you isolate unsolved homicides based on possible adoption records from twenty-five years ago? Any areas where they overlap?'

'I don't know what adoption records to access,' Mank protested. 'We don't have a name.'

'We have three names. Carla, Spencer and Austin Cobb. I believe the birth parents were named Marc and Helen. And we have Friendly Family Adoption Services. There has to be something you can trace there. The Cobbs and the agency won't tell me – literally – anything.'

Mank shook his head. 'Unless I can get a judge to unseal the records of that adoption, and it sounds like everyone signed off on keeping it secret, I can't go any further,' he said. 'You've been here before, Fran. You know sometimes the birth parents don't want to give the adoptee any information and there's nothing even I can do about it. Go back to your client and tell him there's no way to find out anything else.'

That was unthinkable. I spoke at a volume no one but Mank could hear. 'I can't do that. This poor guy is living his life thinking his birth parents rejected him because of who he is. I know about being different and my parents aren't around, but I know they love me and left because they had to. I know they didn't leave Ken and me behind because they were disgusted or uncomfortable with who we were. Austin Cobb doesn't have that level of emotional security. I can't just walk away from him.'

The air seemed to come out of Mank. He slumped back in his chair and his hands went soft on the armrests. He knew me and he knew how I sounded when I'd made up my mind. It was why he hadn't asked me out in months. He didn't know I'd probably have said yes.

'OK,' he finally said. 'With the name of the agency and the adoptive parents, *maybe* I can dig something up. I doubt it, but I'll try. I know a woman at the Adoption Information Registry.'

'So do I,' I told him. 'Her name is Elenore. She already turned me away.'

He seemed to get a little of his energy back and gave me a look. 'Well, the one I know is *not* named Elenore, and if she can, I think she'll answer any questions I ask.'

I regarded him a moment and even raised my eyebrows. 'An old flame?' I asked.

'Not that old.'

Oof! I thanked him perfunctorily and made my way toward the stairwell door. Along the way I had to pass Bendix's desk.

'October the sixteenth,' he reminded me under his breath.

'I'll look into it.'

I couldn't get through that door fast enough.

EIGHT

Austin Cobb looked defeated. He was sitting on a barstool in what passed for his living room, next to a passthrough that led to the galley kitchen in his apartment. The place was, as is typical in New York, a trifle cramped. Don't believe any Manhattan apartment you've ever seen on television.

'So you haven't found out *anything*?' he said, running his left hand through his hair in what I guessed was a gesture of despair, or disappointment in me.

I had pretty much communicated that very message, leaving out the possibility that one of his birth parents might have murdered the other. I didn't know nearly enough about that yet to say anything to the client. It was enough to have to tell him I didn't have any strong leads on where they might be, or what their names could have been. There are only so many ways I can admit to failure at a time.

'I've found enough to keep on digging,' I exaggerated. 'It's only been a few days, Austin. You knew this wasn't going to be resolved that quickly.'

Austin pouted and nodded his head. 'I know. I know. But you said you'd find them.'

'I said I'd *try* to find them, and that is what I'm doing. I want you to understand, again, that there are no guarantees in this kind of situation, so if you're expecting me to magically make your birth parents appear, you should fire me right now. I'm good, but I'm not *that* good.'

My client seemed to shrink a couple of sizes as I looked at him. He drew his arms into his sides and somehow lowered his head so it looked like he had less neck than before. 'I thought that was what you said,' he told me, or himself, in a very quiet voice.

I've been fired off cases a number of times. It doesn't happen a lot, but it happens. I stood up and just sort of strolled around the room, not pacing but without any intended destination. It was essentially a studio apartment and a compact one, the best a medical researcher could afford in the real estate madness that is New York City. It was not exceptionally neat; books were everywhere, there was a laptop computer sitting on a folding table near the reclining chair that was the only major seat in the place (where I had been perched until a moment ago), and the occasional used sock could be spotted on the floor. Luckily no uneaten food was decorating the place. Austin was going to be who he was. There would be no point in trying to attempt alterations, and not my purview anyway. That's true of everybody. Try to get someone to change sometime.

'If you'd like to find another investigator, Austin, I will understand, but I am still doing my best to find your birth parents,' I told him. 'And I want you to know it would have been very unusual if I'd located them in such a short time, especially given the lack of information I've been given to start with.'

That made his head emerge from his contracted neck and he stared up at me, which was a decent amount of up from where he was sitting. 'You think I didn't tell you everything?' he demanded. 'I gave you every piece of data I had, anything I could dig up myself online or elsewhere in my possessions. There are no photographs of me with them, or of them without me present. There are no letters. There is no record of me before the adoption, which leads me to believe that Austin was not my birth name. I told you everything I know, Miss Stein.'

Actually, I prefer 'Ms Stein,' and Austin would have been perfectly within his rights to call me Fran (which I'd explained to him), but none of that was important, so I let it go. 'I didn't think you were holding something back,' I said. 'But I want you to understand why this might take more time than you had hoped. If I even knew where you'd been living before your birth parents were in touch with Friendly Family, that would help.'

Austin looked at me quizzically, as if I'd said something in a language he wasn't able to speak. 'You don't know that?' he said.

That was probably the moment *I* looked like I'd just grown a size or two, and it wasn't because of the chicken parm sandwich I'd had for lunch. 'No, I don't,' I answered. 'Your parents didn't know, or wouldn't tell me, and the adoption agency refuses to discuss it. Why? Do you know where they were living back then?'

The question seemed to have a worrying effect on Austin; he looked meek suddenly and his arms went back into his sides. 'I mean, I don't remember the address or anything. I was just a toddler.'

The first break I was getting in the case and it was coming from my client, but he appeared to be reluctant to discuss it. 'What *do* you remember, Austin?'

He wasn't looking at me; he was afraid he would give the wrong answer, or that he had done something he shouldn't. His mouth opened and closed a couple of times. I needed to be less the prosecuting attorney and more the ally who was serving his cause.

'It's OK,' I said, walking toward him but not getting too close. Austin didn't like to be touched or I'd have put a hand on his arm. 'I'm excited because I think you can help us. Nobody thinks you did anything wrong.'

His eyebrows dove in the direction of his nose. 'Of course I didn't,' he said. But he still wouldn't look in my direction.

I brought my voice down to the tone you'd use on a frightened puppy, and if you're reading this, Austin, I apologize. 'Do you remember something about where you were living?' I asked, despite every indication that he'd already said he did.

His head nodded, almost a spasm because it was so quick. 'I remember my birth father trying to teach me to read, and he showed me a sign with the name of the town on it,' he said.

'Trying to teach you to read? At that age?' I should have let that go, because Austin's eyebrows were not happy with the question again.

His voice reflected a little irritation. 'I was very advanced, and besides, he was just repeating one word over and over, so even if I couldn't sound out the letters, I would just remember it.'

There was a silence because in my mind Austin had left himself a slot in which he'd say the name of the town. Oddly, he did not. He must have figured he'd made his point and forgotten the subject of the conversation. It happens. Sometimes – and I know you'll be surprised – my own sentences tend to get away from me a little bit.

'So what was the name of the town?' I asked Austin.

'Kearny,' he answered.

I felt like I'd heard the name before, but it wasn't adjacent to New York City, and if you're a New Yorker, that meant it didn't matter. 'The one in Ireland?' I asked.

'No. The one in New Jersey.'

NINE

You might think that I immediately bolted for the door to Austin's apartment and caught the next Uber to Kearny, New Jersey, and I don't have any idea why you would think such a thing. For one thing, an Uber to Kearny would probably cost about $50, where a bus to the same location would top out at maybe six bucks. But that's the least of it. The fact was, I still had no idea if anything had happened there and, if so, to whom.

But I did, finally, have something to start with, although why Austin wouldn't have volunteered this information earlier was baffling me. People on the spectrum who are what they used to call 'high-functioning' are easy to misunderstand. You feel like you're having a conversation with anyone else you know, and then their difference peeks its head out and it makes perfect sense to them, but you need to catch up.

I asked him questions for another twenty minutes, but all Austin could recall from his life in Kearny (which admittedly didn't last very long) was his birth father trying to teach him to read the town's name on a sign in the road. Austin apparently did read early, but not that early. He just memorized the name 'Kearny' and moved on, probably to get his dad to shut up about it.

That was enough to text Mank, who grumped at me some and then said he'd look into it. That's how we operate. I didn't go see him because he was still cute and I was being more cognizant of security for my family. That's what I told myself.

I went back to the office and found that Ken had left for the day, which wasn't the least bit surprising, so Igavda and I were alone when Malcolm X. Mitchell decided to amble in and look over the place like he was thinking of buying it. I didn't see him immediately, but I noticed Igavda straighten up in her chair and look to see if we had a new client on the way in. We didn't.

'Mrs Fran,' Igavda began because there's absolutely no way I can get her to stop. 'Mr Malcolm to see you.' She's an equal opportunity name-flubber.

'Tell him I'm out,' I called to her.

Igavda looked at me in wonderment because it was obvious I'd seen Malcolm and he'd seen me. 'He's here already,' she said. Maybe she thought I believed Malcolm had called on the phone.

There was no denying that he was there in the office, so I thanked Igavda and walked to where he was standing. 'I'm asking you to leave,' I said. 'I have nothing for you, and you certainly can't help me with anything, so let's call it a draw and you just leave.'

He grinned the fakest grin I'd seen in quite a while and shook his head as if I'd just said something adorable. 'Is that the kind of welcome you give a member of your own family?' he said, not even attempting to sound sincere.

'There are only three other members of my family and I don't know where two of them are,' I said. 'You're a two-bit grifter who's probably working up a way to monetize that prop port under your arm.' No sense in playing the cards too close to the vest, since I figured I was holding all of them. Igavda, as fascinated as ever by my personal business, was doing a crossword puzzle for children to help her English.

Malcolm's right hand 'instinctively' went to the area under his left arm. 'Prop?' he said. 'That's no more a prop than the one you're concealing, Fran. But I don't know the origins of mine and that's why I'm here.'

'Really,' I said. 'Let me see.'

He raised his left arm and the t-shirt he was wearing fell away in that area. There was indeed a small slit that looked like a USB port. So I reached up and pulled it off. Not surprisingly, he yelped because I'm sure the glue being yanked off stung. 'There,' I said. 'You're cured.' No blood, nothing. Just a couple of stray hairs on the little toy thing, which I threw into the wastebasket next to my desk.

'You were right; that was a prop. My port is in a place you don't want to see. But I'm telling you, my parents are the same as yours, and I want you to help me connect with my family.'

Malcolm's grin had dimmed a bit, but he still had that glint of delusion in his eyes.

I swear, I saw it coming. It was like standing on train tracks in a nightmare. You can see the train coming, you know for a fact it's going to hit you, but you just can't get out of the way. 'I can't tell you anything about my parents,' I said. If I could just move one foot, I could manually lift the other off the tracks. 'Go away.'

'But that's why I came to you,' Malcolm said, never losing that cheesy grin. 'I'm here to hire you. I want you to find my parents. I'd say, "birth parents," but we both know that would be inaccurate.'

'Well, if you'd tell me your real name, I might be able to track down your parents, but I'm certain you already know who they are,' I said. 'And you don't want to do that, so we're not interested in your business. Take your case somewhere else. But I'll warn you now: if you don't tell the investigator your whole story, your *true* story, you'll never find out anything except what you want to tell them. We don't represent frauds, Mr Mitchell. Hit the road.' I gestured toward the office door.

That idiot smile never left his face for a second. I *could* have pushed him through a wall, but we're responsible for damage done to the office. Landlords. 'The name on my birth certificate is actually Malcolm Mitchell,' he said. 'I added the "X" for fun.'

Fun.

'We're not interested in your case, Mr Mitchell,' I said for what felt like the fifteenth time. 'Please leave our offices, and don't return.' I actually started toward the office door, thinking he might follow me there instinctively.

But he stayed rooted to our corridor as if he'd decided to build a vacation home there. 'I don't think you understand, Fran. You're already looking for my parents, because you're already looking for *your* parents. I think you have a way to get in touch with them, and I think it's only fair that you share that access with the only other person on the planet who can use it meaningfully. Face it, Frannie, I'm your half-brother at least, and I'd also like to know what happened to my mom and dad. Since that's your business, I'm offering to pay you for the information. Let's say half a million dollars. To start. How does that sound?'

I will not say that the figure didn't catch my attention, but then I remembered the person I was dealing with. 'It sounds like exactly the kind of lie you would tell to get me interested, Mr Mitchell, but it didn't work. This is a place of business. There's the door. Use it.'

He chuckled lightly, amused by my sass. I guess. 'Not until we have an agreement.' The smirk did not fade. 'You wouldn't want to know what happens if we don't.'

I turned back toward the reception desk. 'Igavda,' I said. 'Call the police and tell them we have a trespasser here who is threatening me and refusing to leave.'

Igavda, whose knowledge of English had been improving but not that much, said, 'Police? Mr Mank?'

It should have been Detective Mank, but there was no point in pursuing that right at that moment. 'No,' I told her. 'The precinct. Tell them we have a problem and they should send officers. A lot of officers.'

Igavda more or less got the hint and started pushing buttons on the console in front of her. 'Officer,' she said.

Mitchell put up his hands as if in surrender. 'No need for that, Fran. No one is doing anything illegal here. We can meet and make an agreement another time.' He started to amble toward the door. I gestured for Igavda to stop, and since she was just looking for a five-letter word for "strange" (WEIRD), it was easy for her to comply. She didn't, but it would have been easy.

'No, we can't,' I said. 'I'll have operatives watching out for you every hour of the day and if you come near me or my brother again, they'll deal with you.' We had no operatives. We couldn't afford operatives. We could barely afford Ken and me.

'Now who's being threatening?' Mitchell's voice had that light, amused quality even as he opened the office door and left.

'Igavda,' I said finally. 'You did well.'

She held out the phone receiver. 'Mr Mank,' she said.

'Tell him I'll call him back.'

TEN

It was against my self-imposed policy, it was against any semblance of common sense, and it was against my own instincts, but I was sitting in a coffee shop across the table from Mank later that day. He was making a show of being concerned without being possessive or sexist, and I was making a show of being *un*concerned and self-reliant. And neither of us was being the least bit convincing.

'Did he threaten you directly?' I'd made the mistake of telling Mank about my encounter with Malcolm X. Mitchell. 'I could write up a report and have a couple of cops visit him at home. Maybe even bring him in for questioning.'

'He didn't make any direct threats,' I said, trying to calm him down with my tone, which would indicate that Malcolm was an amusing irritant. 'There's nothing to charge him with and I'd just as soon forget about it. What I really want to talk about is the possibility of a murder or manslaughter in Kearny, New Jersey, around twenty-five years ago.'

We had chosen to meet at the coffee shop because Mank was farther from my office than to this place, and I didn't want to go to the precinct for fear of being cornered into an answer on Bendix's date request, which I had been trying very hard to forget with little success. I was eating a corn muffin because I figured we have to give the place some business, and Mank had a coffee (actually a latte, but he doesn't like to say that because it belies the macho cop image).

Mank's expression turned to one of fake annoyance, except he didn't think it was fake. 'Is this the same murder you told me about before? Do you think I'm your private research bureau?' he said, almost disturbing the foam on his drink. 'I'm a detective with the NYPD.'

'Of course I know that.' The muffin needed butter, but then all muffins need butter. I put some on. 'I wouldn't ask you to look into stuff if you were an accountant.'

'Don't be cute,' he said.

'I can't help it. It happens naturally.' Why was I flirting? I knew better than that. This was a business meeting. I decided to act businesslike.

'My point is that I'm doing work for the City of New York and I don't have time to drop everything just because you ask me to look into a cold case in New Jersey, of all places.'

I nodded thoughtfully, taking his point of view into account. 'So what did you find out?'

He didn't roll his eyes, but he was probably saving that for a time when I wasn't present. 'There is a case that remains open from that time frame. I don't have access to the adoption records because they're sealed, but it might be the people you're trying to find.'

Wow. That was more than I'd expected. I got out my phone to take notes. 'What are their names?'

'Hang on,' Mank warned. 'We're not sure it's them. Because this didn't happen in Kearny. It was the next town over.'

That didn't *necessarily* make a difference. But if Mank had found evidence of a crime around the right time and near the right place, was that enough to go on from here? When you have nothing, anything at all seems like a step up. 'What next town over?' I asked.

'Arlington. You can't miss it. It's just south of North Arlington.'

I suppressed a grin. 'Don't condescend to New Jersey,' I said. 'Too much.'

'Fine. From what I can tell, there was a couple living in Arlington around that time called Marc and Helen Hawley. She was a tech specialist at Verizon and he was a vice principal at the high school in, yes, Kearny. They had a son named William who is just about Austin Cobb's age.'

'So Austin's birth name was William?'

Mank shook his head. 'William wasn't put up for adoption.'

That didn't seem to add up. 'So they had twins and they put *one* of them up for adoption? How does that work?' I hadn't taken a bite of the muffin for some time now. It wasn't that good a muffin, frankly.

'Look, I said that this wasn't a slam dunk.' Mank sounded testy. Like most men, he really hates the idea of being wrong about anything. 'Let me tell you what happened: Austin was adopted in April thirty years ago. In July five years later, there was a nine-one-one call from their house. It was unclear, according to the incident report, but apparently Helen was dead. So they sent out two cruisers and found her body in the living room. She'd been beaten with a blunt object, maybe a dumbbell. Apparently Helen was into exercising and had worked out every morning with weights. This one, according to the report, was an eight-pound weight. The officers found it on the floor next to her.'

'An eight-pound weight is not light,' I noted. 'That could definitely do the job. What did Marc say when they got there?'

'Nothing. He wasn't in the house and he hasn't been seen since.'

ELEVEN

'What about the son?' Ken asked.

I was watching *Taskmaster* on my laptop and hadn't realized Ken had actually taken an interest in Austin Cobb's case. 'What son?' I asked absently.

'The son.' Oh, that cleared it up. 'The cops went to the house and found the mother dead from being beaten with an exercise weight. The father lit out for the territories and hasn't been heard from again. But they had a son. What happened to him?'

I paused the video because you really have to pay attention to some of the snide comments in the show, which are the point of watching to begin with. I looked over at my brother, who was, in fact, curling a twenty-five-pound dumbbell with his left hand. Ken knows he might need to act as the physical enforcer for our agency at any given moment, and besides, the chicks dig the biceps.

'I haven't had a lot of time to look into this yet, but from what I can tell, his name is William Hawley, and he was seven years old when this happened and was put into the custody of his aunt and uncle, Marc's brother and sister-in-law. It looks like he now works as a ticket sales representative for the Los Angeles Lakers.'

'Cool job.' Ken is easily distracted. 'When can we meet Bill?'

That surprised me. 'What's this "we" stuff, kemo sabe? This is my case. I don't need backup to go meet a ticket sales representative for a basketball team.'

He changed to the other arm. 'What do you know about basketball?'

'What do I *need* to know? I'm talking to the guy about his parents, and I'm not going to see him until I have better facts, anyway. Like, for example, any connection at all between the Hawleys and Austin Cobb.'

Ken didn't say anything, but the look on his face was equivalent to a pout. Then I realized that this was about the chance to fly to Los Angeles and talk basketball. 'I'll probably go see him at home, if I go at all,' I said. 'Which I probably won't.'

That *really* hit badly on my brother. 'Do it your way.' Seriously. I almost went into the kitchen to find a cookie I could give him.

I put down the laptop and sat back on the beat-up futon we call a sofa. It's big enough for both of us to sit and won't collapse even if Ken isn't thinking when he launches himself onto it. 'So let me ask you this: If they had another son, possibly a twin, why would they put Austin up for adoption when he was two?'

Ken stood up, got two heavier weights from his rack and started doing reverse rows. So now I was feeling guilty that I hadn't worked out in at least a week. Siblings can do things to your mind without even knowing they're doing it. 'I thought this was your case and you didn't need any help,' he managed between lifts.

'Don't be juvenile. We always bounce ideas off each other.' Granted, it's usually Ken who's asking me for help when he gets stuck, but that's not a hard-and-fast rule. 'How does that make sense?'

'Maybe it's not them,' he suggested. That was plausible, but it was also the easiest way out of the problem, to do nothing and assume there was nothing there.

'Maybe not, but it's all we have. So let's assume that Marc and Helen *were* Austin's birth parents. What would be their motivation for giving up one twin son and not the other?'

Ken did some more rows, but the fact that he wasn't talking indicated that he was actually thinking, something he tends to reserve as a last resort. 'What if they weren't twins?' he asked.

'How could they not be twins? They were in the same family and were the same age.'

Ken gave me what I'm certain he thought was a triumphant look, with a smile. 'What if one of them was adopted?' he said.

Sometimes his ideas are just nutty enough to work. Not this time though.

'So they adopted one son and put the other one up for adoption?' I said. 'Is that to keep things in balance, or what?'

He decided against more weights and went to the kitchen,

then came back with a bottle of beer because health. 'Don't rule anything out until you have proof it's not true,' Ken said. 'You limit the possibilities.'

'Thanks, Master Yoda. But what we have here is a case where we don't know for sure that these people were involved in Austin's adoption at all, and I think their having a son the same age might make it more plausible that they weren't. Which leaves us right back at our starting point, which is nothing.'

He took a long swig and looked at me as if not understanding what I'd said. 'Don't you want to know who killed Helen?' he said.

'Not especially, unless it turns out that against all odds they *were* Austin's birth parents. He's my client, not the Helen Hawley estate.'

My brother plopped down next to me on the remarkably resilient futon and drained the bottle of beer. 'Then you're leaving yourself with nothing,' he said. 'What's your next move?'

'I'm gonna put a tail on Malcolm X. Mitchell,' I said.

'Of course you are.' Because naturally I'd told Ken about my encounter with our alleged sibling earlier that day.

Actually I had already done that and a bit more. When Malcolm had – finally – left my office, I'd put in a call to my friend Barry Polk, a classmate when I was in the criminal justice program at Fordham University. We'd reconnected about a month earlier. Barry now had a wife and a child and, as it happened, lived three doors down from the building where our offices were located. He was working for a detective agency that specialized in proving your spouse is cheating and was interested in some freelance work. So I gave it to him.

'There's a skinny guy in a W.H.O. t-shirt walking out of my office right now,' I said. 'Let me know where he goes.'

One thing you have to love about Barry is his total lack of propriety. 'On it,' he said, and hung up.

It was some hours later now and I hadn't heard back, so I figured it was time to check in with Barry. But his phone went straight to voicemail. I didn't care for that. 'The guy I sent after Malcolm isn't answering,' I said to Ken.

'How long's it been?'

'Maybe five hours.'

'That's not bad,' my brother said. 'He could just be doing other stuff. Maybe he followed Malcolm home and went to a movie. I realize this is usually the part where you and I find a dead body somewhere, but that probably won't happen this time.'

He was kidding, sort of, but the point wasn't lost on me. We didn't know how dangerous Malcolm Mitchell really was. I'd run online searches of the name and come up with very little, although apparently a football player and a poet each were called Malcolm Mitchell. But there were photos, and neither of them was the one who had sauntered into my office this afternoon.

'You had to say that?' I scolded him.

'I didn't *mean* it.' There are times I think my brother never really got past being eight years old.

'Should I call his wife?' Not that I had the vaguest idea of what her phone number might be.

'No. It's been five hours. When it's five days, then you call his wife.'

But I couldn't leave it alone. I had sent Barry out on a job and he hadn't gotten back to me. I had no idea how dangerous Malcolm Mitchell could be. Mom had warned me in an email months ago to avoid him at all costs, and now both Ken and I had been in close contact with the guy in the course of two days. This, and we were supposed to be on a special security alert. How could I have been so stupid?

I texted Barry: **Just let me know you're alive.**

Suddenly *Taskmaster* wasn't as amusing as it had been before.

TWELVE

I didn't hear anything from Barry the rest of that night, and now I was actively concerned.

Ken had to be rousted out of bed in the morning, something I'm used to doing, and even he was worried when he heard that Barry hadn't checked in yet. He acted like it was no big deal, but he kept glancing at me as if wondering how I'd react when the bad news came in.

I decided I was a detective and if I wanted to know what had happened, I had ways to find out. But exactly what those methods might be was proving to be a little elusive this morning. I checked public records of bodies delivered to New York City morgues the previous night and didn't find anything that set off any alarms.

Then I called Barry's office and was told he'd called in the night before to take a personal day. They would not, or could not, give me his wife's phone number.

Some time was spent trying to remember the name of Barry's wife (Sandra? Cynthia?) to no avail. There were only so many Polks listed in that section of Manhattan, but fifty-four is not a small number and calling a woman to ask if her husband was alive seemed a little ghoulish even for me.

After a while I had to concentrate on Austin Cobb because I couldn't think of anything else to do. I asked Mank (via text) to forward me the incident report from Arlington, New Jersey, twenty-five years earlier just so I could have a look. He, being a cop, refused. But it was a matter of public record, so I could look it up online. It just would have been easier if the guy who wanted to get back to dating me had thought to cut me a break. Men.

The Arlington Police Department's report didn't include a whole lot that wasn't in Mank's snappy synopsis from the day before. Officers Benson and Crawford arrived on the scene, discovered the body of a Caucasian female, approximately forty to fifty years of age, with repeated trauma to the left side of the skull, made with an eight-pound dumbbell, bearing pieces of skull and hair matching that of the victim, next to the body. There had been considerable loss of blood. No one else was found inside the building, although a thorough search of the premises was made. Medical assistance was summoned, but the officers could find no pulse or respiration on initial examination. Medical personnel arrived six minutes later, and the body was placed on a gurney and removed after Detective P. Monroe had arrived and conferred with Medical Examiner Willis.

The body had subsequently (according to the report) been identified as that of Helen Hawley (nee Adubato), one of the owners of the home. The co-owner, her husband Marc, and their son William were not present. William was later located at the home of a friend, Tyler Costigan, whose parents Lawrence and Denise Costigan told the officers he had been invited over for a 'play date.' William was brought to the home of his aunt and uncle, Howard and Janet Hawley, while his father was being sought. (P.S. I contacted the Costigans later. That was the extent of their involvement.)

There'll be a quiz on all these names later. Study up. One thing was certain: what happened to Helen was no accident, and it was not self-inflicted. OK, two things.

And yet Barry had not yet called in. I tried his number again and got the same result: voicemail. The longer it went on, the tighter my stomach felt.

The only thing to do, focusing once again on the business at hand, was to try and track down Howard and Janet, possibly Bill Hawley, and see what they might remember from the time. It had been a good number of years, so possibly the trauma had faded, but in any event, they knew something I needed to know: Did Helen and Marc give their son up for the Cobbs to adopt five years before Helen was killed?

My phone rang and I grabbed at it, hoping to see Barry's name on the screen, but it was Igavda from the office. I answered and said, 'Is something wrong, Igavda?'

'No, Mrs Fran.' You can't talk to some people. 'But someone called looking for you. A lady. She sound maybe worried.'

My stomach tightened up more. 'Did she tell you her name?' I asked.

'Yeah.' That part of English Igavda has down flat. She talks to Ken too much. 'Her name is Sarah Polk.'

Just as I feared. Barry's wife.

'Give me the number,' I told Igavda.

The fact was, Sarah Polk didn't sound 'maybe worried' at all. Truthfully, she sounded just a little amused. But she had not heard from her husband since the day before when he'd told her he was off to do some work for an old friend from college. Guess who. He told her the name of my agency to prove it was legitimate work because, she said, he did like to take the occasional day off to do some online gambling.

'Does he have a problem?' I asked. What the hell, you talk to a woman on the phone for two minutes, you might as well ask her about possible problems in her marriage to a man you knew two degrees and three jobs ago.

'I don't think so,' Sarah answered. 'But he usually doesn't stay out all night, so I was wondering what kind of job you were asking him to do.'

'I wanted him to follow someone for a case I'm working,' I said, more or less truthfully. 'I don't believe the guy is especially dangerous.' But I was realizing with each passing minute that I had no idea about that at all.

'Barry didn't seem worried,' Sarah said. 'But if the person you wanted him to follow was traveling or staying somewhere all night, he might have stayed after him to report back.'

Well, yeah, he could be staking out a place where Malcolm was holing up, but I hadn't asked him to do that. I just wanted to know where Malcolm went. 'But I haven't heard from him and neither have you,' I pointed out, largely because Sarah didn't seem concerned enough and it was clearly my job to alarm her as much as possible. 'I've tried calling him a number of times and I—'

'You keep getting voicemail.' How can you tell when a person is smiling over the phone? 'That's Barry. When he's on a job, he doesn't even look at his phone no matter how much it buzzes. It used to drive me nuts.'

'Well, I'm sorry I can't tell you where he is right now,' I

told her. 'If you hear from him, will you tell him to call me? I'm kind of worried.'

Sarah chuckled. 'Don't be. Barry is being Barry.'

I put down the phone and, oddly, I didn't feel better. I texted, of all people, my brother.

How do I track a guy who was following a guy if I don't know where the guy went?

Ken, being the invaluable asset he is, sent back, **I thought you were the brains of the operation.**

I will not tell you what I texted back. You would think less of me.

THIRTEEN

Janet Hawley was a very neat woman in her fifties, wearing well-pressed clothing and sitting in her immaculate West Orange, New Jersey, living room. She looked like someone whose day would be ruined if a cookie crumb so much as hit the carpet under her coffee table. So I didn't accept the scone she offered.

It hasn't been difficult to find Janet. She and her husband Howard had divorced in the early tens (specifically 2011) and Howard had passed away from a heart attack seven years later. Her nephew Bill had moved to California, she said, and, yes, was working as a ticket sales representative for the Los Angeles Lakers. At least the story checked out.

'Billy was naturally very upset when he first came to us,' she said once I'd given her a vague idea of why I was there (without mentioning Austin). 'It was a very difficult time for all of us.'

I had no doubt that had been the case, but it wasn't answering the question I'd asked, which had been about the state of Marc and Helen Hawley's marriage. Marc was Howard Hawley's brother, and since they lived near each other, I had begun with the assumption that the brothers were close. Janet's manner indicated otherwise, but her ex-husband was dead. They were divorced years before that and that can dredge up a lot of feelings, few of them rosy. I pressed on.

'As I was saying, when all this happened, were Marc and Helen getting along? I'm told there might have been some tension, and I'm wondering if that affected Bill at all.' You can drop in the hint that a man might have bludgeoned his wife to death while making it sound like you're really concerned about their poor young son.

'What are you implying?' Suddenly Janet's tone was sharper and less welcoming. Sometimes you can't hide the nasty motive for your question after all. But it had needed to be asked. 'You're asking if Marc killed Helen.'

'I don't think I was asking that,' I told her. I had definitely been asking that. 'I'm really more interested in something other than Helen's death. I'm working for a client who might or might not have been related to them and he's the reason I'm here today.' All that was true, but I did still want to know what had happened to Helen Hawley. You don't get into the investigation business if you're not at least a little nosy.

'Who is your client?' Janet asked, just a fraction of the hostility out of her voice.

'I'm not at liberty to give his name away, but you can help me if you can answer one question: Did Marc and Helen have any children other than Bill?'

That seemed not just to surprise Janet but to totally baffle her. 'Other children? No!' But her pulse rate had quickened and her respiration was up. She was lying. (Yes, Ken and I can tell, mostly through sound. Don't lie if you ever meet me; I'll know.) 'What would make you ask such a thing?' If she'd been wearing pearls, she'd have clutched them.

'I'm sorry,' I said, when I was not the least bit sorry. 'I guess the information I got from the adoption agency was incorrect.'

As you well know, I had gotten no information at all from the adoption agency. But if I let that slip to Janet, who clearly was sitting on some details she didn't want to divulge, I could stir things up a little. That's usually a decent way to move toward progress in a case. Get the other people to do your work for you when you can't make a connection on your own. They didn't teach me that at Fordham, but I've learned it over the years. Once it almost got me killed. You don't get results like that without ruffling a few feathers.

'Adoption agency? What adoption agency?' Janet didn't stand, but she shifted on the very neat chair she was using, which for her was something akin to a panic attack. Janet clearly prided herself on being as composed as Beethoven's Concerto No. 5.

I tried very hard to limit my smile to the 'confidential' side and short of 'smug.' 'I'm really not able to tell you that. The information I have was meant to be confidential. But I suppose it doesn't matter, because if Marc and Helen didn't have another son, what I was told was obviously incorrect.'

I came wanting to find out about Bill Hawley and if he had a twin brother who somehow became Austin Cobb. It seemed unlikely, since Marc and Helen were clearly not Black people and Austin is a man of color. But there definitely was something that was not being said about this whole entanglement and that made me want to work a little harder on Janet.

It was working. Her jaw was just a hair short of clenched and her eyes were flirting with the idea of being wild. But she was composed, dammit. She'd always stay composed. She spoke verrrrry slooooowly and with careful diction.

'It must have been, because there certainly wasn't another son,' she said. It took a while to get all that out, but she managed. 'Billy does not have a brother and never did. What could possibly have given your resource that ridiculous idea?'

If she wanted to think I was a ditz who didn't know how to conduct an investigation, I was willing to let her believe it. If it got me what I wanted. I fluttered my hands just a little to enhance the effect. 'Oh, there were some adoption records, but I think it's clear the files have been mixed up. I'm sorry to have wasted your time.' I stood up and Janet craned her neck to keep me in her sights, but the last thing she wanted at this moment was for me to leave without telling her anything she could use.

'Adoption records?' I can't tell a person's blood pressure from across the room, but I'd have bet serious coin that Janet's was rising as she spoke.

'The wrong ones, of course. Thank you for your time and patience, Mrs Hawley,' I said. There wasn't a chance in hell I'd be leaving in the next couple of minutes. Janet would have barred the door and held me in check with a carving knife if necessary, but I also had no intention of going.

'Please, call me Janet. Sit down, Ms Stein. I'm so curious as to how this mistake – and of course it *is* a mistake – might have been made.'

'Call me Fran,' I said, but I didn't sit. Let her sweat a little longer. 'Have you heard from Marc since the night Bill came to stay with you?' No sense in bringing up the murder when it wasn't necessary. I could hang onto that until it would be useful.

But Janet's eyes got thinner all of a sudden. 'What does that have to do with a mistake from some adoption agency?' I felt like I was in a 1940s film noir and she was about to become the femme fatale. Then I remembered I was way more fatale than Janet was and relaxed.

'I'm trying to piece out how they might have gotten incorrect information. No one seems to have heard from Marc since then. When I'm investigating a case and a red herring shows up, it's usually because someone heard from someone who heard from someone along the way and information was unintentionally twisted out of shape. I thought if anyone had heard from Marc, there might have been some misinformation about how that happened and what was said. So, have you heard from him in any way since that day?'

Her eyes returned to their normal shape, but suddenly her lips were thinner. Apparently the features of Janet's face gained and lost weight depending on her immediate mood. I gain weight depending on my immediate mood because I eat ice cream. Then I have to work it off.

'No,' she said and her tone could have defined the word *flat* in an online dictionary. And that was it.

I put my hand to my face and stroked my lower lip to look thoughtful. Don't knock it. 'Well, I suppose that's not how they got bad information. The adoption was *probably* legal, but now we'll have to retrace all our steps carefully.'

It seemed that someone examining every facet of some adoption (as yet unnamed) was the last thing Janet wanted to see happen. 'How do you go about doing that?' she asked, as if she were actually interested in my work, as opposed to whatever it was she really did care about. 'Looking into an adoption that took place so long ago?'

Stirring things up is something I do in investigations. I don't do it in the kitchen. Right now I was doing some pretty expert mixing of ingredients, I thought. But Janet, while she was clearly agitated, was not telling me anything I didn't already know, so it was time to increase the pressure just a little. Or maybe more than a little.

'Well, under normal circumstances the adoption agency records, coupled with the memory of the adoptee and his adoptive parents, would be enough,' I said, as if thinking about it for the first time. 'But in this case that's not possible because the adoption records are sealed by the agency and all participants have been made to sign non-disclosure forms. I had to go beyond the usual sources. It makes you think that there was something a little bit unusual going on at the time.'

I let that hang in the air for a bit so Janet could breathe it in. She clearly didn't care for how it smelled.

'So, what do you do when that happens?' she asked. I almost called up the New Jersey State Police website on my phone to let her see the private investigator license application, since she seemed so interested in learning about my profession that it was possible she wanted to join. But sarcastic gestures weren't going to help my cause, enjoyable though they might be.

'Oh, I have a few tricks up my sleeve,' I told her. 'Would you say you and Helen were close?'

Janet looked like I'd asked if she had been friends with a rabid skunk. 'Not at all. The brothers were close, Howard and Marc. I don't think I ever set foot in Helen's house at all. They always came here.'

OK . . .

This time I took a legit step toward the door. 'And I think I've taken up enough of your time, Janet. You've been very kind.'

I was facing away from her, but I'm pretty sure I heard Janet's teeth grinding. 'No, I'm not tired at all,' she said, despite the fact that I hadn't suggested she was tired.

'Got to get back to my office,' I said with as breezy a tone as I could manage. 'Thank you so much for seeing me.' I walked to the door, and if Janet thought she could physically obstruct me, she had disabused herself of that notion as soon as I'd stood up.

'Let me know what you find out,' she suggested, but that was weak and she knew it. She had no connection to whatever fictional case she thought I was investigating.

We both knew something was up with Bill Hawley and with Austin Cobb's adoption. And now that she knew I was suspicious, she'd start making phone calls to . . . I dunno. People.

The wheels were just beginning to spin.

FOURTEEN

In the bus on my way back to New York, I checked in with Ken. He was, uncharacteristically, in the office and asked Igavda if we'd heard from Sarah Polk. We had not. I didn't like that lack of development. It had been almost twenty-four hours since I'd asked Barry to follow Malcolm Mitchell.

'I don't want to think I sent a man with a wife and a small child out to die,' I told my brother. 'I think there's only one thing for us to do.'

Ken, who was concerned and trying not to sound like he was, clicked a couple of things on his phone just to show me how nonchalant he was being. 'What's that?' he asked.

'You need to find Malcolm X. Mitchell,' I said.

I heard his desk chair squeak as he sat up quickly. It's a dangerous move for a man my brother's size. 'Me?'

'You.' It's not easy to have a conversation like this one on a bus. It wasn't packed, but there were other people, and I wasn't crazy about them hearing everything I was doing. On the other hand, this went way beyond texting and I wanted Ken to get going immediately so my mind could stop obsessing on Barry. 'It doesn't matter if you're seen. You're certainly capable of handling old Malcolm physically. And you have tracked down people before. So go find Malcolm Mitchell and get him to tell you where Barry is.'

My brother let out a sigh that would kill a normal man. He has very large lungs. 'There's no point in arguing with you about this, is there?' he said.

'None.'

There was a long pause. Then, 'OK, so given that the only times we've seen this guy he came to us, and the person you sent to follow him has vanished, how do you propose I locate him?'

'You're a professional investigator,' I answered. 'You'll think of something.'

Then I hung up.

Nobody on the bus was paying any attention to me, which is something to say when you look like I do. Usually I'll get at least the odd curious stare. The occasional lech might be ogling a particular area of my anatomy. Not now. Things have changed since smartphones.

Since I had some time on my hands and had delegated the thing I was most worried about to my brother, I could concentrate on Austin Cobb and his adoption, which was seeming more skeezy by the minute. I'd left the ball in Janet Hawley's court, and if I were any judge of human behavior (being very close to an actual human myself), she'd have already begun sending off alarms and stirring up dust . . . but among whom?

Her husband at the time of the murder and the adoption was dead. So was her sister-in-law. Her brother-in-law was missing and had been assumedly on the run for twenty-five years. Her nephew, on the other hand, was not. The best next step was probably to locate and contact Bill Hawley. In all likelihood his aunt/mother (or however he'd identify Janet) had already contacted him about the huge lady asking questions about his alleged sibling and what that meant. He'd be on his guard. Or maybe he didn't know anything at all. So yes, I'd get in touch and get a sense of Bill, but maybe let him settle in a bit first. There had to be more than just him to look into.

Now that I knew who I was talking about and when (or thought I knew), I could start searching for neurologists and psychologists who might have seen Austin before his adoption. But that was something I wasn't going to do on the bus.

So . . . some employment records are made public. Those relating to private adoption agencies are not among them. But I'd been working with adoption agencies, both governmental and private, for some time now, and I'd gotten to know a few people.

One of them was Esmerelda Rodriguez-Cohen, who worked for a very reputable agency whose name I will not mention here because she asked me not to. Esme got into her line of work not just because she had to make a living but because she truly wanted to help people – chiefly children – who needed a better life. She was very good at seeing to it that they got one. But from my point of view, her most valuable quality was that she had been doing this a very long time and she knew *everybody*.

I moved to a seat farther back in the bus just to be away from any possibly curious ears. It's one thing if I'm doing something on the fringes of the rules. It's another if I'm asking someone else to do so. Particularly someone like Esme. See above.

'Fran Stein!' Esme's cheerful voice, which was like that all the time, was a welcome relief after having spent an hour talking to Janet Hawley. 'What's the latest with you and that cop?'

I had made the mistake of letting it slip that I was dating a detective without mentioning any names and now I was living with the consequences of that mistake. 'It's kind of iffy right now, Esme.'

'A shame.' Once she'd married Emanuel Cohen and had two children thirty years ago, Esme had decided she was a Jewish mother, and she was playing the role to the hilt. 'You need a nice guy, Fran.'

'I'm working on it, Es,' I said. 'I'll keep you informed.'

She let a couple of seconds pass, which was unusual for Esme. 'You're saying this is a business call,' she said. Given that every call I'd ever made to Esme was a business call, that was a pretty safe assumption. But what she meant was that I was not in the mood to *kibitz*, as she'd say, and she was right. 'What do you need, Fran?'

You could always count on Esme, or at least, I could. 'There's a guy who's a client of mine,' I started. 'His adoption went through Friendly Family. As far as I can tell they're pretty legit.'

'I haven't heard anything especially shady about them,' Esme said. She wasn't committing, but she didn't have anything bad to tell me.

'That's what I thought. But his adoption, and this was thirty years ago, was basically sealed like a federal indictment and all the principals were essentially sworn to secrecy. I can't find out anything, even from his adoptive parents. They seem terrified someone will find out they talked to me.'

Esme was quiet. Esme is never quiet. 'There's something you're not telling me,' she said.

'Yeah, there is. I'm told that there's evidence one of the birth parents is dead. And that the death might not have been from natural causes.'

'Whoa.'

'Yeah. And I found that about five years after the adoption took place, a woman in the town where my client says he grew up was murdered, and her husband, who was the prime suspect, vanished into thin air, still not found to this day.' I let that sink in with Esme, who likes nothing better than a good story and is disturbed by a bad one.

'That's a lot,' she said. 'But I don't know how I can help you.'

I took in a breath. 'I'm wondering if you know of anyone who was working for Friendly Family around that time who I might talk to,' I said in one gush.

'Oy,' Esme said. Sometimes she overplays the role. 'I'm really not supposed to do this, Fran.'

'I know. But it was thirty years ago. I'm thinking maybe you might know someone who retired from there and so isn't bound by any non-disclosure agreement anymore.'

'They'd still be bound by it and you know that.' She was right; I did.

'Well, maybe you know someone who wouldn't care.'

Esme thought. 'Mebbe,' she said. 'But I don't like it.'

'Neither do I,' I assured her. 'Suppose you call this person and ask if it's OK. If they say no, it's no.'

There was a short, barky laugh on the other phone. 'That's sort of a given, Fran.'

'But you do know someone, don't you?' Esme always knew someone. If she ever retired, I would probably have to hire her as an associate. Actually, that wasn't a bad idea.

'I'll let you know,' she said, and hung up.

It took only twenty minutes for her to call me back. 'She'll talk to you, but it has to be in person, and it has to be somewhere she feels safe, so her place of business.'

Everyone this woman worked with would hear what was going on. 'That's safe?' I said.

'You want the help, or not?'

I did, so we set up a meeting at a liquor store for the next day. Which was just as well because my bus was about to enter the Lincoln Tunnel heading back to Manhattan.

'I owe you yet another one, Esme,' I said. 'This could really help me break this case.'

'Mazel tov,' Esme said.

FIFTEEN

Ken called me at seven that evening and told me he had a lead on Malcolm Mitchell, but that it didn't include Barry, 'necessarily.' Which didn't help me much. I asked him where he thought Malcolm was, and my brother, being my brother, said that he'd let me know when he found out if he was right.

'Just don't go missing on me yourself,' I warned him. 'Keep your phone charged and keep yourself charged.'

'I charged yesterday. I'm probably good until the end of the week.'

I moaned a little. 'You *know* what I'm saying.'

'I'll keep you informed,' he said, and hung up because why say goodbye if you didn't have to? That's what siblings are for; you can be rude to them because they have to put up with you anyway.

But this was the second night Barry Polk was off the grid and I wasn't comfortable leaving that matter solely to Ken. I texted Mank and asked if we could meet. He sent back a message implying that I was using him for cop info, and I didn't deny it. But I said I'd buy him dinner, so he accepted.

Since I had already 'come out' to Mank and had mentioned Malcolm Mitchell (and his alleged connection to my parents) to him before, I didn't have to be cagey about the subject once we settled into our chairs at *Magnifico!*, a fairly standard Italian restaurant in our mutual (my apartment, his precinct) neighborhood. I hadn't been here often enough to be considered a 'regular,' and nobody greeted us by name when we walked in. But *Magnifico!*, despite its name, was not so crowded as to require reservations, so we were seated right away, ordered fairly quickly and got down to what I had decided was strictly business.

'I'm worried about a friend,' I said at the beginning. 'Actually, he's kind of a colleague. I knew him at college and asked him to do some work for me yesterday. And he hasn't been heard from since. His phone goes to voicemail. His wife hasn't heard from him. I don't want to think I sent him to his doom, but the possibility exists, and I wonder if you can check with hospitals and morgues around the city to see if he's shown up anywhere. Jails too, I guess. I never know who you guys are going to arrest next.'

'You sure know how to get a cop on your side.' Mank had a snide side to him. Luckily, I speak fluent Snide.

'I was trying to communicate how important this is to me. I haven't been able to think of anything else since he's been missing.' Breadsticks are a waste of bread. Bring real bread to the table. Sticks are dry and unnecessary.

Luckily, our server brought a lovely loaf of warm Italian bread as we ignored the breadsticks (in a paper bag that indicated they were bought, not made on the premises) as we had been doing. But I dove into the bread. Perhaps this was diminishing the urgency of my message to Mank, that I was distraught over Barry's disappearance and had been for over a day.

'So this guy is a colleague?' Mank had a slight look of skepticism on his face and he wasn't even tearing off a piece of bread yet. It was fabulous with olive oil on it.

'Don't get jealous,' I said. 'He's someone I know from college and a fellow investigator. And he has a wife and a child.'

'I wasn't jealous. I was curious. I know we're just . . . colleagues now. Professional acquaintances.'

'We are not that and never will be,' I told him. 'But it's beside the point. Can you help me find my friend?'

'No. You haven't told me his name.'

Now, pasta is a wonderful thing. It doesn't have cholesterol (if you don't count the cheese) and it is more satisfying than any other type of food. Actual Italians from Italy think of it as one course that is a lead-in to the entrée, but pasta has been the star attraction of many a meal I've eaten, like, for example, the one I was eating now. Rigatoni ala Bolognese. If I weren't so torn up about Barry, it would have been the perfect dinner. And even now it was pretty close.

Needless to say, I gave him Barry's name and whatever contact information (and physical description) I could muster.

I hadn't seen him regularly in years and only briefly when we'd met recently. I was operating mainly on memory. But I knew his name and phone number for sure.

'Give me a couple of minutes,' Mank said, temporarily ignoring his eggplant parmigiana. He picked up his phone, which has a screen larger than my iPhone SE (which, frankly, looks ridiculously small in my hands) and started plugging away.

'You don't have to do this right away,' I said. 'It can wait until later.' Honestly, I preferred it happen immediately, but I didn't want to come across that way.

Mank stared at his screen and didn't look away to make eye contact. 'I am trying to be incredibly impressive,' he said, with a tone that indicated that should have been obvious.

'And doing a hell of a job.' I concentrated on the rigatoni for a while so as not to distract him.

But as I was doing so I also happened to glance out through the front window of *Magnifico!* and noticed a skinny man with a wispy goatee who was wearing a white t-shirt whose black legend read W.H.O. Not the band, the World Health Organization. A man who looked eerily like – although he was not – Malcolm X. Mitchell.

Maybe it was a franchise operation. There were Malcolm X. Mitchells all over the city, annoying perfectly respectable private investigators who happened to be semi-superbeings. It was possible. 'I'll be right back,' I said to Mank, who was deep into his phone and didn't even nod.

I headed for the front door and opened it. The faux Malcolm was about half a block away by now, alone, and did not seem to be looking in my direction. Maybe he wasn't *my* Malcolm and was searching for his designated person to harass. But there was only one way to find out, so I picked up my pace and let out my already-long stride a little. I had come up next to him in less than a minute.

'Malcolm,' I said in a conversational tone anyone would use, just to see if he'd react.

He did not. And it wasn't because I hadn't spoken loudly enough. Maybe he was going by a different fake name.

This was no time for subtlety. If he knew where Barry was,

I wanted to find out, now. I stepped directly in front of him and turned to face the guy. He looked startled, which was expected, but also pleased, which was not.

'Where'd you get that t-shirt?' I asked him. I pointed at the shirt, in case he didn't know that I meant the one he had on.

His voice was a little reedy and nasal. He could have used a good decongestant. 'This?' Clearly that was a time-buying device. He wasn't wearing two t-shirts. 'I used to have a roommate who worked for them.' A little line of perspiration appeared at his hairline. It wasn't that warm out and I was the one who had been walking fast, not him.

'No, you didn't,' I said. 'Does the name Malcolm Mitchell mean anything to you?' I wasn't going to give him Barry's name if he didn't already know it. The man was in enough trouble already.

'No,' the guy said. 'Is it supposed to?'

'He's the only other person I've ever seen wearing a shirt like that,' I told him. People were passing us on the street and faux Malcolm definitely wanted to join them. 'So tell me, without lying, where did you get that shirt, and do you know Malcolm Mitchell?' I was determined not to use the 'X' because I'd decided that was a disrespectful affectation.

The guy in the t-shirt blinked, and if it was possible for eyes to spin in their sockets, his definitely would have been doing so. 'I don't know what you're talking about. I got this shirt from my old roommate and I don't know your Malcolm guy. Now, I've gotta get going.' He tried, fairly vehemently, to do an end run around me, but I wasn't having it.

'What's your name?' I said. Maybe I could bust the franchise that way and see if his name was Rosa X. Parks or Martin X. Luther King.

'I don't want to tell you,' he whined. 'You're crazy.'

What? *I* was the one who was crazy? Just because I was stopping strangers in the street due to their choice of casual wear? Because I thought everyone wearing a certain t-shirt was involved in a criminal conspiracy endangering an almost-forgotten friend of mine? Because the absence of that acquaintance was eating away at me beyond all reason? That made me crazy?

Wow.

'Sorry,' I said, and stepped aside. T-shirt Guy gave me a quick frightened glance and went on his way. I stood there for a moment and let New Yorkers pass me until I remembered from where I'd come and walked back down the street to *Magnifico!*.

Mank had barely moved and just glanced up when I came in and resumed my seat at the table. The rigatoni was getting cold, but then, so was his eggplant parm. He looked up at me, something he's used to doing (Mank is a good eight inches shorter than I am). Then he pointed at his phone.

'I have good news and bad news for you,' he said, and my stomach sank to my ankles.

'Give me the bad news first,' I said.

'I don't know where your friend Barry is,' he said. That was the bad news? I'd expected that.

'What's the good news?'

'He's not in any morgue or hospital in the city, and he hasn't been arrested,' Mank said.

OK, that was good. It wasn't great, because it left open a lot of bad possibilities, but it had eliminated many of the worst ones. 'That is good,' I conceded. 'I have news, too.'

'What's your news?' Mank asked me.

'I think I'm losing my mind.'

'Welcome to New York.'

SIXTEEN

The management at *Magnifico!* had been gracious and understanding enough to heat up our dinners, which were very good. And Mank had heard my story of the non-affiliated Malcolm and shaken his head. 'You're not losing your mind. You're just worried about your friend.'

'He's not even that good a friend.'

Mank smiled, which is something he's very good at. 'You've owned your business for a few years now, but you're not used to being responsible for anyone but yourself and Ken. And you know for a fact that the two of you can take care of yourselves. So this is scaring you because you don't want it to be your fault.'

'It *is* my fault.' I can do maudlin as well as the next girl.

But Mank responded exactly the way I wanted him to. 'No, it's not,' he said. 'You called a friend, a professional, and asked him to do some work for you, for which you plan to pay him. He accepted the job knowing the circumstances and went off to do it. You don't know what happened. In fact, you don't know that *anything* happened. You need to let yourself off the hook and enjoy some reheated pasta.' And his smile was so warm, so understanding, that I could have killed him for making me not want to date him anymore.

'I hate it when you make sense,' I told him. Complying with his advice, I took a forkful of the rigatoni, for which I had regained something of an appetite.

Just as it made its way into my mouth, Mank said, 'So what's this I hear about you dating Bendix?'

Because I was not in a 1940s B-movie, I did not spit out the food in my mouth, but I'm sure my eyes got as wide as silver dollar pancakes and I felt my face flush with mortification. I forced myself to finish the bite of rigatoni and wiped my mouth while I regained normal breath. 'That is so not happening,' I said.

Mank laughed, and I could tell he was sorry for having presented it in that way. 'I apologize,' he said. 'But Bendix was so proud of himself for talking you into going to this wedding I thought he was going to declare himself king and insist we all pay homage to his greatness and give him an orb to fondle.'

My face went from flushed to pale as a white sheet, I'm sure. 'Bendix told—'

'*Everybody.*'

'He told me about this wedding for his sister-in-law's cousin or something and I told him I'd check my calendar because telling him it would make me regurgitate my lunch to even consider the proposition seemed somehow impolite. I *never* said I would go.'

'Well, Bendix thinks you're going,' Mank said. He was halfway through the eggplant parm and I thought I might never eat again. 'You're gonna have to tell him you're not.'

'I just got done tracking a man for wearing a t-shirt,' I reminded him. 'I don't think my social skills are necessarily at their highest level right now. Why don't you tell him we're dating again and you'd be offended if he went on a date with me? Isn't that some macho male nonsense that you guys think is a code or something?'

Mank looked my face over carefully. '*Are* we dating again?' he asked.

'What does that have to do with it?'

He scowled. 'Quite a bit. I mean, I'm not going to tell Meal he can't ask you out no matter what because when did I get the right to do that, but it does matter to me what the status of our relationship is.' The cops call Bendix 'Meal' because his name is Emil and they say he has never missed a meal in his life. It's body shaming and unfair, but Bendix is one guy who comes close to deserving it. And besides, they're cops.

'I can't give you an answer on that right now,' I told Mank. 'I've got heightened security stuff and I shouldn't even be here with you now, but I like you, and—'

'And you wanted me to look some stuff up on the department's site, isn't that about right, Fran?' Mank looked tired all of a sudden. 'Sometimes I think that *is* the status of our relationship.'

Neither of us got up and left, but the rest of the dinner was considerably quieter than at the beginning.

Ken, because he's so considerate, didn't get back to me until 11:30 that night, when I was pacing the floor of our living 'room' and considering calling Mank back to put out a missing person report on my brother. And the only reason I didn't was that Ken hadn't been missing for twenty-four hours. He'd been missing for some hours. That was less.

The text came in as I was charging, lying in my bed and connected to the wall outlet with the help of a charging cable that connected to the USB port under my left arm. Emotional stress can drain me as much as physical activity. I'd never asked Ken about that because he doesn't have emotional stress and he loves physical activity. But that's for another time.

Have tracked Malcolm to AC. Probably spending the night here.

AC? Who was AC? Al Capone had been dead for quite some time. Abbott and Costello were equally deceased. Why hadn't my brother mentioned Barry? Was Barry no longer following Malcolm? Did that mean . . . what did that mean?

Who's AC? I sent back.

Ken sent back an eye-rolling emoji. **Atlantic City.**

Oh.

I didn't want to call Ken in case Malcolm was nearby and would see or hear my brother on his phone. Texting was the best way to communicate, if I hadn't been trying to talk to my idiot brother, who liked to send back cryptic messages because he thought he was funny. But if I was earnest and straightforward . . .

Why is Malcolm in Atlantic City? Where's Barry?

Why is the Eiffel Tower in Paris? Where's Waldo? For some reason my parents had gone ahead and made Ken first. We might never know why.

It's been swell, I sent back and put my phone on silent. I should have charged it, too, but charging me takes priority. I think that's only fair. At least I knew Ken wasn't missing. He was just a pain in the butt. There's comfort in consistency.

But then my phone actually rang, which startled me to the

point of sitting up. I wasn't fully charged yet, but I wasn't fatigued anymore. The sudden call was probably a tiny drain on my energy, but I was still plugged in. I reached for my phone, which was at thirty-four percent.

The screen registered UNKNOWN CALLER, which is always an enormous help. Thanks, technology. Was this just some robocall, at this hour? It seemed unlikely. It wasn't Ken or Barry, both of whom would have registered in my contacts. I took the chance and answered the call, if only to make the ringtone stop. Why did I choose that ringtone?

The voice on the other end, a male voice I did not recognize, did not wait for me to speak. 'Stop asking about Helen Hawley. There was no adoption. You have nothing.' Well, those were three unconnected statements, as far as I could tell.

'Who is this?' I asked. Oh, like you could have thought of something better.

'It's Jack. Keep nosing around and something bad could happen to you.'

And he hung up.

Jack. Who was Jack? He'd just called me randomly and threatened my life? Could Marc Hawley have been using that name now? Was that possible? What a major break in the case that would be!

Wait. Had he threatened my life just now?

SEVENTEEN

The blocked number that had called my phone was untraceable, probably even by the police, so I didn't call Mank right away. I wasn't sure if we were still talking to each other. I texted my brother, but he didn't answer. Either he was hot on Malcolm Mitchell's trail or one of the waitresses in the casino had caught his . . . attention. I couldn't be sure.

Well, I had counted on Janet Hawley to shake things up, and apparently she had done so very efficiently. I'll admit I wasn't immediately terrified by what 'Jack' had said, because it had been vague and I'm pretty good at taking care of myself, but I did want to alert Ken that now we had to be even *more* vigilant about our personal security. If such a thing were possible.

Even though I wasn't cowering in fear at the thought of Marc Hawley (or whoever that was on the phone) coming after me with a grudge, I wasn't going to sleep tonight, or at least not for a while. Adrenaline doesn't care if you're really worried or not once it starts flowing. So I decided to use the limited information I had about Austin Cobb's adoption and Helen Hawley's murder to find any intersections, and maybe make some progress in what had been, until now, a damned frustrating case.

I'd looked into Helen's murder via public records on the case as soon as Mank had mentioned her name. The medical examiner's report had been clear: death had been caused by repeated trauma to the cranium, almost certainly inflicted with an eight-pound dumbbell, and we don't mean a tiny baby who wasn't too bright. The object in question had traces of hair, blood and other materials (skull) on it, leaving virtually no doubt as to what had happened. The only question left was who had bashed in Helen's head, and why. Two questions.

Marc, of course, was the prime suspect, but I've seen prime suspects come and go without being actually guilty. Some of them. OK, one so far. That didn't mean he was a raving serial killer, particularly since he wasn't listed as a suspect in any other crime. That didn't mean a whole lot either, since nobody knew where Marc was or had been for the past twenty-five years.

Except, it seemed, for his sister-in-law, Janet. Because there wasn't anyone else who could have called him and warned him about some very tall (but gorgeous) woman asking questions about his late wife and his adopted son.

Oh, and before you conclude that some massive plot twist is on its way, the police and the medical examiner at the time of the murder had confirmed beyond question the fact that the body on the floor was definitely that of Helen (Adubato) Hawley. This was a straightforward unsolved case.

What I needed to know included: Were there birth certificates on record for Bill Hawley and/or any other child Marc and Helen might have had? Just on an off chance, were there records of any other adoptions by the Hawleys *not* coordinated by Friendly Family? (It seemed very unlikely, but you have to check everything.) Were there lots of hand weights in the house, or did the killer have to bring the eight-pounder with him, as it was likely a man who had killed Helen? I'd definitely want to talk to Bill.

Those were just the first questions to come to mind. What I didn't know about this case could fill an online encyclopedia.

I began with the idea of the birth certificate(s). Those are, generally speaking, not public records and can't be tracked down online. Which is interesting, given that so many other documents, even personal ones, are easily findable, even in the form of photographic images. But rules are rules, and I wasn't aware of effective ways to break them.

There are, however, some techniques that can get around the rules without even bending them. I started with records, or at least announcements in local newspapers, showing the marriage of Helen and Marc Hawley. It took some looking, but there was a one-paragraph paid announcement in the *Observer*, a paper local to the Kearny/Arlington area. It read simply that Helen Adubato had married Marc Hawley on December 22, 1991. The wedding had apparently taken place in the Kearny town hall, presided over by Judge Amos T. Ogden. No witnesses were listed.

That wasn't much. But it was a start. Birth announcements for the time of Austin's birth (give or take, although he knew the birth date his parents had told him was accurate) did not appear in the public records or in the *Observer*. And yes, I did think to look for the name Austin Hawley. No such infant was listed.

The weirdest part was that no William Hawley was listed, either. But there was a record of a birth at a hospital near Kearny of a Harold William Hawley, and it was possible Bill had ditched his first name by choice. There was a record in the Arlington Police Department files of William being taken in by Janet and Howard, a few months after Helen's murder. So there must have been a birth certificate *then*.

The only thing to do when confronted with a problem this perplexing at this time of night was to pester my brother. I sent him another text: **Answer me. NOW.** I felt that was clear enough. An exclamation point would have been superfluous.

I was fully charged, so I unplugged myself and plugged in the phone, which seemed grateful. I got out of bed and walked – OK, wriggled, because my bedroom is small and I'm not – to the window. I like to look out when I'm thinking. Except at the apartment one floor down across the street. Don't ask.

So far I'd found no public adoption records with the Hawleys – any of them – listed as participants. That made sense if the original story was accurate, and Austin was put up for adoption through Friendly Family, which for unknown reasons had sealed the file for thirty years. It also made sense if Austin's birth parents were someone other than Marc and Helen Hawley.

But the way Janet had looked when I mentioned adoption indicated to me that I was on the right path; the Hawleys had some involvement. Besides, it was the only lead I had and it was too late at night to confront the notion that I'd have to start from scratch.

I looked at my phone, which was up to thirty-eight percent. Ken had not responded. That wasn't exactly out of character for him, but it was annoying, and it reminded me of how Barry wasn't answering, either. Maybe I needed a cup of tea.

I went into the kitchen and started poking around in the fridge. No, we don't keep tea in the fridge; why do you ask?

I found some stir fry Ken had made two nights ago and decided it would go great with tea, so I took it out and put some in a bowl to microwave. It was spinning and heating in no time. Now, about that tea . . .

Someone claiming to be a man named Jack, possibly Marc Hawley, had called and made threatening noises in my direction if I should keep investigating Helen Hawley's murder. Or the adoption. Or something. It wasn't clear.

The only way Marc (let's assume it was Marc for the sake of simplicity) could have gotten my phone number would be through Janet. Janet would have to be remarkably stupid to assume that I couldn't figure that out. She did not strike me as being remarkably stupid. A little tight-assed, maybe, but not stupid.

To-Do List for the next day: meet Esme's friend, find Bill Hawley and harass Janet.

On the agenda for the rest of tonight: search all registered births in the area of Kearny and Arlington (and surrounding towns) for the year Austin was born. He had to have been born somewhere. I figured.

Luckily, charging up gives me a feeling of energy, so even if I'd wanted to sleep now, the thought of Barry out in the wind and the fresh charge would have kept me awake anyway. Because it took two hours and forty-five minutes for me to make anything even resembling progress on the search.

There had been, since I was essentially limiting myself to three New Jersey towns (Kearny, Arlington and North Arlington), 604 children born in the year in question. Many of them (in fact, 368) were girls. That left Austin out. So I had 236 children to sort through. On paper.

Of those, 213 had viewable birth certificates or hospital records (HIPAA be damned!) and were clearly not Austin Cobb. That left twenty-three boys, and there was no indication that twenty of them had ever been offered for adoption.

Three left.

The records, when there were records, were vague at best. I could google the names on the birth records (none of which was Austin anything) and see if the now-adult person was traceable online. One was a doctor in Ojai, California. The other two weren't showing up in any capacity in the present day, but there were a lot of explanations for that. One was named Michael Rogers, and that was the fifty-eighth most popular last name in the United States. There were 3.8 million people named Michael. Matching them up would take a mathematical genius or a statistical one. Maybe Austin would be able to help in the morning, but there had to be a quicker way.

The one *not* named Michael Rogers was listed as 'Baby Boy Doe' in the records. Sometimes that happens when the parents don't want to register a name for some reason or when the child has been abandoned. Tracing someone with that kind of backstory is very difficult, but it seemed the most likely avenue for me tonight.

The child was found next to a dumpster at a Dunkin' Donuts on Passaic Avenue in Kearny and the poor kid who was working that night immediately called the police because he certainly didn't want any part of taking care of a newborn child. The cops who responded filed the report I was reading and then contacted what was then called the Department of Youth and Family Services, which sent out a case worker named Roberta D'Angelo (who as it turned out was Esme's friend from the good old days), who took custody of the child in the name of the agency and then set about finding a suitable foster care situation because she didn't want to take the kid in, either. (To be fair, that wouldn't at all be considered part of her job.)

That was where the police report stopped being helpful, and it took another forty minutes to locate a DYFS document dealing with Mr Doe. This one, filed by D'Angelo, did not list foster parents. It merely stated that the child – still given no name – was placed in a licensed foster home in Hudson County.

So I was left with the task I really didn't want: finding a list of all licensed foster homes in Hudson County thirty-two years earlier. It was not considered public information and took some digging on the same back channels I often use to find people whom my clients have suggested were abusive foster parents in their youth. (Sometimes the charges turn out to be true, in which case we alert the authorities. Sometimes the client has been confused or their memories unreliable, and we try to help those clients find the assistance they need. To be fair, it's only happened three times since we opened the agency, but it's jarring and impossible to shake every time.)

The first rays of sunlight were not quite at my window when I found the list I needed, and there were hundreds of names on it. All-nighters aren't entirely out of the question in my line of work, but they're never easy no matter how nervous you are on any given night. Staring at those columns of names was making me wonder if I needed another charge, despite knowing I didn't.

Then my phone buzzed. A text from Ken.

I'm still alive.

Well, I hadn't *really* been worried about that, but it was nice to hear. But he was still being too cute for words, and I didn't have time for that.

Have you seen Barry? What's going on?

His reply wasn't quite as reassuring as the previous one.

Nobody named Barry yet. At the moment I'm tied to a chair, but it's nothing I can't handle.

It was the most Ken thing he'd ever said to me.

EIGHTEEN

"Do you need me down there? How the hell are you texting if you're tied to a chair?"

They seemed like reasonable questions, but my brother wasn't in a mood to answer, or someone had found his phone and taken it. I'd go to him, but I didn't know where he was in Atlantic City, in a casino or someone's apartment. Anything was, believe me, a possibility.

I didn't call Sarah Polk. I figured if she wasn't agitated enough to get in touch, she didn't need me reminding her it was almost two days since she'd heard from her husband. I did what I always do when I feel like I'm walled in and have no options.

I went to see Aunt Margie.

Technically, Aunt Margie is not even our aunt. But she's the closest thing to an in-house mother I've ever had and she sees Ken and me as her (very) grown children. If there's any danger to one of us, don't get between us and Aunt Margie.

But the other thing about her is that she's emotionally intelligent. If I'm feeling frustrated or angry (usually at Ken or Mank) or sad, Aunt Margie is the person who hears about it. Because she'll have a warm, comforting hug and usually cookies. I doubted there'd be any this time because it was only 6:30 in the morning.

Of course, I was wrong. Aunt Margie ushered me over to her somewhat worn but extremely clean sofa and gave me the hug I needed. On the table in front of the sofa there were no cookies. It was breakfast time. There were muffins. I don't know how she does it.

I asked for and got another hug. I wasn't distraught, but I was frustrated and annoyed with my brother. I didn't tell Aunt Margie about his being tied to a chair because I knew that if it wasn't a twenty-foot-tall chair made out of granite, Ken could get himself out of that situation anytime he wanted, so why worry her? But I told her everything else. Then I took a chocolate chip muffin because I'd really been hoping for cookies.

'Do you want advice or sympathy?' Aunt Margie asked.

'I can't have both?' The muffin was delicious, so I knew Aunt Margie hadn't baked it herself. She's a lovely person but a lifelong radio news reporter who had never bothered to learn anything about cooking. Which was evident once a week when she insisted on making dinner for Ken and me.

'Of course you can. Which do you want first?' No one was more flexible than Aunt Margie.

'Oh, sympathy, for sure.'

She nodded, having received her assignment. She took both my hands in hers. 'I won't say I know how you feel because I've never been in your position,' she said. 'But I can tell you about a time I was editing a newscast and had to send a reporter out into the field. And it was the morning of 9/11.'

Oh, wow. I was afraid to ask, but I had to. 'Was the reporter killed?' I asked.

'No. I'd sent her out on a story about an art installation that was happening at MoMA,' she answered, referring to the Museum of Modern Art. 'But everybody was so frantic that morning I forgot where she was and started to think she might be downtown. It was very scary for about fifteen minutes and then we were absorbed with everything else, of course.'

I leaned back in the sofa cushion. It was very soft. The all-nighter was starting to have its inevitable effect, but I stayed awake and kept my eyes open. 'So I feel like I sent Barry out except maybe he went to the towers,' I said quietly.

'Or maybe he's at MoMA. You don't know yet, and you shouldn't let yourself get ahead of the game. The fact is, there are a thousand explanations for what's going on and you don't have enough to go on so far.'

I took another bite of muffin. Sugar gives you energy. It's in books. 'Is that the advice part?' I asked.

'No. My advice is you should make up with Richie.'

It took me a moment to remember who Richie might be. 'Your advice when all this is going on is for me to get back with Mank?' I said. Surely she couldn't mean that. 'He pretty much accused me of only talking to him because he could help me on cases with cop stuff.'

Aunt Margie nodded. 'And you don't want to face it because you think he might be right,' she said. 'But he's a very nice guy and you know it, and frankly, you were happier when you were with him than you have been since.'

To sum up: I was trying to find Austin Cobb's birth parents, one of whom might very well have been murdered by the other. Marc Hawley, or someone like him, had called to threaten me in the middle of the night. Ken was in Atlantic City, tied to a chair in his most recent communication, and Barry Polk was missing after I'd sent him to chase after Malcolm X. Mitchell. But what Aunt Margie thought should be my top priority was making nice with Mank. (Granted, I hadn't told her about Ken, but at this moment it didn't seem like that would matter.)

I don't often question her judgment, but this seemed like a good time to start.

'I've got a few other things on my mind right now,' I said.

'I know. But this will help with all the other things.' Aunt Margie can do cryptic with the best of them. In fact, she might be the best of them.

'OK.' I stood up. The muffin was good, but this conversation wasn't giving me what I needed. 'I've got to go now.'

'Are you going to the precinct?' Suddenly there was only one track in Aunt Margie's mind.

'No. I'm going to find out who killed Helen Hawley.' Which technically was the least of my responsibilities. If Helen's killer didn't lead to Austin's parents, who was I working for? The Kearny police of twenty-five years ago?

Yeah. The Kearny police of twenty-five years ago. That was it. Or maybe DYFS.

Roberta D'Angelo Newman was now in her late fifties, and luckily had moved to Manhattan when she'd married Benjamin Franklin Newman twelve years ago. She no longer worked for any agency, public or private, and was actually the owner of a small business on MacDougal Street, Bobbie's Wines and Liquors, which wouldn't open until noon. But Bobbie – that is, Roberta – was already there getting the store ready for a business day and doing a 'quick inventory,' she'd told me on the phone.

(Yeah, I'd tried texting my idiot brother and gotten nothing back yet. I hoped they'd tightened the ropes on his chair, but I suspected he was long out of that situation and working on being in an even more precarious one after a fun night in AC.)

Roberta was on a ladder checking out six packs of beer being stored above a refrigerated display. It was a small space, and every square inch was covered in beer, wine or the occasional bottle of vodka, mostly SKYY. And since we'd already spoken, she knew why I was here.

'I do remember the baby from the Dunkin's dumpster,' she said. 'Mostly because that didn't happen very much. I was maybe a year from my social work degree and now I was trying to find a home to place this baby that was clearly unwanted. It could break your heart.'

She climbed down off the ladder and dusted off her hands on the apron she was wearing, which had 'Blue Moon' written on it. There were many bottles of wine available in Bobbie's Wines and Liquors, but beer seemed to be the drug of choice.

'I'm sure it did,' I told her, and I meant it. 'But there had to have been security cameras in that parking lot. Wasn't there any footage that might show who had dropped off the baby?'

'Sure.' Roberta walked into a storage room off the main sales area, and I followed her because she didn't tell me not to. 'But it was nighttime and the cameras were not exactly top of the line. The cops and I looked over the footage and we saw someone come over and place the baby on the ground with a pillow under him. He was crying his lungs out. But whoever it was had a dark hoodie on and was being shot from the back. I couldn't tell you if it was a man or a woman.'

'How long was he out there like that?' I asked. A baby next to a dumpster. It made my stomach feel uncomfortable.

'Oh, not long,' Roberta said. 'The time stamp on the video showed it was less than half an hour before the kid working there had come out and found him. He called the cops and the cops called me.'

She counted a number of six packs and then paid some attention to a wall accommodating mostly French reds. She noted whatever it was she needed to know on a clipboard hanging from the wine rack and looked at me, expecting another question. She got one.

'What happened after?' I asked. 'Your report said you were seeking a family to foster the baby, and that eventually you had found one. Do you remember who they were?'

'Oh, yeah.' We walked out of the storage room and back to the main sales area, where Roberta headed straight for the check-out. The cash register probably didn't have very much actual cash in it because everyone pays by card now, but she had to check to see that there was some, in case some freak with real money came in and wanted to buy something. 'It was the Roosevelts.'

I stopped and stared at her and Roberta laughed. 'Not *those* Roosevelts,' she said. 'There was a couple called Todd and Julie Roosevelt who lived in the area and were licensed to foster kids. They were lovely, but they didn't want someone long-term. They were kind of a halfway house for kids who needed a place to stay.'

'Meanwhile, you were still looking for a permanent adoption, or is the process to find the birth parents first?'

Roberta finished programming the register and walked to a small display of what bar owners will refer to as 'salty snacks,' meant to keep the clientele drinking. This was a freestanding display with bags of chips and other such products clipped to it, impulse purchases for those who came in to find drinks and needed something to wash down. She rotated the display, looking for empty hooks, and found none. She sighed lightly.

'The chips aren't selling so much these days.' Then she looked at me. 'The first thing you do is, you try to find the parents. But we had a grand total of nothing to go on and in those days, you couldn't do DNA testing. There was no pediatrician we could call. It wasn't a hospital; it was a Dunkin' Donuts. So after a few days we had all admitted that this was probably a waste of time. The baby stayed with the Roosevelts.'

I was trying to stay out of Roberta's way, and while the shop was small, it wasn't put-out-your-hands-and-touch-both-walls small, not even for me. But I did have to make a few quick swerves like now, when she walked back toward the refrigerated display with the clipboard, counting six packs again.

'But not permanently,' I said.

'No. They weren't going to go for that, and I didn't want to try it,' Roberta answered. 'They were more like grandparents, a little older and more indulgent. The baby, especially, needed someone to raise him. So I started contacting first the state and county agencies and then a few of the private adoption agencies.'

'The public ones couldn't find a home for him?' It seemed like they would have had the best, and most, resources. A healthy newborn baby shouldn't have been, please pardon the expression, a hard sell.

'Well, you want to cast a wide net just to find the best possible situation,' she said. There seemed to be a small shortage of Heineken in bottles, so we headed back to the storage room to fill that need. I followed and listened as Roberta plowed on, expending more energy than me, and I was fully charged. It was still morning. 'So you ask everywhere and see what answers you get. With that little boy, it was harder than it should have been.' She pulled four six packs off the shelves and handed two to me. I carried them without being asked. It was almost literally the least I could do.

'Why?' I asked.

'I think because of the way he'd been found. Agencies get antsy about abandoned babies. They figure the mom is going to have a change of heart, and they'll have to stand between the birth parent and the adoptive parent. They try to avoid those situations.'

I had to cut to the chase. Roberta reached the proper door and opened it to put the beer inside. I handed her my two six packs. 'So where did the baby end up?' I said.

'With a couple called the Hawleys,' she said. 'Normally I wouldn't remember the name, but it's from a movie I really like.'

Somehow I'd known it would end up with the Hawleys. 'Do you remember their first names?'

Roberta stopped and looked at me, clearly trying to think. 'Not really,' she said. 'I just remember the last name because of that movie.'

'What's the movie?' It didn't matter, but you ask.

'*Silverado*,' she said.

NINETEEN

I got to my office about eleven, had a quick chat with Igavda that I understood at about a thirty percent rate, and sat down at my desk to do something I'd been waiting a full day to do: harass Janet Hawley. Because she was the only Hawley I had available.

But first I did some research into psychologists and neurologists Janet might have contacted about Austin before the Cobbs adopted him. There were only two in the Kearny area who were practicing at the time and still living. Dr Adam Kenton said he had no records of Austin, and Dr Lucille Baker refused to divulge any patient records, after saying she had no evidence Austin had been a patient of hers.

Doctors.

Janet's phone answered on the second ring. No doubt she'd been expecting me to call about 'Jack's' phone call the night before. But I had more pressing issues than a vague threat from a guy who didn't have the nerve to tell me his last name.

'Ms Stein!' You'd think she was an Avon representative and I was calling to find out where my delivery of blush might be. 'What a pleasure to hear from you again!' So that was how we were going to play it. Well, that was how *she* was going to play it.

'Hello, Janet,' I said. 'Do you want to tell me why you were lying yesterday?'

That had the desired effect. Janet fumfered for a long moment and finally managed, 'Lying!' No doubt she was lying back on a white rattan chaise lounge and reaching for a sweet tea to calm her offended nerves.

'Yeah,' I said. 'Lying. You told me there was no adoption involving a little baby boy in your family, and now I know that's not the case. So maybe you'd like to fill me in on exactly what *did* happen before I call a friend of mine on the NYPD and see if he's interested in investigating what happened to that child. Possibly after one of his parents was murdered.'

There was a very long silence on the other end of the call. I waited. Twenty seconds . . . thirty seconds . . .

'It's your turn to talk, Janet,' I said.

'I don't know what to say.' It's a fairly standard stalling tactic, but I was worrying about my college friend, my brother and my client, perhaps not in that order, and I wasn't in the mood for stalling tactics.

'Try the truth,' I told her. 'It'll be a whole new experience for you.'

'Ms Stein, I believe I might have to call the police myself and report you for harassment and terroristic threats.'

'Funny you should bring up terroristic threats, especially since I haven't made any,' I said. 'But a friend of yours called me late last night, told me his name was Jack and threatened my life unless I stopped asking about this child.'

Janet seemed confused. 'So why didn't you stop?' she asked.

'Because my client wants to find his birth parents and I believe that they were involved with your family, or were members of your family. That's my job. If you could be honest with me for five minutes and tell me what I need to know to do my job, I won't bother you anymore.' (If there were crimes involved, I would instead see to it that the police or the FBI bothered her.) 'So why not just answer my questions truthfully and we can part company for good. How's that?'

Her tone was less frightened or intimidated and more annoyed, like a customer at the returns counter who *really* wants to talk to a manager. 'I don't have anything to tell you because I don't know anything more,' she said.

My tone was considerably less weary and more aggressively annoyed. By design. 'Janet, the only way – and I mean the *only* way – the guy who called me last night could have heard about me or gotten my phone number was through you. So clearly you *do* know more than you're telling, so I can only conclude that you enjoy my company so much you'll be happy when I start calling or texting you, or showing up at your door, every hour on the hour.'

By now Janet's voice didn't so much have a tone at all. It was like hearing a mannequin speak. 'Ask your question.'

'Don't sell yourself short, Janet. It'll be *questions*, plural.

First and most to-the-point: Who put Austin up for adoption?' With the answer to that I could put this whole thing to bed and let some ancient retired cop who couldn't stand cold cases find out who killed Helen. Or was that just a TV thing?

'Who's Austin?'

'I'll talk to you in an hour, Janet,' I said, and disconnected the call. I put the phone down on my desk and gave serious thought, for the first time since I'd opened the agency, to resigning from Austin's case because there were too many brick walls in my way. Even my status as a mostly-human superbeing wasn't proving to be an advantage this time, and that's rare.

But apparently I had underestimated my status as a world-class pain in the butt, because less than a minute after I'd hung up on her, Janet Hawley called me back. Just to annoy her (more) I let it ring three times before I picked up.

'K&F Stein Investigations,' I said.

'You hung up on me.' Because apparently Janet thought I didn't know that.

'You weren't answering my questions. I had made it very clear what would happen if you didn't answer my questions,' I told her.

'I couldn't answer that question. I don't know anyone named Austin.'

Maybe she didn't. It was possible Austin had been named after his adoption, despite the Cobbs telling me his first name had been his first name since birth. Maybe Janet hadn't known him before he was adopted. Maybe, again, I was chasing in the wrong direction and the Hawleys had nothing to do with Austin Cobb at all.

'OK,' I said, tossing Janet a bone. 'I might be wrong about that. But apparently there were two little boys, and your son Bill was one of them. Who was the other?'

'Bill is my nephew,' Janet corrected. She was starting to feel like she was in charge again, and I'd have to take steps to dispel that in a minute.

'Great. Your nephew. Who was the other little boy? And if you say that there was no other little boy, I'm going to hang up on you again. So choose your words carefully.'

Like that.

'But there really was no other—'

I hung up on her. You have to do what you say you'll do.

But I had no time to enjoy the moment because the office door opened and three large men walked in. They weren't wearing matching suits, but they should have been. They all had shaved heads, broad shoulders and faces that indicated they had not just left a meeting of Mensa, although you can't tell intelligence by appearance or you'd think my brother was an idiot. Which he is.

They walked right past Igavda, who stood and protested, and came directly to my desk, which didn't take a lot of thought because I was the only other person in the office. I did not stand, which might have been seen as confrontative, but noted that my phone hadn't started ringing again. Janet knew they were here and she was done keeping me occupied.

'Can you gentlemen please check in with our receptionist?' I said as they approached. 'She gets very upset when she can't do her job.' Igavda, who Ken initially hired because he enjoyed looking at her, had passed her citizenship test and was working on a bachelor's degree in sociology. But her English was still spotty. Checking in with her would buy me some time, and again, it was about me and not my visitors being in charge.

'We don't need to check in,' said the middle one, whom I decided was called Moe. (He just looked like a Moe.) I half expected him to tell me then that they didn't need no stinkin' badges, but he didn't. 'We're here to give you a message.'

I was already planning what to do when things got physical, because they were going to. 'It takes three of you to deliver a message?' I said. 'Isn't that a little inefficient for your business plan?'

They looked back and forth at each other for a few moments. My initial impression had been right; none of these guys was an Ivy Leaguer. Or a high school graduate.

Moe clearly decided that he'd been given instructions and he was going to carry them out no matter what incomprehensive babble I might spout. 'You're gonna stop asking questions about kids up for adoption,' he said.

'But that's *my* whole business plan,' I told him.

The guy to Moe's right, who in my world was called Larry,

narrowed his eyes to the point that I wasn't sure they were still open. 'Did you hear him?' he asked. So he wasn't asleep, at least.

'Yeah, but I didn't really care about what he was saying,' I answered. I tensed my glutes because I'd be standing soon, maybe in a hurry. I looked at Moe. 'I'm sorry; what were you saying?'

He seemed stumped for a moment and that was alarming because he appeared to be the brightest of the bunch. 'I *said* you've gotta stop asking questions about those kids up for adoption.'

I shifted my weight to my toes so I could be standing faster. 'Which kids?' I said. 'Most of my clients were adopted.'

It was Curly, the third guy who hadn't spoken yet, that started all the trouble or, more to the point, incited me to start all the trouble. 'That's it,' he said, as if that meant anything. 'Are you gonna stop poking around in our business?'

'I don't even know what your business is,' I told him, and that was at least eighty percent true.

With a face dialed to livid, Curly reached into his jacket and that was enough for me. I leapt up out of the chair and grabbed him, across the desk, by the front of his jacket. 'There better not be anything resembling a weapon in your hand,' I said. Then I patted down his chest and sure enough, there was something metal and heavy where he had put his hand. 'Oh, bad for you,' I told him.

I picked Curly up with one hand, still holding his jacket and with my hand positioned so he couldn't move the gun out of his clothes. Then I turned my wrist to the right and flicked him – that's the word, 'flicked' – to the side. The other two stooges were just starting to react, given their quick-witted personalities.

Now, normally I'd have just tossed everybody around until they were either unconscious or more agreeable, but this was my office, and I was responsible for any damage to the premises, so I had to be more precise than I might have otherwise. Igavda was holding the reception telephone and pointed at it, asking if she should call the police. I shook my head. The last thing I needed was for these three to squeal to the cops about

Superlady, or to my landlord about anything that might get broken. Best to handle these jerks myself. Igavda put the phone down.

I stepped in front of my desk and slapped Moe hard in the face. Not hard enough to fracture any facial bones, but hard enough to do more than get his attention. 'Who sent you here?' I demanded.

Moe made a gargling sound, and I wasn't even touching his throat. Meanwhile Larry had produced a pair of brass knuckles from his pocket and was drawing his elbow back.

I was still slapping Moe every few seconds, so it made the most sense to deal with Larry with my feet. I kicked him in the stomach at about a third of my strength and he fell backwards, dropping the brass knuckles and landing in Ken's desk chair, which was purchased with Ken in mind, so it wasn't at all damaged. Larry just sat there looking perplexed, arms dangling at his sides.

But now Curly, having shaken himself back to what passed for consciousness in him, was rising off the office floor. I figured Moe knew the most out of the three, so I just pushed Curly back down, but he had managed to get the gun out of his jacket and into his hand, so that was going to be an issue. He was lining it up to aim at me.

In all honesty, that was probably the last thing his employer would have wanted. They didn't need me dead with all those cops investigating and my massive brother, if he was out of the chair yet, tracking them down. And frankly, I have no idea if I could survive a gunshot wound or if my semi-constructed body would have extra defenses against one. I had no desire to find out, either.

So I did what was necessary. I stomped down on the gun hand and heard a crack or two. Curly yelped and I reached down for the gun.

All this had forced me to pause slapping Moe, which had so far been the highlight of my day. I looked at Curly and yelled, 'Stay!' Curly, looking convinced, fell back on the floor and closed his eyes. I figured he was taking a nap.

Moe, having witnessed the treatment his companions had undergone, wasn't doing anything too threatening at the moment.

I loomed over him and dropped my voice an octave. I also lowered the volume. 'I asked you a question,' I said. 'Who sent you here?'

'Nobody.' Being the brains of this outfit didn't amount to much. 'Nobody sent us.'

'You just ambled in off the street to deliver vague threats?' I said. I didn't have enormous faith in logic in this situation, but it was really all I had left short of pushing Moe's head through the dropped ceiling, and that would require repairs. Best to avoid.

His eyes bulged a little because thinking was something of an underdeveloped skill with Moe. 'No,' he said. I waited for more and nothing came.

'Who. Sent. You. Here?' I would have leaned over to be more intimidating, but then his eyes would have been at my chest level, and I have found that not to be especially frightening to many men.

'A guy named Jack. And that's all I know, I swear. We never got a last name.' His voice, the opposite of mine, was rising in pitch to the point that he'd gone from baritone to alto.

'How did "Jack" contact you? You guys have a website?' Sometimes I'm a riot.

'I get a call. That's all I know.' Moe was never a riot.

I heaved a very theatrical sigh. 'I just threw your two buddies around the room, probably broke one of their hands, and disarmed you without even breathing hard,' I said. I felt the scene needed a recap. 'So don't give me any more stupid answers that I'm not going to believe. How were you contacted to come here, and by whom?'

Moe's eyes were about twice as wide as they had started out; he was convinced. 'I get a call from a go-between,' he said. 'I don't know who called them. They said to come here and put a scare into you about some kid who got adopted a long time ago. That's everything I know, I swear!'

It probably was, because I figured he'd forgotten his times tables by the time he'd started high school. 'What's the go-between's name?' I growled. Oh yeah, I can growl when it's helpful. Ask Mank. Better yet, don't ask Mank.

'You've never heard of them,' he said.

I put my left hand under his chin and lifted him up to a fully standing position. He made a yelping sound. 'Great,' I said. 'I get to make a new friend. What's the name?'

Larry was still dazed and confused in Ken's desk chair. Curly was lying with his eyes open on the floor to my right, counting the tiles in the dropped ceiling, one of which I would have to replace. Moe knew, therefore, that he had no reinforcements. 'Patty McCloud.'

'Patty? Short for Patrick?'

I let Moe off the hook on my left forefinger, so he could shake his head negatively. 'No. Patricia.'

Cool. Women moving up in the criminal ranks. Soon she might hit the glass manhole. 'How do I find Patty?'

Moe looked properly terrified. 'I don't know, I swear! She always calls me!'

I nodded like the patient teacher I never was. 'And when she does, her number shows up on the screen of your phone. I will now allow you to reach for your phone and bring up your recent calls so you can show me which one is Patty.'

Something happened to Moe's face in a rapid succession. First terror, then resignation, then defiance. 'Sure,' he said, and reached into his pocket. He pulled out a small handgun. How I'd missed it before was a source of embarrassment, but there was no time for that now. I tried to reach for the muzzle, but he pushed it up so it was aimed at my face. 'Don't,' he said. So I didn't. 'Now, you're gonna agree never to deal with this adoption thing again, and I'm gonna let you live. How does that sound?'

From behind him there was an animal noise, and I looked up toward Igavda and saw only a man's chest.

My brother Ken had arrived, and he was not in a good mood.

'There's two of them,' Larry moaned. So he was kind of conscious.

Ken snatched the gun out of Moe's hand, hit Moe over the head with it and then – I swear – bared his teeth at Moe like a German Shepherd confronted by a Doberman Pinscher. Ken looked at me. 'Is it OK if these three leave?' he asked.

I nodded. Moe wasn't going to give me Patty McCloud's phone number anyway. I doubted that was her real name.

Ken looked down, and I mean down, at Moe. 'Take your two buddies, get out, and never come back. Was that clear enough?'

Moe didn't answer. He just patted Larry on the face until he seemed conscious, got Curly off the floor, and the three of them shuffled out the door. Curly was cradling his left hand in his right and Larry just looked like someone had surprised him enough that he'd be surprised forever. Moe looked back a couple of times to take in the spectacle that is my brother and me.

Once they were gone I took a moment to assess Ken. He didn't look all that worse for wear after having spent time tied to a chair, but on closer inspection his shirt was torn at the seam on the left shoulder and he had a small bruise under his right ear. His hair, however, was absolutely perfect. You never know if you're going to meet a cute woman on the bus home from Atlantic City.

'So, what'd I miss?' he asked.

'Not that much.'

TWENTY

For the record, I never found any evidence that there actually was a Patty McCloud. There was no one by that name listed in Manhattan, which is rare, and I never was contacted by anyone with that name again. So all in all, I figured Moe had been lying about Patty.

Despite the situation Ken had walked in on, I had far more questions for him than he had for me, so I explained what had been going on for the past day in about five minutes and then Ken took his seat at his desk, adjusted it because apparently Larry had somehow changed the height, and looked at me with the blandest, most innocent face I'd ever seen, except that I knew him and his face was lying.

'So you followed our pal Malcolm to Atlantic City, got tied to a chair and didn't find Barry, which was what I'd asked you to do in the first place,' I said. 'That about right?'

'Give or take. Except Malcolm still doesn't know I was there. Probably.'

'Who tied you to the chair, Penn and Teller?'

My questions seemed to be something of an irritant to my brother; he closed his eyes and sighed for effect. 'Very funny.'

'Who tied you? To the chair? And while we're at it, how'd you get out of the chair?'

Ken opened his eyes and looked at me, realizing I wasn't, after all, being unreasonable. 'OK. Here's what happened: I followed Malcolm to AC. Mostly, I saw that he was taking a limo that was licensed in Atlantic City and figured I could pick him up there. Which I did. I took New Jersey Transit down to the boardwalk, which is awful, by the way, and waited in front of the Borgata hotel.'

'How did you know to go to the Borgata?'

Ken looked amused. 'It's where a guy like Malcolm would go.'

'My God. There are other guys like Malcolm?'

'Lunatics who think they own the world and everybody else is from Central Casting? Yeah, there are a few.' Ken didn't luxuriate in his desk chair, which had cost twice as much as mine because he wanted to be able to lean back almost to a prone position. But he did lace his fingers behind his head, a signature move that he would probably have learned in business school if he'd gone to business school. He probably did learn it from reruns of Nineties sitcoms. 'But I have a thought about what he was doing down there.'

I went over to Igavda's station because I wanted to make sure she wasn't traumatized by what she'd seen. I don't know how much she's figured out about the people she works for, but she was currently applying snap-on fingernails with floral patterns, so I guessed she could make it through the rest of the day. She looked up at me. 'Something, Mrs Fran?' she asked. I shook my head. Apparently I was the only one traumatized by my throwing three men around.

Because I wanted it to seem like I wasn't interested, I called over my shoulder. 'OK. What's your thought?'

Ken stood up because he *wanted* me to be interested. He has a thing about not being a college-educated investigator, although he did get a bachelor's degree in psychology. Barely. 'Malcolm seemed to be using something, maybe an app on his phone, at the roulette wheel,' he said. 'Roulette was all he played, and he never lost.'

That's almost impossible, so I started back toward my desk. And my brother. 'He *never* lost?'

Ken came just short of smirking, but he sat back down to watch me take my chair behind my desk. The damage to the office was minimal and we could pay for it out of pocket, which eliminated the need to let our landlord know. Ken didn't seem to notice the hole in the ceiling or the skid marks on the carpet.

'Not once,' he said. 'Whatever app he had on the phone made the ball land wherever he told it to.'

No. That couldn't be correct. 'There's no app, even if it's connected to WiFi, that can change the path of a solid object in motion. Couldn't he have just been lucky?' And yes, I know how stupid that sounds.

'Nobody's that lucky,' my brother said, charitably leaving

out the 'duh.' 'He kept playing with his phone. Everybody stays on their phone now, so it didn't look like anything, but I'm telling you, Malcolm was intent on his. Seems like he's really good at tech.'

There was so much more story yet untold. 'So if Malcolm didn't spot you, how did you end up tied to a chair, and did you get out the way I imagine you got out?'

Ken shrugged as if to say he had no idea what I imagined. 'I was staying nearby, pretending to watch another guy at the next roulette table, and these three guys appeared all of a sudden, one on each side and one behind me.'

'Aw, that's sweet.'

'Yeah, it was like they were worried about me.' Ken stood up and walked to our office mini fridge, where he found an energy drink that I wouldn't use on my worst day. He pointed at me to ask if I wanted a bottle of water and I nodded. So he got one out for me. 'I'm there minding my own business, or really Malcolm's, and then there are big hands on my shoulders. Both of them.'

'And you didn't pulverize these two because . . .?' He gave me the water bottle and I nodded thanks. I hadn't realized how thirsty throwing three grown men around had made me.

'I was in a public place and I've been told to be very careful about doing anything that only we can do,' he said. 'Besides, I was watching Malcolm and didn't want to draw attention to myself.'

That made sense. I hate it when he makes sense. It makes it more difficult – although far from impossible – for me to be snide.

'Did you stand up?' I asked.

'Well, yeah. These guys put their hands on my shoulders and told me not to turn around. I *had* to turn around.' Ken sounded vaguely offended.

'If you stood up, you drew attention to yourself. You know that.' The water was helping. I was starting to regain some of the oomph I hadn't realized I'd lost. I mean, it was just three men. I'd have to make it a point to work out every morning. (The fact that I hadn't slept at all might have had a little to do with it.)

Ken waved a hand to declare my comment irrelevant. That

was OK; I was being snide just to prove I could. 'Yeah, whatever. But as soon as I was standing, there was something very hard pressing into my back, and it wasn't a gold ingot.'

'They had a gun on you?' This might have been a little more serious than he had led me to believe the night before. Forget where he came up with a gold ingot. My brother's mind works in mysterious ways.

He nodded and spread his hands; yes, that was what had happened. 'They said they didn't want any trouble, and for that moment, neither did I. So they walked me off the casino floor and into an elevator. I would have messed them up there, but there were two other people with us.'

'Other people are such an inconvenience,' I said, sympathizing with him. I put my feet up on my desk. This story was taking a while.

Ken ignored the comment, which was probably smart. 'The doors opened on the fifth floor and they maneuvered me into a hotel suite, with the gun in my back the whole way,' he went on.

'Is that when they tied you to a chair?' I was hoping to avoid more unnecessary details and cut to the chase.

Ken seemed annoyed at the attempt to accelerate his story. He frowned and folded his arms. Then he remembered he wanted a swig of the energy drink, so he unfolded his arms and took one. Then he folded his arms again. It was a very expressive few moments. I sat and watched without commenting.

'They didn't just tie me to a chair,' he said with a little extra sauce on it. 'But they didn't grill me for any information about anything, which was what I thought I should expect. If they were with Malcolm, they'd ask me about Mom and Dad. If they were attached to some case we're working, they'd poke around about that. But they didn't ask me anything.'

OK, that *was* odd. 'What did they do?' I asked.

'They took turns punching me. That seemed to be the game, to see if they could hurt me or get me to come after them. So I didn't.'

That explained the bruise on his face and the tear in his shirt. 'Why'd they want to do that?'

Ken flattened out his lips to show me he had no idea. 'Beats me. If you'll pardon the pun.'

It wasn't a pun, but I let it go. 'And *then* they tied you to a chair,' I said.

'They took a chair from the dining table in the suite, and they put it in the closet,' Ken went on, as if I hadn't actually asked. 'Then they did their best to force me into the closet, but they never would have been able to if I hadn't let them; I wanted to get a better handle on what their game was, and after all, I figured that they couldn't really hurt me. They pushed me onto the chair, which was fine with me, and then they used packing tape wrapped around my chest and my arms and legs to keep me there.'

I laughed. 'Like that was going to work.'

'Yeah, but they didn't know that. So they closed the closet door and I was out in about two minutes. I was being careful that they didn't hear the tape ripping.'

This was interesting, but it seemed to have no direct connection to Malcolm X. Mitchell or to Austin Cobb's case/Helen Hawley's murder, which were the two subjects foremost in my mind at the moment. 'And Barry never showed up?' I asked.

Ken looked at the ceiling as if expecting divine assistance. 'I keep telling you that guy wasn't there! But if you *want*, I can tell you what I found out from the three knuckleheads in the suite.'

So he *had* gotten some information! Who would have known from the rambling tale Ken was telling? 'OK. Please. Tell me what you found out.'

'Once I was out of the chair, and I texted you so you'd know I wasn't dead, like you'd care, I waited until I heard voices right outside the closet door. And I kicked the door open, hard. That took care of one of them. The other two were fairly easy.'

Exactly what I'd expected. 'I don't suppose it occurred to you to ask why they'd attacked you to begin with, and who they were working for,' I said.

My brother tried very hard to look humble, but he shook his head. 'Mostly they were unconscious, but I did manage to get a little something out of one of them,' he said. 'The biggest one, he hung in there the longest. He said they were working for a guy named Jack.'

TWENTY-ONE

Because I'd mentioned the phone call from the man who called himself Jack, and of course had brought up the name Marc Hawley more than once, we sat and looked at each other for the better part of a minute.

Finally I cleared my throat. I don't think my throat necessarily needed clearing, but it seemed a way to break the silence. Ken's eyes met my stare and I said, 'All the way to Atlantic City? You didn't see them on the bus going down, right?'

Ken seemed insulted. 'Of course not. Three guys like that, I would have been on my guard right away. They had to know I was coming.'

'How?'

'They had to know you called me and told me to follow Malcolm, and they had to either know Malcolm was going to AC or see him get in the limo.' Ken stood up to pace. He says it gets blood flowing to his brain. I say, do what works for you.

How could these three anonymous musclemen have known I asked Ken to follow Malcolm Mitchell? My favorite thing to do these days was to blame Janet, but the only way she could have known about Ken, or Malcolm, or anything was to have gotten the frequency on my phone or my brother's, and that just didn't seem to be within her capabilities. She made cookies; she didn't hack people's cell phones. But Malcolm, he was 'good at tech.'

Jack? Whoever he was?

'Come with me,' I said. I stood up and headed for the office door. Ken, already on his feet, followed, but slowly.

'Where are we going?' he asked.

'To rent a car. Both of us have spent too much time on the bus lately.'

The drive to Kearny took a lot less time than a bus ride, largely because we didn't stop anywhere once we had rented the most generic vehicle offered that would still accommodate two people our size. You'd be surprised.

'What are we going to do when we get there?' Ken asked me just after we exited the Lincoln Tunnel.

'We're going to harass a suburban housewife,' I said.

'Sounds like fun.'

We pulled up to the front of Janet Hawley's house at about two in the afternoon. It had already been a long day, and I'd had no sleep the night before. It's not an excuse; it's an explanation.

'She's not what she seems,' I told Ken at the front door.

'Neither are we.'

I looked him up and down. He looked like if the Leaning Tower of Pisa stood up straight. 'We kind of are,' I said.

He looked at the doorbell to indicate that I should press it. I considered looking back to ask why it was my job, and then figured somebody had to do it, so I did. And we stood there.

And we stood there.

And then we stood there some more.

'I guess she's not home,' Ken said. 'Let's go back.'

'There's a car in the driveway,' I pointed out.

'It's not her car, maybe.'

'She lives alone, Ken.'

He let out a breath and pointed to the left side of the house. 'You take that side,' he said.

I moved around in the direction, noting that my brother had reached into a pocket somewhere and pulled out the small handgun he supposedly only uses when we're out on a dangerous part of a case. I hadn't considered this to be that no matter what Janet's buddy Jack might have said on the phone. Then I remembered that Jack had allegedly sent three bodybuilders each to beat up Ken and myself, and I understood his precaution, even if I didn't agree with it. We can handle ourselves pretty well without help.

There wasn't much on the left side of Janet's house. It was fairly large for just one person, which led me to wonder why she hadn't sold and downsized when her husband Howard had died some years ago. It seemed unlikely she was being sentimental. Maybe she just liked having a big house.

Windows lined the whole downstairs, so I could see the dining room clearly as I walked toward the backyard, and there was no one present. My eyes are pretty far off the ground, but not far enough for me to determine if there was anyone, living or not-so-much, on the upper floor because let's face it, that's what Ken and I were both wondering about. I jumped up a couple of times to try and catch a glimpse, but without a ladder or an attempt to scale the wall (something I was not interested in doing), it was a pointless gesture.

I reached the far end and took in the backyard, which I had not seen the last time I was here. It was not terribly large, as none of the houses on this block had a big lot, and most of this land had been devoted to the house. But it was impeccably maintained, mowed and trimmed, with the hedges around each side (next to a chain link fence that enclosed the space) perfectly level and even. Give me a pillow and a blanket and I could sleep on top of those hedges. Especially today. What was I thinking, staying up all night? That my brother was in Atlantic City tied to a chair?

I made a right turn and headed across the rear of the building. The windows were somewhat lower here, and there was a small deck on the back with glass doors leading to it. I walked up the five steps to the deck and looked inside.

No murder victims, which was something of a relief. Everything was, of course, in its place. There was nothing in the dish drainer, which led me to wonder why she needed a dish drainer. Cleanliness wasn't next to godliness here; it was an absolute to be enforced at all costs.

But while I was peering into the kitchen I caught a glimpse of movement behind it, in the dining room, about fifteen or twenty feet from where I was standing. Was Janet inside and just ducking her doorbell when it rang? Had she known I was outside? Or was someone else moving around inside the house?

I tried the glass doors, but they were locked, and forcing them would have caused too much damage to even make an attempt. I ran down the steps of the deck and toward the right side of the house to see what Ken might have caught while he was walking toward me. Something must have grabbed his attention because he wasn't back here yet.

I turned the corner to run to Ken but stopped in my tracks. My brother wasn't there. I picked up the pace on my walking and kept my eyes on the windows into the house as I approached the side door, which seemed to lead down to a basement and up to either the front room or the dining room; it was hard to tell.

But then I caught that movement again in the dining room and took a few steps back to see inside better. And then I was simply livid.

My idiot brother was inside the house, prowling around the dining room and heading toward the front of the house, to a room I couldn't see, but which had to be an area I'd seen the last time I was here, which was more or less a mudroom or a walk-in closet. It was full of various detritus of family life, but because it was Janet's house, they were extremely well organized, and everything was absolutely spotless.

I rushed to the side door and found it, of course, open. I couldn't tell if Ken had forced it or if Janet had uncharacteristically left it unlocked, but I used my sleeve to cover my hand and pulled the door open, then walked up onto the staircase. It was only four stairs from here to the living room entrance, and I used them. Well, I used two of them.

Once inside I ran, flat-out ran, to the storage area and of course found my brother there with a silly grin on his face. He was at eye-level for a shelf I'm fairly sure Janet wouldn't have been able to reach without a step stool, and what he was seeing seemed to delight him no end.

'She has *Hungry Hungry Hippos*!'

'How did you get in?' Even if she had *Chutes and Ladders*, possibly the stupidest game ever invented, I wasn't that interested in the games Janet might be keeping for the grandchildren she didn't have . . . or did she?

'How do you think? I breathed heavy on the side door lock and what do you know? It just opened magically. Look! *Stratego!*'

I looked up at the shelves. There were the usual family mementos, snow globes from trips to very standard tourist areas, high school yearbooks and one from Rutgers. There was a little exercise equipment, like bands for resistance exercises and a rolled-up mat that hadn't been used in years but was free of dust. There was something green, maybe plastic, barely visible in one corner and Ken went to reach for it. 'What's that?'

I slapped his hand, making him turn to face me. 'It's something we don't need. Leave everything *exactly* as it is, understand? If we're lucky, we can get out of here and there won't be any security cameras, so we'll stay out of jail.'

Ken waved the hand at me as a message: *Don't hit me.* He's such a baby; it was barely more than a pat. 'Jail,' he said. 'Nobody's sending us to jail.'

Well, that made me feel a bunch better. 'We need to leave. I don't know why we're here to begin with. Janet isn't home.' Unless she was upstairs in one of the bedrooms, but she'd probably have heard us and come storming down – or called the cops – by now.

'There's something black up there.' He pointed to a shelf even he couldn't reach. 'Doesn't look like much of anything. Small. Maybe a wrench or something.'

'I don't care about a wrench,' I told him. 'I don't care about any of this stuff. Why are we here?'

'We're here because she has *these*,' my brother said, and he ran his hands up and down one shelf like a model showing off prizes on a TV game show. It was, incongruously, a tall shelf filled with VHS tapes, the kind I didn't think anyone had anymore. Leave it to Janet.

'You thinking of putting together a video collection from the Nineties?' I asked.

'No, but maybe you should look at the titles,' Ken suggested with a hint of superiority in his voice.

The titles? I figured it was a collection of the *Home Alone* movies and maybe a Jim Carrey comedy or two. What did I care about the titles of Janet's ancient videos?

All but two of them had handmade labels on which had been printed (printed!) with just one word: FAMILY, with dates ranging from twenty-seven to fifteen years before.

'I bet we can find out a lot about how many kids there were and how long they were here,' Ken said. 'Especially since a couple of them go back before Helen was murdered.'

Yeah, but there had to be thirty VHS tapes here, and I hadn't seen anything resembling a VHS player in my quick scan of the house. Again, we hadn't been upstairs yet, but this didn't seem like a room Janet visited regularly, except to dust. The tapes were immaculate.

'How are we going to see them?' I asked. 'There have to be thirty hours or more of video here. I don't want to stay another thirty *seconds*.'

'Go into the kitchen and get a garbage bag,' Ken said.

No. 'She'll notice if we steal them,' I said.

'I'm willing to bet she doesn't come in here and watch home movies three times a week,' my brother answered. 'And we're not going to steal the boxes, just the tapes.'

I hated it, but Ken's plan might have been our best option under the circumstances. More than that, I hated it because it was Ken's plan and not mine. But also the possibility of being busted for breaking and entering was something of an issue for me. So I took almost five full seconds before I went and got a garbage bag from under the kitchen sink.

We were very careful to put each box back on the shelf in exactly the same position it had been, and put precisely to the edge as they had been displayed before. We left the ones that were actually professional VHS tapes, one of *The Poseidon Adventure* and one of *Psycho*. I didn't speculate.

I literally had one foot out the side door before I turned back, looked into the living room, then at the staircase. 'We should look upstairs,' I said to Ken. 'Maybe there are records she's hiding or more videos.'

'Or a dead body,' he warned.

'Don't do that. Don't ever do that.'

'OK,' my brother said. 'I'm taking the tapes to the car in case she comes back.' And out he went.

I started for the stairs. But yes, the comment about a dead body was living inside my head now. There was a car in the driveway but no sign of Janet. Was that Janet's car? I hadn't checked to see what she might be driving the last time I'd been here. For all I knew she'd never sold Howard's car, although they weren't living together when he died. Maybe it was the car of the friend she drove off with to go shopping or to a movie or something. Maybe I was hesitating because I didn't want to find a dead body upstairs in the bedroom. All these were possibilities.

There didn't seem to be an alternative, so I put my foot on the first stair and started climbing. And now, the silence in the house didn't speak to me of emptiness but of a lack of life. Why hadn't I gone into the frozen yogurt business or something? Why was I following my brother into a house illegally and worrying myself about a woman who was probably out getting a frozen yogurt?

There were twelve stairs leading to the second floor. Yeah, I counted. When you're taking an obscene amount of time to climb a staircase, the first thing that pops into your mind is to count the stairs. Twelve. I went back down and climbed again to be sure.

At the top of the stairs was a landing and a hallway led in either direction. I went right first. There was a linen closet behind the first door, then a bathroom (nobody in there) and then the main bedroom. The door was open.

Absolutely nobody was lying dead on the bed, or the floor. It was almost a disappointment. But there was still the other side of the landing.

Sure enough, there was a powder room there sharing plumbing with the main bathroom. Then there were two smaller bedrooms, assumedly one that had been for Bill and another that was an office or a guest room.

What I assumed was Bill's former room did not, alas, have a slip of paper bearing his new phone number; that would take a little digging. And it sported no family photos, which I guessed he had taken with him or had been moved elsewhere in the house. It was a fairly generic room with a twin bed and a desk. No personal effects to speak of or, for that matter, to say nothing about, either.

The guest room, as I'd decided to call it, was last to be checked. And I will admit to hesitating when reaching for the doorknob. I'd so sold myself on finding a corpse in the house (despite the lack of any indicator) that with only one room left, I'd decided it had to be here.

What was there was weirder.

The room was laid out much like Bill's: it had a twin bed

but no desk. There was a closet and a small table, as if someone were going to ask a friend in for lunch. There was a wooden dresser, with no personal items displayed on it. There were curtains (blue) on the windows and a rug (equally blue) on the floor.

And there were a boy's dress shoes and sneakers next to the bed, alongside a pair of slippers for bedtime.

I checked the closet, and there was a full wardrobe of boys' clothing, I'd say age three-to-eight. Blue was the favored color. There was one suit of clothes, in case the boy who lived here (?) had to go on a job interview, some slacks, no jeans, no t-shirts and no shorts. It was like looking into a young boy's bedroom if he lived at IBM.

It startled me when my phone buzzed. There was a text from Ken: **Get out now! She's back!**

No time to lose, so I didn't look in the dresser. I did make sure everything looked untouched and ran for the stairs, then the side door. Before Janet, whom I could see walking from a taxi to the house in double-time, could make it inside, I was out the door and watching from the side of the house.

'Who's that?' Ken asked in a whisper. As much of a whisper as my apartment building of a brother could manage.

'I've only seen pictures, and it's been some years, but I think that's her brother-in-law, Marc Hawley,' I said.

'The one who killed his wife?'

I tilted my head affirmatively. 'Allegedly.'

'This is getting weird,' Ken said.

'Getting?'

TWENTY-TWO

'So she was with a man who might have been her brother-in-law,' Mank said. 'Are you sure it was him?'

I know, I know. Mank and I had a lot to discuss, but it wasn't going to happen now. Ken and I had driven back into town, dropped off our rental car and then taken the subway back to Mank's precinct (where thankfully Bendix was nowhere to be found) without calling ahead because I'm a coward. I was *consulting* with him, the very thing he'd said was all I'd ever wanted from him, because I wanted some clarity on what the scene we'd witnessed at Janet Hawley's house might have meant and if it constituted an illegal action.

'I can't say for certain,' I answered, after considering the possibility of saying it was Marc for sure. 'Also, she had a whole room devoted to a boy, an entire closet of clothes for him. There was a winter coat and wool sweaters in it. But there was no boy.'

Mank looked at me sideways. 'A winter coat and sweaters? Like she'd have for a *guest*?' he asked. 'And by the way, what were you doing in her house if she wasn't there?' I'd been hoping to avoid that question.

I cleared my throat. It didn't need clearing. 'Acting on an anonymous tip,' I said.

'By breaking into a woman's home?'

Ken, stepping forward because he thinks he can protect me, said, 'The door was open when we got there.' Well, we got there and then the door was open. It was all in how you looked at it.

'Uh-huh.' Mank wasn't the Kearny, New Jersey, police, and he wasn't at all interested in arresting Ken and me for something that allegedly happened when he wasn't around to see it. Compassion makes a good cop better. 'Still, having a room for a child in your house isn't illegal, and it's not in New York City, so it's been nice catching up, but I have actual police work to do.'

I had a hunch and I was not able to research it as well as Mank could. 'Can you just check and see if any boys between the ages of three and eight in that general area have been reported as missing in the past month or two?' I noticed my voice reaching the upper register of its range as I finished that question. Maybe Mank had a valid point when he said this was the basis of our relationship. I didn't like to think that.

He looked up to meet my eyes. Even sitting down I was taller than Mank. 'You've decided a room decorated for a small boy means that one has been abducted, and that a man you've never seen before is a murderer on the lam?' The language was meant to be somewhat snide, which I did not appreciate.

'I'd just like to eliminate those possibilities if I can.'

Mank looked at me, then at Ken, who was registering amusement, then back at me. I was not registering amusement. 'If I look into it, will you leave?' That was kinda cold.

'If that's what you want.' I can be a jerk of an ex-girlfriend if the situation calls for it.

He nodded once. That's what he'd do, then. The laptop was opened and the keyboard was utilized with a good deal of enthusiasm. It took a few minutes, during which I looked around the squad room, saw Bendix walk in, which was all I needed, and Ken took a few long swigs out of the Slurpee he'd bought at a 7-Eleven on the way here. It was blue. Don't ask me what flavor that is.

'OK,' Mank said. 'The last reported sighting of Marc Hawley was seven years ago, in Buffalo, New York. None in any county in New Jersey since the night of the murder. Here's a photograph of him they had from the time.'

He turned his monitor to show me the same picture I'd seen of Marc before. It was still blurry. I shrugged.

'Any abducted children?'

'You think I have immediate access to every kidnapping that's taken place in an unspecified section of New Jersey for the past thirty years? That's the best I can do. Now let me go to work for the City of New York, OK?' I didn't think I'd ever seen him this prickly before.

'OK,' I said. I sounded meek and wounded. I thought about putting myself out of my misery and then I remembered I wasn't a gerbil. 'We'll get out of your way.' I stood up, trying to look fierce.

But Ken didn't move. 'What's going on here?' he asked Mank. (Mank!) 'Are you both going to give up on finding a possible murderer because you're having a *tiff*?'

Mank, being a full foot shorter than my brother, probably didn't consider taking him on in a fistfight, but his face indicated that he'd like to. 'A tiff?' he repeated.

'Yeah. You and my sister are having a rough time admitting you still like each other, so a woman's killer gets away and our client never finds his parents. Nice priorities.'

And that, of course, was when Bendix decided to waddle on over, a complete lack of understanding in his smile. 'What have we here?' he asked. 'You're not going back on me for the wedding, are you, Fran?' He put his beefy hand on my left shoulder. He had to reach way up to do it.

I have never wanted to kill a person. But I could see myself making an exception for Bendix. 'I'm not going back on you because I never said I would go,' I said in what I was hoping was a low enough volume that no one past Mank's work station could hear. 'I said I would check my schedule and guess what – I can't make it. Now take your hand off my shoulder or they'll be calling you Lefty for the rest of your life.'

I've never seen my brother look so amused in his life. By the same token, the look of utter disappointment and, yes, betrayal on Bendix's unattractive face actually had me feeling bad about what I'd just done. Even Mank looked sympathetic, and he probably hates Bendix even more than I do.

Bendix immediately removed his hand and took two steps backward. 'OK,' he said. He sounded like a seven-year-old caught with his hand in a box of Oreos. 'I won't bother you.'

He walked back to his desk on the other side of the bullpen.

I swear, I almost went after him to apologize and tell him I'd be his date for the wedding. Almost. I do have limits to my empathy. I won't say my eyes teared up, but they gave it some thought until I looked at my smirking brother.

'Get up,' I said. 'We're leaving.'

Ken, recognizing the tone of my voice, stopped grinning and stood in a nanosecond, not an easy thing for someone with legs like tree trunks. I took a step toward the door and Ken was right behind me.

'Hang on,' Mank said. I didn't want to, but I turned to look at him. 'I'll do some looking into the Hawley thing. If it's him, there'll be an APB. I'll let you know.'

It was me getting him to do cop work for me again. 'You don't have to do that,' I said.

'I know. Give me a call in about three hours.'

I smiled at him and it felt like it had been a while since I'd smiled at anybody. 'Thanks.'

'I serve the residents of the City of New York,' he said.

Ken and I could walk to our apartment from the precinct, so we did. Half a block from the cop shop, my brother, without looking at me, said, 'Did I mess up your relationship with Mank?' Oh wow, he was being sincere!

'No,' I said. 'I don't have a relationship with Mank.'

'Uh-huh.'

I'm sure it would have gone further than that, but my phone, currently in the hip pocket of my jeans, buzzed. I chose to ignore my brother, which is usually the best course of action, and pulled it out for a look.

The screen had the same message as it had shown the night before. UNKNOWN CALLER. Made me wonder why Mr and Mrs Caller had chosen to name their child Unknown, but you can't figure some people. But what if it was my pal Jack again?

I answered it, fully prepared to hang up on any robocall. No such luck. It wasn't the voice from the night before, but as soon as I indicated there was a human (of sorts) on my end of the line, the voice on the other end had an interesting message for me.

'This is Marc Hawley,' he said. 'I hear you've been asking about me. I didn't kill my wife.'

This day just kept getting longer and longer.

TWENTY-THREE

I stopped walking in the middle of the sidewalk, something absolutely guaranteed to annoy all New Yorkers in my general area. They were all on the way to something vitally important and I was taking up valuable walking space just staying immobile with my phone next to my ear.

'How do I know you're Marc Hawley?' I said, so Ken would know who I was allegedly having a conversation with. My brother's eyebrows rose a bit. He indicated I should keep walking, but I had a nice clear signal here and I wasn't moving. You have to have priorities in New York.

'I don't know how I can prove it to you,' said the voice, which could have been that of a man about Marc's age, if I'd calculated correctly. I'm not great at math. 'I used to live in Arlington, New Jersey, with my wife Helen and our son Billy. Then Helen got killed by somebody with a dumbbell, a workout weight, and the police were going to think it was me, so I ran.'

'Where did you run to?' I asked.

'There's no statute of limitations on murder and the cops never looked for anybody but me, so you can't really think I'm going to answer that question, Ms Stein.' Marc Hawley, whoever he was, definitely was not stupid.

Ken gave me a light shove on my right shoulder, so I pointed at my phone and mouthed, *four bars*. He looked impressed and took a step back.

'Why did you call me, Mr Hawley?' I asked. It seemed a logical question. He had eluded the authorities for twenty-five years; why call up a random private investigator because his name had been mentioned a couple of times to . . . 'Did Janet tell you about me?'

Marc Hawley – and I was starting to believe this *was* Marc Hawley, which made me wonder who had called to threaten me the night before – made a low sound in his throat at the mention of his sister-in-law's name. 'I've been sworn to secrecy,' he said. 'Yes, she did.'

'I'm not investigating your wife's murder,' I told him. 'I'm trying to find the birth parents of a client of mine, and I have suspicions that he was involved with your family at some point. Have you ever heard the name Austin Cobb?'

Ken shook his head slightly, disagreeing with my tactic. I shrugged, because it was too late to do anything about it, and besides, he was wrong. People still looked pissed off as they passed me, but I managed not to let it interfere with my self-esteem.

'I don't believe I know that name,' Marc said. 'Should I know it?'

'The truth is, I don't know,' I answered. 'He was adopted a few years before your wife was killed and his birth parents lived in or near Kearny. There's some circumstantial evidence that he knew you or your brother, but I have not been able to confirm that yet.'

When Marc spoke again, his voice was spacier and less friendly than before. 'That doesn't sound familiar,' he said.

I decided, against the advice that Ken would give if he knew what I was thinking, to push a little harder. 'He would have been just about the same age as your son Bill,' I said. 'Maybe they used to play together. Austin is of mixed race and on the autism spectrum. Does that ring any bells for you?'

Because I'd only seen *someone* running into Janet's house, I had no idea what Marc Hawley might look like today. But I pictured him pulling on his collar, perspiring and widening his eyes. I think I was picturing Rodney Dangerfield. What? I saw *Caddyshack*.

'No.' All of a sudden Marc's answers were getting a lot shorter. Maybe I'd pushed him a little too hard after all. 'Billy was only seven when Helen died. I was working full time and I didn't see who he was playing with all the time. I don't know. No.' Maybe not shorter, but certainly less sincere.

'Mr Hawley,' I said, trying to sound as friendly and solicitous as possible, 'did you have another son? Have you ever put a child up for adoption?' I didn't bring up the possibility that the second son, presumably Austin, might have come from an extramarital affair Marc might have had with a Black woman. I could hold on to that for a later question if necessary.

'No,' he said again. Then he hung up.

I tried not to move either my facial muscles or my iPhone, but Ken looked at me with a touch of pity and said, 'He hung up, didn't he?' I nodded, put the phone in my pocket, and we moved on. People all over downtown Manhattan breathed a sigh of relief.

'So we didn't find out anything, did we?' Ken said finally.

'Oh, no. We found out something very significant,' I told him. 'We have cemented the link between Austin Cobb and Marc Hawley.'

Walking beside me, my brother didn't give me the side eye, but even in looking straight ahead he managed to imply it with his eyebrows. 'Really. And what is that connection?' he asked.

'At the moment, it's cement.'

Neither of us spoke until we had reached our apartment. The sun was starting to set and I was feeling the effects of being up for thirty-six hours straight. 'I need some sleep,' I said when we walked into our kitchen through the apartment's main door. OK, its only door.

'Fight it,' Ken said. 'You don't want to wake up at three in the morning and think it's time to start the day.'

'*You* don't want that because I'll wake you up,' I pointed out.

'Come on.' Ken was trying to keep me awake. 'I'll make supper. You sit at the kitchen table and we'll try to work out this Austin Cobb thing.'

My brother, when he decides to cook, is actually a very good intuitive chef. I don't think he's ever read a recipe in his life, except during a two-week period when he was 'dating' a food writer for the *New Yorker*. And let's be real, he was just feigning interest in the recipes. But they served his purposes well.

Now, he was rummaging through our undersized refrigerator for something to base his mealtime ambitions on and found a small (for us) package of chicken breasts that we'd been smart enough not to freeze in our minuscule freezer after bringing it home from Trader Joe's. He put it on the countertop, then removed two cloves of garlic, some asparagus, bell pepper and a jar of Paul Newman's spicier marinara sauce, which to me tasted like Paul Newman's regular marinara sauce, but Ken says it's better. OK.

'Can you get some water boiling?' he asked.

'You told me all I had to do was sit at the kitchen table,' I whined.

'Fine. I'll do it.' I had started to stand, but Ken was already on his way to the cabinet to get the large pot and take it to the sink. I figured he'd do that, but the gesture is important. I learned that in Passive Aggressive 101.

'So what we have,' he began, since I could tell he was about to start a lecture, 'is your belief, backed up by nothing, that Austin Cobb was the child of Marc Hawley and some as-yet-unnamed woman of color, and was put up for adoption because Marc didn't want to tell his wife Helen about it. Five years later Helen shows up murdered, the cops immediately suspect Marc and nobody else, but he says he didn't do it and has been on the lam for twenty-five years. We can't prove *anything* here, and we seem to be losing our focus on our job, which is to find Austin Cobb's birth parents and ask them why he was put up for adoption. Is that about it?'

I didn't need to charge, but I needed desperately to sleep. It's not the same thing. I closed my eyes and let out a long breath. 'It's not backed up by nothing,' I told my brother. 'Marc immediately clammed up when I suggested he had a second son, and he hung up on me when I mentioned adoption. That's not nothing.'

'It's nothing-adjacent.' Ken had filled the pot with water and was putting it on the stove. He went back to the countertop to start dealing with the chicken. This apparently required pounding, since he took out a mallet from one of the drawers, put the chicken breasts in a large plastic bag and started wailing away on them. I'm told it's a good way to release anger. 'It's all guesses, Frannie. You got threatened on the phone and I got beaten up, sort of, in a casino in Atlantic City and then you beat up those other guys. Somebody's playing hardball here, and so far, it's not us.'

And then, when I was an inch and a half from putting my head down on the kitchen table and taking a nap, my phone buzzed again and that familiar UNKNOWN CALLER screen greeted me.

I didn't even get in a 'hello.' Marc Hawley's voice was now kind of familiar and he was operating on adrenaline by the sound of it. 'I'm very sorry I hung up on you, Ms Stein,' he said. 'That was very rude of me. But the talk of another little boy and an adoption got me upset.'

Interesting choice of words. 'What made you upset about it, Marc?' I asked. 'Is there something that happened all those years ago that makes you sensitive to the subject of adoption?'

At the name 'Marc,' my brother turned away from the stove, where he was sautéing chicken, and looked, for once, interested.

'I don't know why I reacted that way,' Marc said, and in my head, I was replying, *Yes, you do. Just tell me.* 'But I want you to understand that we had only our one son, and not having seen him for all this time is extremely upsetting to me. He won't answer my phone calls and I don't have an email address, for obvious reasons. It's killing me that my own son thinks I killed his mother.'

Did you kill his mother? The conversation in my head was much different. Instead, I said, 'You've tried to get in touch with Bill?' That was something I would very much have liked to do.

'Yeah, he's out there on the West Coast and he's doing OK from what I can tell, but he believed what he was told about his mother, so he thinks I'm responsible. And he won't talk to me, so he can't hear my side of the story. I didn't kill my wife, Ms Stein.'

After all the brick walls in this case, finally an opening! 'Would you like me to tell him that?' I asked. 'If he won't answer your calls, maybe he'll talk to me.' Knowing what Bill remembered and what he'd been told would be invaluable. Especially if he remembered anything or had been told something true.

'You would do that for me? How do you know I'm telling the truth?' Marc seemed genuinely surprised and touched, and not at all clued into me wanting a way into this case, even if it turned out he *had* killed Helen. I'd be happy to turn him in if that were true.

'I don't,' I admitted, 'but I'm willing to tell your son that you say you're not responsible, and to communicate to him the pain you feel that you haven't been able to talk to him for all this time.' And then I couldn't help thinking about my own parents, and how we hadn't seen them in even longer, and that led me to thinking about Malcolm X. Mitchell, and who needed that?

Ken turned back toward the stove because dinner was dinner no matter who was on the phone, and during that time, Marc seemed to be thinking over what I'd said, because I could still hear generic background noise behind him (he appeared to be outdoors), but he said nothing.

I chose not to prod him because I wanted him to think this was his idea if he came around to the way I was thinking. Ken took a glance over his shoulder to see if I'd put down my phone, if Marc had hung up on me again.

But Marc was doing anything but that. I heard him sniffle a bit and then he cleared his throat. His voice was a little raspy. He was crying.

'I'd really appreciate it if you could do that for me, Ms Stein,' he said. 'Please let me know what Billy says to you.'

'I promise I will,' I said. 'But you're going to have to give me his number.'

It took seven more minutes to persuade Marc Hawley, after which I had Bill Hawley's phone number.

But when I said, 'I saw you at Janet's house,' he hung up on me again and didn't call back.

TWENTY-FOUR

I didn't call Bill until the next day. I was tired enough to consider myself incoherent, and even though my brother offered to make the call – just what I needed – this was something I'd do myself. In my office. Where I did business as an adult investigator.

Ken, I knew, had spent a decent amount of time the night before watching VHS home movies from Janet's house, but I'd been too tired to join in. They probably would have put me to sleep anyway.

Before I got the chance this morning to dial the number Marc had given me (assuming that was Marc, because I didn't have to believe him when he said that's who he was), my phone rang, and Austin Cobb was on the line. I sighed a bit, knowing I had very little of substance to report.

'Good morning, Austin,' I said.

'Hello, Miss Stein.' It was too late to correct him now. 'I am calling for my regular progress report.'

Of course he was. He had waited, probably staring at his phone, until the very stroke of nine a.m., the beginning of the K&F Stein Investigations business day, and had hit *Call*. This was Austin believing he was being incredibly patient, and in a way, he was.

'I don't have huge breakthroughs for you yet,' I told him, anticipating a groan from the other side of the conversation, which I got. Patience was not Austin's strong suit. 'But I have made some progress.'

Austin sounded a little stern. 'Well, that's what these reports are supposed to be about,' he said. 'What progress have you made?'

'I have been in contact with a man named Marc who says he is not your biological father, but I believe it's possible – not certain, by any stretch – that he isn't telling the truth. He also has a son about your age named Bill and I'm about to call Bill to find out what he can tell me about his childhood and possibly yours. How old were you when you started living with your adoptive parents?' I already knew the answer to that question. But having Austin start with a piece of information I knew might keep him from being annoyed with me for not having solved every mystery of his childhood in less than a week.

'I was thirty-five months old, one month before my third birthday,' he said, in case I was completely incapable of doing arithmetic. Which was actually a decent assumption.

'And the only time you remember from your life before was your birth father teaching you to read the name "Kearny" off the town's welcome sign? Is that right?'

'That is correct.' Austin wasn't being snippy; that's how he talked.

'Austin, if I brought you a picture of a man, do you think you'd know if he was your birth father?'

The other end of the phone line remained practically silent. I took that to mean that Austin was thinking and seriously debating the question in his mind. 'I can't say for certain,' he answered finally. 'But I will know better once I see the picture.'

Now all I needed to do was find that picture of Marc Hawley, and then make sure that the guy on the phone was the same man.

'OK. I'll get a picture and then I'll call you. Don't worry. We are making progress.' Sort of.

'I suppose you are,' Austin said. He could be painfully honest.

I disconnected and then did some more arithmetic. It was 9:10 a.m. in New York. That meant it was 6:10 a.m. in California. If I called Bill Hawley now, he was not likely to be thrilled to hear his phone ring. I needed to wait at least two hours.

And suddenly I felt like I had been inside for too long. Yeah, it had only been twenty minutes, but stop being so judgmental. I told Igavda I was going out for coffee and asked if she wanted anything. Igavda has never wanted anything. I was surprised she accepted her paycheck (via direct deposit) every two weeks.

So now I didn't even have to get coffee if I didn't feel like it and I could stay out in the city for as long as I liked (within reason). I would have gone to the Jewish deli downstairs from my office, but they didn't open until eleven. So *Coffeé*, the café down the street, would have to do. I could pretend to write a novel like everyone else there, but they'd be on laptops and I had only my phone. I'd check the three emails I'd gotten this morning. And maybe I'd get a mocha just to fly in the face of adulthood a little.

I was reaching for the handle to the café door (the *Coffeé* door?) when I felt something in my back. Something very much like a gun barrel. And there was a man, about six-foot-two (so a little shorter than me) behind me, not so much whispering as soft-talking into my ear.

'Come with me or I'll shoot you.' That seemed pretty direct. I let go of the door handle, with every intention of hoisting this guy off the street and possibly throwing him down the stairs of the nearest subway station, three blocks away.

But there was another man with him, perhaps the same size, and he also appeared to be pointing a weapon at me. 'We don't want to hurt you,' he said.

'So why didn't you bring a Nerf gun?' I asked him.

Now, I have the same instinct for self-preservation as anyone, but I'm harder to kill than most everyone else. I didn't want to get shot, just because I thought it would hurt. On the other hand, I agreed that even with Malcolm Mitchell roaming the streets freely, I had to adhere to our agreed-upon security protocols, which were pretty much based on the idea that I not decorate the streets with assailants whenever possible.

Besides, if I went along with these two jerks, there was a decent possibility that I'd meet someone higher up in their organization and maybe find out what exactly it was they wanted from me in the first place, so I could aggressively not give it to them. And if they took me somewhere indoors, I'd be able to decorate the walls with them and that would be satisfying.

'She's funny,' the first guy said to the second. The one who had originally talked to me was wearing, believe it or not, a navy-blue polo. It was like being abducted by a Best Buy employee. Then he turned toward me. 'You're coming with us,' he said, trying to add some authority to his voice.

I shrugged. 'OK,' I said. 'Lead on.' I gestured toward the street.

'C'mon,' polo shirt said. His friend, in a cheerful short-sleeved plaid shirt (green), followed, scowling. I guessed I was supposed to have put up more of a fight. That, I assumed, would come later.

Given that I'd already agreed verbally to going with them, I felt polo shirt's comment was redundant, but there was no point in arguing the question. Some people won't admit when they're wrong. I was feeling quite normally charged and not especially concerned about anything about to happen. 'Where's the car?' I asked. The last time I was kidnapped, there had been a van and I was tranquilized. Apparently this time I'd get to stay awake for the whole thing.

Plaid shirt chuckled. 'Car,' he said. Perhaps he'd never heard the word before and thought it sounded funny.

'There's no car, lady.' Polo shirt was less easily amused. He just kept walking uptown and his colleague and I kept following him. I decided at this point that if I didn't discover something really important either about Austin Cobb or Malcolm Mitchell, I would have to mess these boys up badly. All I'd wanted was a cup of mocha and a little time to myself.

Two blocks later I was a bit surprised to see polo shirt head toward the entrance to the 6 train. 'The subway?' I said. 'You're abducting me to the subway? What kind of low-rent kidnappers are you guys?'

Polo shirt stopped at the top of the stairs and turned to stare at me. 'Keep your voice down! And get down these stairs!' He pointed, as if I didn't know which stairs he might have meant. He didn't know it, but he had just added a hard backhand to the jaw to his eventual punishment.

We trudged down the subway stairs, polo shirt first, then me, then plaid shirt, single file. They wanted to make sure I wasn't going to bolt on them. Not a chance of that now; I wanted to speak to the manager. Whatever stop he was at.

(I apologize for assuming the manager would be a man. I sincerely hoped the criminal mastermind involved here would not be a woman, out of sisterhood and all that.)

I headed toward the turnstiles to get to the train, but plaid shirt stuck that damned gun in my back and herded me to the left. On the wall beyond the MetroCard machines there was a door that I probably wouldn't have noticed under any other circumstances, painted the same color as the wall, if you wanted to call that a color. Polo shirt pulled a card from his pocket and tapped it on a sensor at the door, then opened it. The door.

They worked for the MTA? I was being kidnapped by subway employees? This was a lot. It was going to take me a while to clear my head.

'What goes on in there?' I asked polo shirt (because he seemed to be in charge). 'You going to revoke my MetroCard?'

He didn't answer, which was probably wise on his part. I was already thinking of breaking his leg. No sense in adding on.

Plaid shirt nudged me through the door, not buying himself any good will. I looked into the room and walked in carefully in case there was something sinister in there. The subway is sort of famous for rats. I'm not a fan.

But it was just what appeared to be a staff room of some sort. There were no monitors of the station, which you might have expected, especially if you were me. It looked like a very low-tech conference room from 1982. There was a small wooden table in the center with four chairs around it that didn't match each other. There were no windows, which was not my favorite feature. If you can't see out, they can't see in.

Plaid shirt was very deliberate about locking the door as soon as we were inside. The place had a general dankness to it because, let's face it, we were below street level and near a very loud subway track. Not the kind of area where you want to spend a large amount of time.

'Have a seat,' polo shirt said. He gestured toward the table because, once again, he felt that I didn't know what chairs were for or how to find them. These guys were starting to wear on my nerves. To be fair, they had started to wear on my nerves as soon as they stopped me from going into *Coffeé*.

I sat, if just to speed up the proceedings. 'What now?' I asked. 'Hors d'oeuvres?'

They just both looked to the far side of the room, which wasn't that far, and into a shadow, where a figure was . . . I was going to say 'lurking.' The figure wasn't *lurking*. It was just standing there. Then it moved forward and into the admittedly sparse light.

And it was a man I'd never seen before in my life. Probably. His face was in shadows. All that suspense, and then this. Worst kidnapping I'd ever had.

'My name is Jack,' the guy said.

TWENTY-FIVE

I did sort of recognize the voice from the other night. It's not like you immediately commit every nut case you hear on the phone to memory, but he had a voice that couldn't definitively be categorized, and I'd noticed that. Sometimes it rumbled and other times, like now, it tried very hard to sound reasonable and almost friendly, but failed. This man was a problem.

'Hi,' I said. 'I'm Fran. Nice place you have here.' I stifled the impulse to wave my hand around the room because I thought he'd gotten my point and that would have made me seem more like polo shirt. 'Why am I here?'

'I told you to stop asking about adoptions.' Jack turned out to be a somewhat underweight man in his late fifties, I'd guess, of average height, with longish brown hair that had been washed in the past month. He was wearing, completely incongruously for this setting and this season, a wide-brimmed hat and a brown duster that hung off him loosely, adding to the illusion that he was in fact a scarecrow. 'You didn't stop. I told you there would be consequences for you and those you care about. There are consequences.'

Just to recap: I'm sitting at what is essentially a card table in what is definitely a folding chair. There's a man in a green plaid shirt sitting across the table from me, and he has a handgun. Another, in a blue polo shirt, is standing near the door in case I decide to stand up, walk over and leave, which I could easily do at any minute. And a guy who had called to threaten me two nights earlier, now dressed in clothes that Sam Elliott must have donated to a thrift shop somewhere in the last three decades, is telling me these were the consequences for me trying to find out who Austin Cobb's birth parents might be.

Sometimes life is funny. This wasn't one of them. This was just stupid. I decided to piss him off just to see what would happen. I took my phone out and snapped three pictures of Jack. With the flash on.

He went straight to shouting. 'STOP THAT!' Mission accomplished. I smiled at him, I think winningly.

I wasn't as tired as I had been the day before, but I was annoyed and under-caffeinated, sitting in a room next to the 6 train and just a bit on edge about rats. 'So what you're telling me is that unless I stop doing my job, you're going to make me suffer?' I said. 'Or is this the suffering that you had in mind?' And this time I did sweep my hand around the room just so he didn't think I meant the chair, which was starting to hurt my butt a little. I should move to a padded one, I thought. The one to my right looked like it might be better. Or would that be a sign of weakness?

'Ms Stein, I am not playing a game. You have been meddling in affairs that are *not* your job and that has been causing me some . . . inconvenience. I don't see the harm in *asking* that you stop.' Jack's face was largely in shadow under the rim of his hat, but I could see it all right. My eyesight might be a little better in the dark than yours. Or not. He looked, anyway, like an actor trying very hard to look menacing. Not a very good actor, either.

I stood up, with two purposes. First, I wanted Jack to see me standing and realize I was not like most women he knew. Second, if I pretended to be defiant, I could maneuver myself to the better chair. You've always got to be thinking in my business.

'You're not asking,' I said with what I hoped was a chillingly calm voice. 'You're threatening, and I don't take kindly to threats. If my trying to identify and locate my client's birth parents so he can ask them questions he's been thinking about his whole life is interfering with some criminal – I assume – enterprise you're involved in, I apologize for the inconvenience. But there's no chance I'm going to stop until I get the answers I've been hired to find. So are we done here?'

I didn't get the chance to turn toward the door. Jack, however retro his outfit might be, was quick to act in the present; he took three steps toward me that seemed measured and urgent at the same time. That's not easy to do. 'No, we're not,' he said. 'I told you there would be consequences.'

I made a point of looking around the room. 'There are only three of you here,' I said. 'I wouldn't advise you to try and overpower me. And if your buddy over there wants to use his gun, I promise you it'll be less effective than you might hope.' I really had no actual information on that last part, but there was no reason to think I was wrong until the theory was tested, and I was determined that wouldn't happen today.

'What makes you certain I was talking about harming you?' Jack said. 'There are people you care about. There's your brother and your aunt, aren't there? And I believe there's a police officer you have some involvement with. Wouldn't want anything to happen to them, would you?'

The only one I was worried about was Aunt Margie, and she has the ability to take care of herself quite neatly. 'My brother is bigger and stronger than I am,' I told this guy, who was getting more annoying by the minute. 'You sent three more of your goons to bust him up in Atlantic City and I take it they came back somewhat damaged. So you should know better. Now, the police officer and I are not in any way associated, and besides, being a cop, he carries a gun. And people have tried in the past to get to me through my aunt.' (No names here.) 'The ones who didn't go to the hospital have been dissuaded.' That was technically true, even if I was exaggerating Aunt Margie's involvement a bit. 'So why don't you stop trying unsuccessfully to scare me and get to the negotiations. I'm not going to stop trying to help my client. What will it take to get you to stop being a pest?'

Jack's eyes came close to bulging out of his skull, which would have been very unattractive. 'A *pest*?' he squealed, probably not the sound he was going for. 'I'm telling you that people you love might face very serious harm and you think I'm a *pest*?'

'More and more,' I admitted. 'Look. How about you help me find my client's birth parents and then I won't ask any more questions about the Hawley family? How would that be? Or I could keep digging there and find out something illegal has been going on, which might or might not involve you. And you can rest assured that if I do find something like that, I will not hesitate one second before I report it to the police and, if applicable, the FBI or Interpol. Wouldn't that be a bigger problem? What's your best offer, Jack?'

'My best offer is that you stop what you're doing and I won't cause any harm to you or people you love.' But Jack's shadowed face was worried; he was threatening me and I wasn't quaking with fear, as he'd expected. This was an issue for him and he'd have to find a way to cope with it. I could see what his choice of coping mechanism might be when he glanced toward plaid shirt, and I tensed my left shoulder and arm below the elbow to prepare for it.

'This is the problem,' I told him. 'Men don't listen when women are talking.'

'The problem is that women don't comply when men explain the world to them.' Oh, now Jack was *really* asking for it.

And he got it. He nodded toward plaid shirt, who took his hand off the table to reach for his gun. All I had to do was yank the table off the floor with my left arm, hitting him hard in the gun hand before he could reach the firearm, and then continue to swing the table to the right, catching Jack in the face and pushing him back. I think he probably got the most upset because his hat fell off and I could see that he had no hair on top of his head that hadn't been bought and paid for. Plaid shirt, wringing his right hand, tried to rush toward me, but I hit him with the back end of the table and he sat down. He did not look eager to stand up again.

Polo shirt, behind me, had a little more time to react, but it didn't do him tons of good. He reached for a crowbar that was sitting on a shelf next to him – because apparently subway workers need crowbars on a regular basis – and managed to get it into his right hand before I threw down the table, picked him up by his belt and spun him over my head a few times, making him drop the crowbar. He started to make sounds that indicated he might lose whatever meal he had most recently eaten, so I dropped him heavily on the floor and he stayed there.

Jack, having shaken himself back to full walking-around-human status, headed toward me again. I raised my right hand in a defensive pose I learned in tai chi training and he stopped in his tracks. 'This isn't over,' he said.

I let out a sigh. 'No, I suppose it's not, because you're going to go on being a pest,' I said. 'But what you just saw is what I can do without thinking about it. You don't want to see what happens when I can think about it.'

He took a long look at me. 'What *are* you?'

'Just another small business owner in New York City,' I said.

I walked to the door. It was locked, but from the inside, so it would have taken perhaps two seconds to open it. But the lock was old and rusty and I wanted to make a point. So I tore the door off its hinges and tossed it aside, landing just to the left of plaid shirt. I looked back toward Jack.

'Don't make me do this again,' I said. Then I left. Luckily, I was right near the 6 train.

TWENTY-SIX

There was just no point in making a big deal out of being abducted. Sure, that sounds funny, but I'd never been the least bit worried about myself and had gotten out without much trouble. Maybe Jack, and I never did get a last name out of him, thought this wasn't over, but I knew where he'd gotten my phone number and what he looked like, so I could be very careful about avoiding any future contact.

In the meantime, once I actually managed to get a mocha from *Coffeé* and returned to my office, I'd managed to kill a few hours, and now was a perfect time to give my old pal Bill Hawley a call out on the coast. Good ol' Bill.

He answered, strikingly, on the first ring. I wondered if Janet had given him my number, because he would otherwise have thought the random sequence of digits on his screen were a wrong number or someone trying to bother him about the warranty for a car he didn't own. I was leaning forward, elbows on my desk, and noticed myself feeling a little anxious about what I might hear in the next few minutes. But I couldn't be specific about what was worrying me.

'Hello?' Either he didn't have my number in advance or he was being some version of polite; it was hard to tell.

'Mr Hawley? Is this Bill Hawley?' I felt the need to say 'Bill' because a telemarketer would ask for Mr Hawley.

'That's me,' Bill answered. 'Is this Fran Stein?' Aha. So Janet had passed on my contact info.

'It is,' I said. I've trained myself never to say 'yes' on the phone to a stranger because it can be recorded and used in any variety of scams. No, I didn't think Bill was going to do that, but it's become a reflex. 'Bill, I'm calling in connection with a client who's trying to find his birth parents.' I've found that people tend to open up more if they think they're helping someone other than me.

'Who?' Bill said.

'I'd rather not share my client's name right at the beginning,' I told him. 'I might be following a bad lead, and then there would be no point in your knowing his name.'

'But you know my name,' he pointed out. 'That doesn't seem fair.' Bill was going to be a cagey one. That's good, because they tend to be interesting, and bad, because they rarely tell you anything you don't already know.

'You know my name, too,' I said. 'And if it becomes necessary, you'll know my client's name. But right now it is not necessary for my investigation or for your needs.'

Bill seemed to consider that. 'That's probably not fair, but I can't figure out why. What are you calling about, Ms Stein?'

I gave him the usual spiel about having a client looking for his birth parents and how he might have some information that could help. But the tricky part was coming up next because it was going to involve a very difficult part of Bill's childhood and there was no way to ease into that politely. 'I'm wondering if you remember another little boy in the house when you were living with your birth parents,' I said. 'Just about your age?' I didn't mention Austin's race because I wanted to see if Bill would remember Austin independently.

'You mean someone I played with?' Bill was going out of his way to be obtuse.

'Someone who lived there,' I said. 'Like a brother, or an adopted brother.'

Bill didn't stop to think. 'No.'

That's it? 'You don't remember anyone like that? You never had a sibling?' He'd answered the question, but I got a very strong feeling that he was lying, especially since he wasn't the least bit thrown by my asking about such an odd thing. A sibling he didn't remember?

'No,' he repeated. Suddenly Bill had a very limited vocabulary.

This had his adoptive mother's fingerprints all over it. 'Janet told you I was going to call, didn't she?' I asked in a less friendly tone. I wanted him to know I was aware he was lying. About what, I couldn't be sure.

'Janet?' I must have thrown him.

'Janet Hawley. The woman who raised you.' Oh yeah, her.

Bill's voice was suddenly very haughty. 'I call her *Mom*,' he said.

'She let you know I'd been to see her and she probably told you not to give me any information, didn't she? What's puzzling me is why nobody wants to talk about the other boy in your house when you were a kid. What's the problem with talking about him? Does it have something to do with your birth mother's murder?' It probably didn't, since Austin would have been out of the house for a few years before that happened.

'I'm not talking to you about that.' Bill sounded genuinely angry, but he didn't hang up, which was telling. So I could press on, in a different direction.

'That's fair enough,' I told him. 'I don't want to make you talk about anything you don't want to talk about.' A blatant lie. I wanted him to talk about *everything* he didn't want to talk about. Politics. Religion. The world's best ice cream flavor. But mostly, about Janet and her still-unclear connection to Austin Cobb. 'So instead, tell me about your birth father, Marc Hawley.'

Bill didn't talk for what felt like a long time. I pictured him reading through the prepared notes Janet had sent him and finding nothing. 'I haven't talked to him since I was little,' he said.

'I saw him yesterday,' I told him. 'He was with your mom walking into her house and then he called me on the phone. There's also an extra room in the house you grew up in that's set up for a small boy. Do you know anything about that?'

'I don't know what you mean,' he attempted. But I wasn't buying; it was time to go in for the kill. So to speak.

'Here's what I know, Bill,' I said. 'There was a room for a boy in your aunt and uncle's house, because that's who they were, with no boy in it, and it wasn't your room. I know that when your mother was killed, you were brought to your aunt and uncle and you stayed there. But if there was another boy living there, he would have been gone by then. I also know that Janet Hawley is refusing to talk about those days, that she is clearly hiding something about that boy. I know there's a man named Jack who is *not* your father Marc Hawley, and he's running around threatening anyone who even inquires about adoptions your aunt and uncle or your parents might have been involved with at the time. And I know that you are not speaking to your birth father and haven't been for years, and he wants me to tell you he had nothing to do with what happened to your mother.'

That was a lot to say, and Bill had listened quietly until the end. Once I'd mentioned Marc, he'd groaned a little and cleared his throat, but didn't say anything until I'd finished.

When he did speak again, his voice was closed and deeper. 'I don't know anything about another boy in my mom's house,' he said. 'My *parents* did foster kids every now and then when I was young, but as far as I know there hasn't been anyone else living in that house since my dad died. And that, Ms Stein, is all I'm going to say to you, today or ever.' And he hung up.

I was young when I got my first mobile phone, but I do still kind of miss the sound of an actual phone receiver hitting the cradle. It was so satisfying. Now it doesn't even feel rude anymore. Hardly worth cutting someone off, really.

But I didn't have much that was new, except that one or other of the Hawley couples was fostering kids thirty years ago. And now I had no choice.

I had to go to the cops. If he'd have me.

TWENTY-SEVEN

'You asked me out on a date,' Mank said.

We were at a very classy American restaurant (a diner) on 22nd Street having a relatively early dinner. I didn't want to bother Mank in the precinct because I didn't want this to be a work thing for him and also Bendix might be there, and I hadn't left that plotline going well. I was treading very lightly because I did like Mank and I didn't want to reinforce his idea that I only sought him out to get information on a case.

But here I was with him, hoping he'd give me information cops would have on the Austin Cobb case. I am, in case you hadn't noticed it yet, a bad person.

'Yes, I did, because I don't like where we've been lately,' I told him. I was having a cheeseburger, non-deluxe, which meant there were no fries. That was turning out to be a mistake on my part, so I was contemplating flagging down our server and getting a side of fries. Deluxe be damned. 'We've been saying hurtful things to each other that I'm hoping neither of us meant.'

Mank, eating a cheese omelet with hash browns and rye toast (because diners serve breakfast all day), was loading up on carbs with no mention of 'deluxe' in his order. Sneaky.

'I think I meant everything I said,' he told me, and my heart dropped about an inch. 'But I think it's possible I was mistaken when I said it.' That was something. It wasn't much, considering why I'd called him, but he didn't know about that. Yet.

'I hope so,' I answered. The cheeseburger was good and I should stay away from the starches. 'Excuse me! Can I get a side of fries? Thanks!' The server nodded and headed for the kitchen to tell the cook that the crazy big lady wanted the deluxe after all. I looked at Mank. 'I do like you, and I don't want us to be mad at each other.'

Mank is always a detective. That is to say, he notices things most people would not give a thought. For example, he notices when I'm being less than trustworthy. Like now. 'What aren't you saying?' he asked. I didn't answer, largely because he didn't give me any time to do so. 'Look, Fran. I've never been vague about what I want. I think you're very special and I want to be more than a friend. I don't know if you want that, but there was a time when it seemed like you did. And when I said I thought you only came to see me to get cop help on a case, I meant it. I felt hurt that you didn't see anything else in me than being a detective with access to the NYPD database.'

The server brought the fries and I didn't want them anymore. I just looked at them on the table and they looked very well cooked. I didn't want them. I was exactly the awful woman Mank thought I was but I didn't want to be. Should I just stay at dinner and never ask him about the Austin Cobb case? I had already ruled out telling him about being abducted because I was afraid his response would have been, 'Again?'

I couldn't look him in the eye. 'I can't sit here and tell you there's no truth in that,' I said. My voice was less forceful than I had intended. I felt like someone had punched me in the stomach, but not very hard because I'm a superbeing, but that seemed irrelevant now. 'I do come to you for help when the police have information I don't have access to. That's true.'

Mank looked at me – I snuck a glance – and his expression wasn't one of disgust, which I took to be a positive. 'I'm really hoping the next word is "but,"' he said.

'It is. But I really like you. I think you're funny and caring and a very good man. And I come to you for all those things and more. But as a private investigator, I can't pretend that you're not a wonderful resource at times I'm hitting a wall. I called you today because of both those things, but I've decided to ignore the second one and not ask you for anything tonight. Because I'd like us to start getting back to where we were, too.' I ate one fry. One wouldn't hurt me. It was very good. I had two more.

Mank sat quiet and I was afraid he would stand up and leave, carrying his fork. It wouldn't have been the first time. But he just looked at me for a while like he was deciding. When he spoke, it wasn't even with an exasperated sigh. 'What's the case?' he asked.

'What about all the other stuff?'

'Later,' Mank said. 'What's the case? You're a good investigator and you do it for the right reason, to help people. The NYPD should give you assistance when it can. What do you need?'

'Honestly, advice,' I said. 'It's not a question of police information, but I can't promise it won't be later. Right now, I'm just trying to figure out how to get unstuck.' I gave him the rundown: everything I'd learned from Janet, from Marc, from Jack (without mentioning the whole being held against my will thing) and from Bill. 'It all seems to be pointing somewhere, but I can't figure out where.'

'Well, I did some looking, and there has been no report of sighting a runaway killer in that area of New Jersey in the past six months, but it was twenty-five years ago, so that's not a terrible surprise. So I don't know who the man you saw might have been.'

I held up a hand. 'Advice, Mank. Not information.' I really wanted to hold to that. I was asking a friend – at least – for his expertise, not for anything he had to steal from work.

He sat back and looked a little dreamy, clearly thinking. 'OK, advice,' he said. 'You've been spending all your time talking to people involved with this murder in New Jersey. But you don't have any actual solid evidence that the murder and your client's adoption are tied together. You've made that assumption based on your impression that everyone you've spoken to is hiding something. But people who had something to do with a murder tend to have something to hide. What if you're looking in the wrong place?'

I've heard of tough love, but tough like was getting through just as brutally. 'If I've been looking in the wrong place all this time, I have nothing,' I told him.

Mank bowed his head a little and held up the finger of his right hand in a gesture suggesting I calm down a bit. 'Hang on,' he said. 'First of all, are you eating those fries?'

'You have hash browns,' I pointed out.

'They're soggy.'

I pushed the plate with the fries closer to Mank and he took one. He bit it in half and used the unbitten portion as a pointer for emphasis. 'I'm not saying that everything you've done has been useless. It's very possible, given the timing and the location, that Helen Hawley's murder *does* have some connection with the adoption, especially since the word *adoption* seems to trigger everybody you talk to. But I think you've been spending too much time trying to solve the murder, which isn't your job, and not enough tracking your client's adoption, which is. That's advice.'

'Won't one lead to the next?' I said, contemplating whether I liked him enough to let him keep eating my fries.

Mank nodded and took another fry. Too late to stop him, given that I hadn't decided if I wanted to yet. 'Likely it would. But your expertise is in tracking down birth parents for your clients, not in solving murders. Why not do what you do best?' OK, he could have fries.

'I've done most of the things I usually do and come up dry,' I said.

'Then do things you *don't* usually do.'

Now, that was a thought.

TWENTY-EIGHT

The offices of the Friendly Family Adoption Service were located in Yonkers, New York. I could have rented another car to drive there, but the subway will get you there, even if you do have to transfer to a bus just before you arrive. Which is what I did, and it took me less than an hour to get there. I will admit to taking a cab once I got to Yonkers because my map app (I don't make these things up) told me it would be another forty-five minutes to walk, and seven minutes by car. Which was accurate.

Friendly Family was housed in a flat-looking two-story building on the banks of the Saw Mill River. Well, a block from the banks. The whole building was dedicated to the agency, and there was security at the front door. That's not wildly unusual for adoption agencies because a lot of sensitive personal business is conducted in their offices. The guy with the gun was a little over the top, but not a cause for alarm, particularly for me.

'You got an appointment?' Not only armed, but urbane.

'No,' I said. 'You got any extras?'

He looked absolutely stumped, which was not a huge change from his resting face. 'Extras?'

'I need to get inside and talk to someone in records,' I told him, because the witty banter that would have become necessary otherwise would have been too time-consuming. 'Who do I talk to about that?'

'You don't.' My armed pal was going to play this one by the numbers. Well, the number 1, anyway. 'You go home and you call for an appointment, and if they give you one, I let you in.' He was bordering on quaint.

I put my hand on my hip to give him the impression that I was processing what he had said. I had no intention of pushing the guy through the door and then past the inevitable locked reception station, but I like to keep my options open. 'Yeah, that doesn't work for me,' I said, noting that his gaze was more on my hip than on my face. 'I really need to talk to someone now. How can you help me?'

Always ask them how they can help you because it carries with it the assumption that they have agreed to do so. The dimmer bulbs will just go with it because it's what you said. I was hoping this one, who wasn't a Mensa member but probably had graduated high school, would go along with me because he liked the way my hip looked, although his gaze had drifted somewhat higher, still not near my eyes. He was one classy guy.

If I'd shown him the USB port under my left arm, he probably would have invited me in and asked me out to dinner. But I felt that would be going a tad too far.

The guard did seem to be considering my question seriously. His mouth silently repeated back to me, *Help me?* And then his lips twitched back and forth like he was trying to figure out which magic spell to use to get me to go away. 'I can't help you, lady. You can't come in.'

'Stop me,' I said, and walked past him into the building. Hell, the door was open.

'Hey!' the guy shouted, and started after me. I just kept walking until I reached a reception area just inside the front door. The woman behind the glass partition was about forty, of South Asian descent and a little confused when she saw my armed buddy rushing in behind me. Her body tensed.

'You have to help me,' I said to her. 'My only crime is that I don't have an appointment and there's no time for me to get one.'

The guard, having caught up and huffing his breath a bit, did not, to his credit, pull his gun. But he did say, 'You have to leave.' He took a second to catch his breath. 'Now.'

I stood my ground and ignored him. The woman behind the glass held my fate, except that I really held it myself. If I wanted to get arrested for trespassing, it was certainly within my capabilities to do so.

'With whom do you need an appointment?' she said. That was good; that was positive. She was allowing that maybe I *could* have an appointment.

I had to choose my words carefully. 'I don't have a person's name to tell you. I need information on an adoption that took place quite some time ago and it's very important I find it. Who is the right person for me to talk to about something like that?' I thought I'd handled it well.

The woman, who was not wearing a nametag (and for that matter, neither was the guard), appeared to disagree. 'I'm sorry, but we are not allowed to give out that kind of information to anyone,' she said. 'I couldn't let you in even if you had an appointment because you wouldn't get what you're after in any event.'

I might not be Sherlock Holmes, but I'm not so bad at the investigation business that I had expected any answer other than that one. So I'd already prepared a backup plan of attack. I started to cry, quietly. (Yeah, they gave us tear ducts and everything.) 'You don't under*stand*,' I blubbered. 'My brother has a medical condition and we need to find out if it's genetic. It could save his *life* to get this background. You have to let me in!' I didn't even do any acting in high school, but I believed I had nailed the part pretty decisively. I hear the theater community is very welcoming of all sorts, but they'd never run into my kind before.

'I'm sorry,' the woman repeated, with very little change in her tone. 'But that is information we don't give out to anyone.' Apparently my heartrending performance had not rendered anything in her. Maybe I shouldn't apply for the Actors' Equity card just yet.

I let the sobbing get harder. And louder. A young man had entered the lobby (there was, after all, no security guard at the door) and was looking puzzled. The woman behind the glass noticed him and was starting to look at me as a problem, not just a visitor. 'His life is in your hands!' I shouted, and dropped to the floor in what I hoped looked like an emotional swoon. Not that I'd know; I'd never swooned before. There's not that much to it, I was finding.

Lying on the floor, which was refreshingly clean, I let big, heaving gulps of air out in the guise of weeping. I can't really gauge how effective it all was because the woman said, 'I'm sorry' again and the security guard reached down to pull me up by the arms.

As he did, I reached up gently and grasped him on each bicep. His eyes grew a little larger, but I knew I wasn't squeezing enough to hurt him. I drew his head close to my face. 'Do you believe that I can kill you with my hands if I choose to do so?' I hissed at him. 'Just nod if you do.'

The guard nodded.

'Good. Now. I'm not going to do that because you don't deserve it and I don't want to go to jail for the rest of my life. But you know I can, so you won't get crazy with that gun. And you'll do what I suggest you do.' I tightened my grip maybe one percent and his eyes got bigger again.

He nodded a second time.

'You're going to tell your friend there that I can come through. Tell her you've checked my ID and I'm all right.'

I stood up, pretending it was with the guard's help. He stood next to me, his eyes still registering something like awe (which, let's face it, was warranted) and I wiped my eyes (which were dry) and walked to the reception station. 'Please,' I said. 'I'm sorry I got so emotional. It's just that so much is riding on this.'

The guard, after I had surreptitiously shot him a glance, stood next to me at the window. 'It's OK, Dorothy,' he said. 'I've checked her ID. We can send her in to talk to Brittany.'

Dorothy, now that I knew her name, looked at him with a questioning expression. 'You know we don't give out adoption information,' she said. This struck me as odd, since this was an adoption agency. What kind of information *did* they give out?

'We'll straighten it out in there,' he told her. 'I think we can keep things calm out here. I'll get Bob to cover for me at the door.'

She didn't shrug, but her face wanted to. 'If that's what you're saying, but we never do that.' She pushed a small plastic badge marked VISITOR through the slot in the glass and didn't break for a second. She looked at the young man who had entered and said, 'How can I help you?' He, having witnessed my debut performance as an actress, just walked up and pulled his driver's license from his wallet. But Dorothy had clearly pushed a button inside the booth because a buzzer on the door sounded, and the guard reached over and opened it. He even held it open for me like a gentleman and we walked inside.

'I'm going to take you to the director of adoption records,' he said. 'Then I'm going to turn around and walk back out and I won't be a witness for what you're going to do.'

'Fair enough. Just give me fifteen minutes before you call the cops.'

'I'll give you twenty because you didn't kill me,' he said. We stopped at a door marked, *BRITTANY PASTERNACK, RECORDS*.

'I was never going to do that and you knew it,' I told him.

He reached for the doorknob. 'Whatever you're looking for, it must be important.'

'Matter of life and death.'

The guard knocked, then opened the door and let me walk in ahead of him. Behind a desk in the neatly appointed, but not ostentatious, office, sat a woman in her late thirties (?) with her hair back in a very efficient bun. She looked up, somewhat startled. 'Yes?' she said. That was interesting, because no one had asked her a question.

The guard indicated me and said, 'Ms Pasternack, this is Fran Stein. She has gone far out of her way to ask you for help.'

Pasternack's eyebrows dropped with concern and maybe a little annoyance. 'You know I can't give out records, Lester.' So his name was Lester!

'Yes, I do,' he said. 'I'll leave Ms Stein to explain.' He backed toward the door.

I nodded to him. 'Thank you, Lester,' I said.

Under his breath: 'Twenty minutes starts now.' Then he closed the door and was gone.

I turned my attention to Pasternack, who was looking at me with the air of a woman who had been asked the same question hundreds of times and had never varied with the answer. 'I have a very special situation to discuss with you,' I told her.

'I know.' It was like the exhalation of a very tired fire-breathing dragon, all smoke and no flame. 'You *desperately* need information on an adoption and I'm the only person who can help you. But I won't. Because I can't. These documents are kept sealed for a reason. If we start giving out records to everyone who asks, our reputation will be severely damaged and no one will want us to help them with their adoption needs. You can understand that, can't you, Ms Stein?' I think 'their adoption needs' was where I decided to crush her spirit if I had even the slightest chance. This wasn't a lawn care situation; Austin Cobb needed to know about this to protect his self-esteem. And besides, I really wanted the dirt on Helen Hawley's murder. But of course this was all about the client.

'Yes, I can,' I said. Agree with them first. Then crush their spirit. 'But this adoption took place thirty years ago and it's very likely it is tied to a woman's murder.' I got my investigator license out of my bag and put it down on Pasternack's desk, open. Sometimes that makes people think you're a member of some law enforcement agency.

Sometimes it doesn't. 'I'm sure the circumstances are extremely serious,' Pasternack said. 'But my agency's rules are absolute and I've kept my job for twelve years by never violating them, no matter how serious the circumstances are. So no, Ms Stein, I will not ask your client's name and I will not be opening *any* of our files for you. Even if I'd run an extensive background check on you and determined you are trustworthy, which I doubt, I would not open those files. I don't do that for anyone. Ever.'

Now, you might think that was the end of the confrontation, but I hadn't crushed her spirit yet, and I certainly wasn't leaving without getting more information for Austin. 'I understand your point of view,' I said. 'You're a corporate automaton who must follow the rules without question even when they are in desperate need of questioning. I get that. You like your job and you want to keep it. I don't blame you. Most businesses would require humanity out of an employee who deals so intimately with people's lives.'

'Ms Stein.' Pasternack's jaw might need rewiring after this and I hadn't laid a finger on her.

'Ms Pasternack,' I countered. 'My client believes that it's his fault his birth parents put him up for adoption. He thinks it was because he presents as being on the autism spectrum. He's been carrying that around with him most of his life. You can help alleviate it. Now, suppose I suggest a way you can do that without giving me any files.'

'What I think you should do is leave.' She was probably a lot of fun at parties.

'I respectfully disagree.' But I did stand up. 'You can see how tall I am.'

Pasternack blinked a couple of times, but then she was looking up directly into her overhead light fixture. 'I don't see how that is at all pertinent.'

'I'm also very strong.' I decided to go on as if she hadn't spoken, because what she was saying wasn't going to help me, and I don't believe in negative feedback. 'If I wanted to, I could lift your desk up and throw it out your office window. Now, I'm not going to do that, because I don't think you want to see it and neither does anyone who's currently in the alley next to your building. And as much as I think it would look kind of cool, I don't want to see it, either.

'So I'm not going to threaten you because I'm not that kind of person, and besides, it's illegal. But I'm giving you an idea of exactly how much restraint I'm using right now because my client, his dead possibly-birth-mother and I have invested in my getting the information in his file. Is that message getting through to you?'

Pasternack just nodded.

'Good. I have, as I said, an idea for how you can help me without giving me any files.'

She didn't look excited, but perhaps she was looking for a safe way out. 'What is that?' she asked.

'*You* look through the files, show me nothing and then answer questions I have that will cover only some of the file and not all of it. You will not have shown me anything.'

Her head shake was not large, but it was visible. 'Oh, no. I don't think so.' That wasn't the most adamant refusal I'd ever heard. She needed a little more persuasion.

I reached over and picked up a small object from her desk, a snow globe that was apparently a memento of a trip to Vail, Colorado. Pasternack's eyes flashed anger, but she said nothing before I could ask her, 'Is this very important to you?' I held it in my right palm, fingers stretched over the top.

'Yes.' Her voice was slightly choked. 'That's a gift from my daughter.' The emotion she was trying to quash was an indication that her daughter might have died, or they were estranged. I didn't need to ask. I put the snow globe back where it had been.

Pasternack stared at it for a moment. 'You were going to crush it, weren't you?' she asked.

'Yes, I was.'

She looked me in the eye, which she hadn't been doing previously. 'All right,' she said. 'Tell me your client's name and I'll look up their file. But I'll only disclose what I can.'

'Why?' I asked. 'What made you change your mind?'

'You didn't crush it because it was important to me,' she said. 'That means something.'

I told her Austin's name. Because it meant something.

And Lester never called the cops. He tipped his cap to me when I left.

TWENTY-NINE

'It turned out she couldn't tell me much, but some,' I told Ken. It was one of those rare times when both of us were present at the office. I almost took a staff selfie just to commemorate the occasion. 'She could confirm that Baby Boy Doe became Austin Cobb. She knew about the Roosevelts, but said they both passed away since Austin's adoption and no, their heads weren't busted in with exercise weights. But what was interesting was how Austin got from the Roosevelts to the Hawleys to the Cobbs. If that's what happened. I'm still trying to sort it out.'

'Was the adoption through Friendly Family? Did her records say they had processed the adoption?' Ken asked. He had lately given up ogling Igavda because I'd yelled at him enough, and besides, he knew it was wrong. Instead he was juggling his dating calendar on his iPhone, which was already full enough. Besides, Igavda had met someone in 'Citizen Class' who actually spoke her language, and you can say what you want about my brother, but he will not intrude on someone else's relationship. Unless you count heckling me with Mank 'intruding.'

'She wouldn't give me names, but she didn't seem to dismiss the name "Hawley" at all,' I answered. 'She said he'd moved from the Roosevelts because his behavior had gotten him kicked out of nursery school and they didn't know what to do with him. He was in another foster home, but only for about five months before the Cobbs adopted him. I'm not sure I believe her about the Hawleys. She looked nervous when I asked about them.'

Ken looked confused, which was not unusual. 'But the Cobbs said they met with his birth parents when they were applying for the adoption. If Austin was abandoned as a baby, how could they have done that?'

'They couldn't. That's the point. What's interesting is that the adoption agency's records note that he had been abandoned, but then indicate – again, no names – that the birth mother had come back to claim him, gone through various legal machinations and then, less than two years later, applied to Friendly Family to find a family that would adopt him.'

'Was she with a guy?' Ken asked. 'Because Austin remembers his dad showing him the sign for Kearny, New Jersey.'

'Pasternack couldn't say, and I think it's because some of that file was classified even from her,' I said. 'I need to get Austin over here and show him pictures of the Hawley brothers.'

Ken stood up. 'Let's go find Austin,' he said.

It wasn't the worst idea I'd ever heard, so I moved to follow. I almost didn't check my phone when it buzzed, but a habit is a habit, so I dragged it out of the hip pocket on my jeans, which was nowhere near my hip. They lie.

I stopped and gasped when I saw the text, to the point that Ken looked at me and said, 'What's the matter?'

I read the text again two more times and then showed it to him. It was from Barry Polk, and it read: **Finally free in AC. If you don't hear from me in two days, either I'm filthy rich or your pal Malcolm has had me killed.**

I called him immediately, and he didn't answer. When I called Sarah, she didn't answer either.

'The longer this case goes on, the less I understand it,' I said.

'What case? Malcolm isn't part of Austin's adoption.' It's a sad state of affairs when Ken is the sibling making the most sense.

I waved a hand at him as if he was wrong, which he wasn't. I immediately texted Barry back: **Where are you? Your wife is worried.**

There was no answer. I waited an eternity – two whole minutes – and texted him: **You're fired. Come home.**

Nothing.

'Maybe he's filthy rich,' Ken tried.

THIRTY

'The Roosevelts?' Austin Cobb asked me. 'Like, Franklin and Teddy?' He looked, understandably, puzzled.

Ken and I had gone to Austin's place of business, Pharmation Labs, in Astoria, Queens, to question him about photographs I could have sent to his mobile phone and didn't. Sometimes you have to get out of the office, like when an old friend of yours is texting you like a madman about a mysterious figure your mother has told you to avoid and refuses to answer your increasingly frantic pleas to respond. Times like that.

After Austin had told the people at the lab's entrance that we were OK, and after a few of the people we passed on the way to his work area looked like they wanted to take tissue samples from my brother and me, we found Austin in a rather open space, a lab where he had a cubicle that seemed like a place he didn't visit very often.

'No, Austin,' I said. 'Your first foster parents were a couple named Todd and Julie Roosevelt. You weren't with them very long, but I had hoped maybe you had even a little memory of them.'

Austin looked baffled. He sat behind the small desk in his cubicle and looked at Ken, who might as well have been King Kong in this setting; he loomed over everyone. I did too, but Ken loomed over me as well. 'I remember my birth father at the sign for Kearny,' he said. 'I don't remember any Roosevelts. Do you have photographs of them? I might recognize those.'

I had been unable to find any pictures online of Todd or Julie, both of whom had been dead for more than fifteen years. 'I'm sorry,' I told Austin. 'But maybe I have a picture of your birth father. Do you think you would recognize his face?'

This made Austin frown with concentration. 'I'm not certain. Mostly I remember his hands pointing at the sign and his voice telling me, "It's CARNIE, not KIERNEY!"' He seemed very intent on my getting the pronunciation right, when I thought he was teaching me how to read.'

'Was he a very intense man?' I asked.

Ken caught on to where I was going. 'Did he yell at you a lot?'

Austin squinted his eyes in thought and then shook his head. 'I don't remember,' he said.

I took my phone out of my jeans pocket and opened the photograph I had of Marc Hawley. I turned the phone toward Austin. 'Do you remember this man?' I asked.

Austin, to his credit and exactly as I would have expected, stared at the picture closely for quite a while. He moved the phone to various angles and looked at it, perhaps trying to recreate the few seconds of memory about his birth father that he had left. 'I don't think so.'

Disappointing, but not a shock at all. I hadn't intended to go past that picture, but I did have one other on my phone, so I found it, blew it up as well as I could and showed it to Austin. It was a little grainy, but certainly visible. 'How about this man?' I asked.

Austin gave this one the same treatment as the first, and as it had been before, it was a time-consuming process. His pursed lips moved back and forth a little as he considered. 'I think I do recognize him. Do you have a better photograph?'

If I'd had a better picture of Howard Hawley, Janet's late husband, I would have shown it to him first. This was, in fact, a picture of a picture Janet had left out on a side table, that I had snapped when Ken and I were in her house. It had been strictly for background purposes. I hadn't expected to show it to Austin, but now he was suggesting he had known Howard.

'You think you know him?' Ken said. 'Is that your birth father, the man who showed you the Kearny sign?'

I could see the pressure building in Austin's head. He closed his eyes tightly and his lips moved lightly into his mouth. His hands, clenched, made little circles at his sides. The researcher at the next cubicle, a young Asian woman in a set of white scrubs, noticed it as well and she took a few steps toward Austin. But she stopped short of reaching out to touch his shoulder.

'You OK?' she said in a very low volume. 'Austin?'

Austin's eyes shot open and he looked at her. 'Yeah. Yeah, Mika. I'm OK. Don't worry.' She backed off, seemingly upset that she had intruded. I didn't touch Austin's shoulder, either. I didn't know how he'd react.

I tried to have a soothing tone in my voice, which is not my best thing. It's not easy at my size. 'Do you recognize the man, Austin?' I asked quietly. 'Is he your birth father?'

Austin shook his head. 'I think he might be my uncle,' he said in a matter-of-fact voice. 'I remember someone calling him Uncle someone.'

I didn't want to mention the name 'Howard' because Austin could just agree to that without having an independent memory. 'But he didn't show you the Kearny sign,' I said.

'No. That was definitely my father, but he's not in either of those pictures, I'm pretty sure.'

Now, that was a stumper. Austin didn't recognize either Marc or Howard Hawley as his birth father, but he knew Howard as his uncle. Howard was Marc's brother. Was Marc *not* who we thought he was? If, as Pasternack had said, Austin's birth mother had returned to claim him and he had a memory of his birth father, was Helen not his mother, either?

This wasn't getting any clearer.

'OK,' I said to Austin. 'I get it. I don't want to stress you out. You've given us all the information you can, and we appreciate it.' Ken was giving me incredulous looks, suggesting that he thought I should push Austin a little more strenuously. But I wasn't going to do that.

It was Austin who changed the dynamic. 'Wait,' he said. 'I don't want to quit now. I remember some of this, and it's so close. What are the names of these two men?'

As I said, I didn't want to mention them for fear of prejudicing Austin's memories, but my brother didn't have those issues. 'Marc and Howard Hawley,' he said.

Austin, seemingly discouraged, just shook his head.

Don't ask me why, but I remembered the pictures I'd taken in the subway station room where I'd been 'held' by three men and left in a somewhat less orderly condition than it had been when I'd arrived. I took the phone back from Austin and went through my photos, finding the clearest one of the three I'd snapped.

'What about this man?' I asked Austin.

He looked at it and did not go into a state of deep concentration or stress. He simply pointed at the phone. 'That's him,' he said. 'That's my birth father.'

Jack.

THIRTY-ONE

We left Austin back at work, having reverted immediately to medical researcher mode after a brief – out of necessity, because I had damned little verifiable information – explanation of who Jack was and why I might have a picture of him dressed in a nutty outfit near the 6 train. Austin, having seen the man he knew as his birth father, did not feel the matter had been settled completely, but he said it had lifted a lot of the doubt from his mind. The doubt, in all probability, had rested in whether he had hired the right investigators for his case. I wondered that, myself.

Ken and I went back to the office, where I could use my desktop computer, linked to our database, to upload my picture of Jack and see if there were any matches in our files that might help identify him.

While I was waiting and hoping (probably in vain) for a match, my cell phone buzzed and showed Mank was calling. We appeared to be back on good terms, so I answered. He sounded more excited than usual, which was unexpected. We weren't on *really* good terms. Yet.

'I think I have a line on that murder in New Jersey,' he said immediately. 'The woman whose head got bashed in.' He *was* excited, as only a homicide detective would be.

'Tell me,' I said, giving Ken a look of interest. He looked back and waved a hand at me as if I was leaving on the afternoon train. Then he looked back at whatever was on his phone.

'It didn't look like anything to start,' Mank said. He clearly had worked out how he was going to tell his story and would not vary from the script, so there was no point in my asking questions or diverting him in any way. No doubt the story would be worth it. 'I was going back over the incident report from the scene of the murder, and something was just a little off. The eight-pound weight that they assumed was the murder weapon was the only one in the room.'

I didn't see how that led to a huge break in the case, but again, I had decided not to ask questions and let Mank deliver his monologue.

'It sounds like it wasn't an elaborate set of weights, or a really unusual exercise area in the den, but there were two-pound weights, four-pound weights, five-pounders and a pair of twelve-pounders. But they were all in pairs, mostly shaped so you could put your hand around them, with the heavier part away from your fingers, what they call grip weights.'

Not that this tour through the home-fitness catalogue wasn't fascinating, but I was starting to wonder where Mank was going and how it would help us find out who killed Helen Hawley. Nonetheless, I held to my convictions and said nothing. He wanted to talk. If we started dating again, I could teach him this technique to use when I was talking.

'And that was what set me off. All the other weights in the room, which apparently either Marc or Helen, or both, used pretty regularly, were grip weights and in pairs. But the one they found next to the body, which was confirmed to be the murder weapon, was a standard dumbbell shape, eight pounds, and had no partner on the rack.' He waited a few seconds. 'Don't you think that's odd?'

That let me out of jail. 'Yeah, it is, but what does it tell us about the murder?' I asked. 'Are you saying the man who killed Helen brought the eight-pounder with him? Why? The others wouldn't have done the job?'

'There's more.' Mank had wanted that break so he could show off how additionally smart he was. 'Maybe the *person* who killed Helen brought the weight along, although that seems weird and unnecessary. But the medical examiner, or the team that came to look at the scene – because forensics might not have been a thing there yet – were either incompetent or covering for someone.'

'How do you figure that from a weight?' Since I could talk again, it seemed worth asking.

'There was blood on the rug in the room, and it matched Helen's,' Mank said. 'But there wasn't enough of it. And there were marks on the rug, that somebody tried to cover, based on the pictures I saw, that indicate to me Helen had been dragged into the den.'

Dragged? 'Before or after?'

'After she died,' Mank answered. 'Well, maybe after the attack, but before she died. There was still blood.'

My head was back into its swirling mode. 'This just adds more questions,' I said mostly to myself. 'Why would someone go out of their way to kill Helen and then bring her into the den? Was there blood anywhere else in the house? How come the cops didn't see any of this at the time? Who wanted her dead that bad? And if you saw all this stuff after a short time and the cops at the time didn't, does that mean someone's covering it all up?'

'Those are all good questions, and I've been looking into it,' Mank said.

'Why? This isn't your case. It's not even *my* case and it's twenty-five years old. Coldest case I've ever had. What made you so hot to solve it?'

'Because I'm in love with you.' Just like that. No build-up, no elaboration. Boom.

I sat there not staring at my phone because I didn't even have the presence of mind to do that. It was so out of the blue that my mind wasn't even searching for a response because what my ear had heard hadn't registered completely yet.

A while passed. Maybe a week. 'Fran?' Mank sounded a little worried. OK, a lot worried. Had his bold gambit failed miserably?

'Yeah.' That was the best I could do at that moment.

'Did you hear me?'

I don't seriously believe my hearing was in question right now. I knew he wanted a response. I even knew the response that he wanted. I just didn't know what to say or do. Given the opportunity to cement a relationship with a really good guy who had just said the 'L' word regarding me, I punted. (Which I believe is a football term.)

'So you think you can solve Helen's murder?' I said.

This might not be the time to point out that what I'd just asked was possibly the worst response I could have offered. Just take pity on my astonished brain and rest assured that I believed I would have a better response after I could think about it for a year or two.

It was Mank's turn to sit silent for an extended interval. 'Maybe,' he said a day or so later. 'Maybe.'

I had to rally. 'Mank, I know that wasn't what you wanted to hear.'

'No.' He cut me off. 'I always want to hear the truth and that was the truth. I get it.'

'I don't think you do. I just haven't had time . . .' For what? I didn't know what.

'It's OK, Fran,' he said. 'Take all the time you need.'

And he hung up.

Ken walked over to my desk looking at his phone. 'So how do we find this guy Jack again?' he asked.

Let's be clear: my brother's hearing is more precise than most instruments operated by the CIA. He had caught every word of what I'd said and in all likelihood the bulk of what Mank had said, including the most devastating part. By changing the subject, he was doing three things: he was avoiding having to talk to me about Mank's declaration; he had avoided making *me* talk about Mank's declaration; and he had made sure to ask me a question to which he knew I had no answer. We have a close relationship, but it's not without its sore areas.

'He's only ever contacted me,' I answered. 'I can't trace the number he used because it was labeled UNKNOWN CALLER, and then he just had his goons pick me up off the street.'

'And take you to a subway substation, which you might have mentioned to me before. Remember how we're supposed to be concentrating on security? A little heads-up wouldn't have been an awful thing.'

If we were going to indulge in a recital of everything I'd done wrong, I could take the rest of the day off. 'But that's the point, isn't it?' I said. 'It was a subway substation.'

'Well, that's *not* the point at all, but sure,' Ken said. 'What are you getting at?'

I stood up. Sitting had done me no favors lately. I would have walked over to get a bottle of spring water, but I already had one on my desk. I took a swig. 'Jack's boys, the ones who thought they were kidnapping me—'

'They *were* kidnapping you,' my brother helpfully pointed out.

'I let them,' I said. 'Anyway, they had a key card for that substation door. They didn't have to break in and nobody batted an eye at them as they led me inside.'

There are times I try to pretend my brother isn't intelligent, but he is. Except right now he wasn't picking up on me at all. 'So?'

'So somebody in that operation works for the MTA, and that means we might be able to track them down.'

'Yeah,' Ken said. 'We could do that.'

THIRTY-TWO

Our company database had come up with no matches for the picture of Jack, which wasn't a surprise. We hadn't dealt with him before and he probably had kept his face out of the online feeds of any notable newspapers, media outlets or socials. It had been worth doing the check, but it had been destined to fail.

So once we started on finding records of Manhattan Transit Authority employees, who are hired by the state and not the City of New York, and so therefore are part of the public records, held a little bit more promise in finding either Jack or one of his minions. I started by finding the MTA's employment records, but had to keep in mind that they might have been ex-employees who had not, as I'm certain they were instructed to, handed in their key cards. Finding the name and designation of the room in which I'd been 'imprisoned' (according to my brother) was the first step.

Because I knew what stop on the Lexington line the station was, and because I knew where the room itself was situated (and records of recent repair crews installing a new door), it didn't take long to figure out that it was listed in MTA records as a custodial supply conduit, which meant it was a storage area for the things teams who clean the subway stations (and yes, they do that) would use in their daily duties. Now, matching employees to that *conduit* should have been easy, but this was a New York State government database, and those are designed to confuse, confound and discourage anyone who accesses them other than the person who designed them, who no doubt believes them to be clear as a bell.

I was about to dive in when I noticed an incoming email on the top right corner of my screen. It was from an unknown source and I usually ignore those, but this one began, *Dearest Daughter*, and that was how my mother always started an email.

But this one was not as flowery or affectionate (or long) as usual. It read only: *Stay away from Malcolm Mitchell. Some of our friends in clandestine agencies are saying they've heard he's getting close. Stay away. Will get in touch soon.*

'Ken!' I yelled.

Once my brother read what was on my screen he sat down in the client chair that sat in front of my desk, and nearly broke it. It's made for normal people. 'I left Malcolm in Atlantic City,' Ken said, a little weakly, which is a big difference for him. 'Those three guys came after me, and when I was done busting them up I just caught the bus back here. I should have followed him more.'

I was shaken but more coherent. I actually read what Mom had sent. 'Nobody is blaming you for anything,' I told my brother. 'There was an abduction attempt on me and we're not trying to decide whose fault that was.'

Ken was looking at the floor. 'No, that was clearly your fault for not being aware of your surroundings.' Statement of fact. No equivocation. I had a choice: I could argue with him about how he was blaming the victim or I could ignore it and focus on our parents, who appeared to be in more immediate danger.

Because I'm more mature than my *older* brother, I chose the latter path. 'But it happened here and it wasn't Malcolm who tried to take me,' I reminded him. 'We don't even know what country Mom and Dad are living in right now.'

Ken hates it when he doesn't have the answer, or more to the point, when he doesn't have some harebrained solution he thinks he can sell me. He balled up his fists and hit them – lightly, thank goodness – on the arms of the guest chair, which valiantly held up under him. 'Why don't you tell me something I don't know?' he said. Classic deflection.

'Do you think there's any chance Malcolm and Jack know each other?' I said to myself. Ken just happened to be in the room. 'He's in Atlantic City and Jack's goons find you there. Jack tried to take me hostage and we know Malcolm, or someone working with him, has been trying to find Mom and Dad, and Jack tried to kidnap me. That's an awfully big coincidence, isn't it?'

'The last one is a reach,' Ken said. I'd forgotten he was there for a moment, so I started a bit at the sound of his voice. 'Mom says to stay away from Malcolm. We already knew that. Then

Jack's buddies thought they could beat me up and found out otherwise. It's not the same thing as Jack's guys walking right up to you and dragging you off the street.'

I growled a touch in the back of my throat. 'They didn't *drag me off the street*. I went along with them so I could find out more. And what I found' (because I knew he'd ask) 'was Jack, who apparently might be Austin Cobb's birth father.'

'Where's the connection?' Ken asked.

That was, and I hated to admit it, an excellent question, and one to which I had no answer at the ready. Malcolm X. Mitchell was some guy who had popped out of nowhere, first calling Ken on the phone and then trailing me in the subway, in an obvious attempt to find our parents, and most likely not to send them flowers. Now he was claiming to be another person like us, and Ken had seen a port like we have (or something that looked like one) under his left arm, like ours. I'd ripped it off his skin and found glue on the back of it. Malcolm was a con man.

Jack (no last name), on the other hand, had called *me* out of the blue to threaten my safety and that of all the people I care about if I didn't stop investigating Austin Cobb's adoption, which I didn't. We knew virtually nothing more about him except that Austin thought he recognized Jack's face as that of the birth father who had tried to teach him to read via a street sign at a very early age.

What Venn diagram existed where the two of them intersected?

There was another element in this story, particularly one that knew about both men, I was guessing, in Atlantic City. Since it was now clear that Barry Polk was alive and functional, I decided I didn't have to wait for another day to go by. I was his employer. I got out my phone and texted him.

Report on your movements and your findings immediately. This is urgent. I'm your boss. I require that you answer me right now.

I did not sign it affectionately. You don't sign texts.

While I was communicating with people who preferred to get in touch on their own terms, I answered the email from my mother.

I understand you're under duress, but I need more information about Malcolm, and I need it quickly. Knowing where the two of you are wouldn't hurt either. All sorts of things are going on here and I'm willing to bet you have knowledge about them that can help me. Please get in touch ASAP. This one I did sign. *Your loving daughter.*

My newfound aggressive attitude paid off by the time I had hit 'send' on that email. There was, sure enough, a buzz from my phone. And the caller ID showed Barry Polk on the other end. He wasn't even texting now. Maybe he was afraid I wouldn't pay him (I definitely was going to pay him). I picked up.

'Barry, I need to know what you know. Things are going crazy here. So tell me all you know about the guy I sent you to find, and if there's someone else you've run into, I need to know about them, too. Lives are at stake.' Maybe lives were at stake. I didn't know. But it sounded urgent, and that was the goal.

But the voice that came back was more familiar from a subway storage facility than my alma mater. 'Your friend isn't in a position to answer at this moment,' Jack said. He still had that movie-evil-genius turn of phrase, and I wondered why he thought it was helpful. He sounded like someone doing very bad cosplay. 'So you'll have to talk to me.'

'Where's Barry?' I demanded. 'If he's been harmed, there's no point in talking. I'll just find you and kill you.' OK, so I probably wouldn't have killed him. But when I turned him over to Mank, he would not have been in original factory condition. That was for sure.

'Your friend is perfectly healthy and I see no reason why he won't stay that way, Ms Stein.' Jack liked to address me by name. He was one of those formal movie evil geniuses. Although 'genius' might have been a bit of a reach.

'Then put him on the phone. I need to talk to him about a job.' Technically, the job I'd hired Barry for didn't have anything to do with Jack, but that no longer seemed likely.

'I'm afraid he's a little tied up.' I remembered how Ken had been treated by Jack's employees (I assumed they weren't family).

'I'm going to hang up now unless you tell me your last name

and prove to me that Barry is OK,' I said. And I definitely would do that. I wasn't going to call Sarah and tell her that my personal arch nemesis had hurt her husband while I spoke to him on the phone.

'Neither of those is possible at this moment.'

So I hung up. That had been a completely useless conversation. The only piece of information was that Jack knew who Barry was. And had his phone. I could assume that meant Jack was holding Barry hostage, but thinking that wasn't going to help me find them. Maybe I should have questioned him more about that, but based on the number of new facts I had after our chat, I did not have high hopes for . . .

My phone buzzed again. Barry's number. I took my time picking it up.

'I'm not going to continue to have these pointless conversations where you call me up and pretend to be Lex Luthor,' I told Jack. 'If you want to talk to me, use your own phone and have something to say other than, "Ooh, I'm spooky and you should be afraid!" Because you aren't and I'm not. So hit the road, Jack.'

'It's not Jack,' Barry said. 'I got your text.'

THIRTY-THREE

I was getting seriously tired of being confused. Strands of Austin's case were bleeding into Helen's murder, Malcolm Mitchell was involved even as Mom warned us about him, Mank was mad at me (again), I was starting to rethink the whole notion of being an investigator for people who were adopted, and on top of that, I was starting to feel like a charge wouldn't be an awful thing again. It had been a few days, and that was normal. I wasn't depleted yet, but it's better to top myself off (which is a lot less dirty than it sounds) ahead of needing energy badly.

But this, with Barry on the phone and Jack apparently nearby, was just too much.

'What the hell kind of game are you playing?' I barked at him. 'I've been worried sick about you.'

'Gee thanks, Mom,' Barry said. 'I didn't know you cared.'

'What the . . . who do you think . . . just what have you been doing on my dime, Barry? I want a full report and I want it now!' The Boss Lady thing had gotten me this far and I was going to ride it for all it was worth.

Barry's voice took on a more serious tone. 'I'm being watched,' he said.

'Really?' Was Jack keeping him in check?

'Of course not! I'm messing with you, Fran!' I wished, suddenly, that I had recalled Barry had an annoying sense of humor. And had a really bad sense of when to exercise it.

'Give. Me. Your. Report.' I was in no mood. No, that's not true. I was in a rotten mood. That's a mood. I was in a mood.

'Let me move a little away.' The sounds behind him might have been those of a casino. Not near the slot machines, because those are louder than you think, but out on the floor where it's just a lot of shuffling and people talking under air conditioning. No windows. Casinos had always sounded like torture chambers to me.

'Where are you, Barry?' I asked.

'I followed that guy Malcolm you told me to follow,' he said, which wasn't at all an answer to my question, but at least was *something*. 'We ended up in Atlantic City at the Borgata. I've been here all this time.'

Good Lord. 'Does your wife know?'

'Sure! She came down yesterday. She's up in the suite right now.' I wasn't hearing any prominent voice, like for example Jack's, talking to Barry. I wondered if that was good or not.

'The suite? I'm not paying for a suite, Barry.' I mean, worry only gets you so far.

'The suite is entirely on me, Fran. I've been winning like I never have before! Just yesterday . . .'

I cut him off. 'No. Don't tell me how lucratively you've been indulging your gambling problem. I don't have the time,' I said. 'You followed Malcolm to the casino. Then what? What have you found out about him?'

I'm pretty sure I heard him take a sip from a drink, then exhale with pleasure. 'Ahh. OK. Malcolm. He seems to be a guy who doesn't have a real job, but I've only seen him down here. In the city he could be the CEO of Citibank for all I know. I haven't gotten close to him because I didn't want him to see that I was tailing him. Once I met Jack . . .' And it was going to be necessary to interrupt Barry's strange story again.

'How, exactly, did you meet Jack, and has he hurt you in any way?' I asked.

Igavda waved to indicate she was closing up the front desk for the day, and I waved back. Ken was in his desk chair working on his laptop, or playing solitaire. It was hard to tell.

There was a pause before Barry responded, and there had been each time he'd spoken. 'Of course I'm not hurt, Fran!' he said. 'I met Jack here at the casino and we've been great friends ever since.'

I waved to get my brother's attention, then threw him a question I'd written on a piece of scratch paper on my desk and crumpled up. It was very low-tech but still proved effective. Ken looked at my message, did a little inquiry on his keyboard, looked back at me and nodded.

'And how do Jack and Malcolm know each other?' I asked, just to be sociable and see how far this could go.

The pause, again. 'Malcolm seemed to know Jack as soon as he got here,' Barry said, or his voice did. 'They embraced when they first met and they've been talking on and off since I first saw them.'

'Is Malcolm planning some action against people I know?' I asked. Malcolm's purpose in life seemed to be finding my parents, for reasons he had only lied about until now.

'Oh, I don't think so,' came the response after the requisite breather. 'He hasn't said anything about it and he's just not that kind of guy.'

OK. It was time to end the stupid game. 'What's your wife's name, Barry?' I said.

There was a longer than usual gap. 'Sarah.' Then another gap. 'Why?'

'Because you're using AI to simulate Barry's voice. Is this Malcolm or Jack? I'm betting Malcolm, because he seems to be more technologically savvy.'

There was no pause and the voice that came back was indeed Malcolm's. 'How did you know, Fran?' No apology, no explanation, no new information. This guy was a real annoyance.

'If I told you that, you'd be able to avoid it in the future,' I told him. 'Now put the real Barry on the phone, Malcolm, or I'm hanging up. Again.'

Ken walked over. *Malcolm?* He mouthed the name. I nodded. 'Put him on speaker,' he said quietly. For him.

I didn't feel like arguing and there might be some value in letting Ken hear what Malcolm had to say. Of course, it was going to be a very short call if Barry didn't take the phone quickly.

'He's not here at the moment,' Malcolm answered.

'Get him. I'll wait.'

'Look,' the little weasel said. 'I've got some information about where our parents are, and I thought you'd be interested.' So we were still on that scam, were we? Mom had said she thought he was getting close, but he couldn't have been *too* close if he was still trying to get information from me.

'They're not *our* parents, pal. And I don't believe you because you've never told me the truth once. Now, is Barry there, or isn't he? Because my finger is right over the disconnect button and I'll know if you try using a trick to pretend it's him.'

'OK.' Malcolm actually sounded miffed. 'You don't want to talk. I get that.' And this time he disconnected the call.

Well, that hadn't just been a waste of time; it had been an irritating waste of time. Now it seemed more likely that Malcolm or Jack had Barry's *phone* as a hostage, and not so much Barry, or they wouldn't have had to play electronic games with his voice.

I looked up at my brother. 'He should have figured out by now that we don't know where Mom and Dad are,' I said. 'Why does he keep pushing us on that? What's his motivation?'

Ken didn't need time to think about it. 'Best guess is that he's after the medical technology that created us,' he said. 'He seems to be the tech guy, but he's never hit it big. Somehow he found out about us and he knows *we* don't know how to make more people. He wants to get into the superbeing business.'

I sat there, stunned. When I could speak again, I said, 'That is without question the most frightening thing I've ever heard.'

'It fits all the facts,' my brother said, defending himself.

'That's what makes it so scary,' I told him.

THIRTY-FOUR

I called Barry's phone again in the hope that Malcolm, or Jack, or some other maniac I hadn't met yet, might have given it back to him. There was no answer. I envisioned Barry working undercover, trying to steal his phone back. It helped quell the panic because there wasn't much else I could do.

'Helen Hawley's murder seems to be at the center of everything we're doing these days,' I told Ken and Aunt Margie at our weekly dinner at her apartment. Meat loaf and mashed potatoes. Aunt Margie is old school. Ken loved it (and had made dinner). 'And Mank seems to have made it his hobby.' I hadn't mentioned his declaration of love for me to anyone because I hadn't processed it myself yet, and I figured if I hadn't told me, it wasn't fair for me to tell anyone else.

Aunt Margie spent years as a crime reporter and she absolutely adores a good cold case. 'You know the murder weapon, and from what you've told us, you know it was brought to the crime scene, along with maybe the victim herself, but that's not clear yet. You know the husband high-tailed it out of town the minute the cops got involved and hasn't been back, but he insists he didn't kill his wife. He just left his son to be brought up by other people.'

Ken, stuffing potatoes into his mouth, did not immediately chime in, to the relief of everyone else in the room. I took the opportunity to get there ahead of him. 'To be fair, Austin had already been adopted by then, and wasn't Marc's child. He's supposedly Jack's son.'

'Either way,' Aunt Margie said, 'Marc ran out and left his son Bill behind. Now Bill won't talk to him, which I understand, but that's because Bill thinks Marc killed Helen. And the only reason we think he didn't is because he says he didn't. Maybe Marc is lying about committing murder. I know it's a wild theory, but shouldn't we look into it?'

Ken and I looked at each other because we were thinking about how stupid we'd been not to do that. So I had to turn the tables. 'So what would you do, Aunt Margie?'

She looked a little surprised to have been asked, which was both fair and unfair. I often come to Aunt Margie for advice, but I'll admit that her background as a crime reporter was somewhat buried in my mind because for most of the time I'd known her – all my life – she'd basically been reading the news a few times a week for the local all-news radio station. Investigating crimes wasn't something I associated with her.

'Well,' she said, seeming to give herself time to think, 'I'd start with the official police report, assume it doesn't tell the whole story, and try to come up with questions from that, but your detective friend has already done most of that.' Aunt Margie sat back in her chair. 'If I was on this story, I'd have two very important questions that haven't been answered yet.'

'Only two?' Ken thinks he's witty.

Aunt Margie, being wise, ignored him. She held up her index finger. 'First, you need to find out what the killer's motive might have been. You have some vague notion that there was trouble in their marriage, but nothing very solid. Why did someone want Helen Hawley dead?' Then Aunt Margie joined her middle finger to the index. 'Second, if it wasn't her husband, who had access to the house? There was no sign of forced entry, you said from the police report. How'd they get in?'

'I got in by pushing on the side door lock of Janet Hawley's house and forcing it,' Ken said.

'I think we can rule out the idea that the killer was someone like you,' Aunt Margie said. Because apparently that wasn't obvious enough.

'I also want to know what Jack has to do with this, if he's Austin's birth father,' I told them. 'And I want to know why he's so intent on not discussing Austin's adoption.'

'And what he's doing with Malcolm X. Mitchell,' my brother threw in.

'We are way too late in the game to have this many questions in this many directions,' I said. 'How would you proceed, Aunt Margie?' Which was, to be frank, what I had asked her to begin with.

'First, I think you should make up with Richard.' She never wants anything more than for me to be nice to Mank. Maybe she thinks he's my last chance, or something. 'Then I think you need to talk to the detective who worked the case all those years ago.'

P. Monroe. Whoever that was.

I looked over at my brother. 'I'll find P. Monroe and you get what you can from the NYPD,' I said.

It was a weak try and it got the reception it deserved. 'Not a chance,' Ken said. 'The NYPD isn't in love with *me*.'

Aunt Margie's eyes lit up.

So the next morning I was back where I didn't want to be, in the local precinct, watching Bendix walk around with a sad/angry grimace on his face, and sitting across the desk from Mank, whose face wasn't a lot friendlier. 'I really think we should talk somewhere else,' I began.

'You want to talk about the murder in Jersey. I've told you what I know.' This was not the most romantic meeting we'd ever had. On the other hand, it wasn't the least, either.

'Any idea how the killer got into the house?' I asked.

He shrugged. 'Best as I can tell, she let him in.'

'Got an idea about a motive?'

Mank's face got more serious. 'I have a theory, but I don't have any facts to support it,' he said. 'Yet.'

'What's the theory?' I'd take what I could get.

'Not until I have facts. But it's in your line of work.'

'You're so exciting when you're cryptic,' I said, and his face went back to being impassive. 'So let's talk after this, OK?'

'Not today, Fran.'

'Tomorrow?'

He didn't respond in any way.

Time to switch gears. 'Do you know who P. Monroe is, or was?' I asked.

He didn't have to refer to his laptop, his desktop or any notes he'd jotted down. 'The detective in Kearny?'

'Yeah. I thought I might ask them for their memories of the time. It's certainly not all in the incident report. And then, please, can we go somewhere else to talk?'

Bendix slapped a file down on Mank's desk, glowered at me and walked back to his desk.

Mank's face softened a bit, but only a bit. He'd bared his soul to me and I had, in his mind, rejected him. I didn't think that was what I'd done at all.

'As far as I know, Philip Monroe is still alive. He retired more than fifteen years ago, and I did some looking for him but did not have a lot of luck because he doesn't talk much. He has a daughter who lives in Edison, New Jersey, if that helps. Dinah.'

'I can probably find a phone number,' I said. 'Thanks.'

He made a noise in the back of his throat. 'I have it.' He gestured for my phone and I gave it to him. Mank put Dinah's number in my contacts. 'Good luck.'

'Is her name still Monroe?' I asked him.

'Last I heard.' He looked at me like I should leave.

So I stood up. 'Can't we . . .' I began.

'Not now. Not here. I'll call you.'

'Will you?'

'Probably. Now get going.'

I passed Bendix on the way out and stopped to face him. 'I never said for sure that I would go to that wedding,' I said.

'Go home, Gargantua.' Great. I was on excellent terms with everyone in the New York Police Department.

Aunt Margie wasn't working at the station today, so I went straight to her apartment when I got back to our building. Being Aunt Margie, her first words on seeing my face were, 'I take it things didn't go well with Richard.'

I put up a hand like a crossing guard. 'Not now, Aunt Margie. I have to find a retired detective who probably won't want to tell me anything, connect a murder he botched to an adoption procedure, and then tell Austin Cobb exactly how twisted and weird his childhood was, before trying to find a friend of mine I sent out on a two-hour assignment five days ago.'

Aunt Margie sat me down on her sofa, which is her thing, but did not offer cookies because I wasn't actually in tears yet. 'So why did you come here first?' she asked.

'Because I want you to tell me that I'm not a complete

failure.' I'm not above reverting to my sixteen-year-old self when necessary.

She smiled at me as if I'd said I wanted to fly to the moon by flapping my arms. 'Oh, Frannie,' she said. 'You get like this whenever there's a snag in a case. You'll figure it out. You always do.'

Aunt Margie always seemed to be on top of everything. I couldn't remember a time when we were growing up (and yeah, we grew up just like anyone else, except more) that she couldn't handle a situation. I looked at her on the sofa, older but not weaker, grayer but not at all slower in the mind (her legs were another story). She was who I wanted to be when I grew up.

'Did you ever feel like that, when you were on a story?' I asked her. 'Like you never should have gone into reporting at all because you were certain to screw it up?'

She put her head back and laughed a little. I thought it was for show. 'Of course!' she said. 'It happened all the time.'

I was sincerely flabbergasted. 'You?' It was hard to imagine.

'Me. Who do you think I am, Lois Lane? I remember this one story, a murder in the Village. I read the police report and it sounded fishy. This woman drowned in her bathtub, one of the ones that sat in the middle of the kitchen, you know, on feet. But there were marks on her shoulders and forehead that made me think someone had held her down.'

'The NYPD listed it as an accident?' I asked. That was a little hard to believe.

'They said it was probably accidental, not a suicide. At least they got that part right. So I went down there and started talking to neighbors. Nobody saw anything, nobody heard anything, nobody knew anything. Except I could tell they did. But I couldn't get anyone to talk.'

She just stopped talking then, when there was clearly much more to the story. 'So what did you do?' Clearly she needed a little prodding.

'I wallowed in it for a while, like you are now,' Aunt Margie said, her eyes looking past me to a time decades earlier. 'I knew all about Ellie Kowalski by then, and I had no idea why anybody would want to kill her.'

'Did you give up on the story?' I really wanted to give up

on the Austin Cobb adoption right now because it was too hard. I wanted to get Mank to follow Barry's cell phone to Atlantic City and track him down, except I knew he probably couldn't do that. I wanted to crawl into bed and stay there for six days. I wanted a charge.

Aunt Margie seemed to think the question was funny; she actually giggled. 'Oh Lord no, Frannie, you know me. I kept digging at it, but first I thought about why anyone would want Ellie dead. And you know how this works.'

I knew; she had drummed it into my head since I'd stopped watching *Teletubbies*. 'The only motives for murder are love' (later she would say sex) 'and money.'

'That's right!' Aunt Margie was pleased her hard work training me had paid off. 'And I knew it wasn't sex, because Ellie was rather famously uninterested in that. All her friends knew it.'

'So it was money,' I said.

'No, it was sex. She'd been lying to all her friends and had a jealous lover named Ralph who thought she was cheating on him when she wasn't. But money was involved, too. They had a business together selling heroin to people in Washington Square Park, and Ellie was skimming from the top, saving up for the wedding dress she wasn't going to need. Ralph didn't care for that, but I caught him when one of his pushers in the park squealed on him.' Crime reporters can seem remarkably without empathy, but they have to be because of all the misery they see. Cops can be like that too.

I stood up so fast Aunt Margie made an 'ooh!' noise. 'That's it,' I said. 'That's what I have to do.' I headed for the door.

'Sell heroin in the park?' She didn't think that, but she likes to point out imprecise language. She writes for a living.

'No! Thank you, Aunt Margie; you're a doll!'

I almost made it out the door before she could say, 'I'm not. Dolls are made of plastic.'

THIRTY-FIVE

It took four phone calls before I found P. Monroe's daughter because the phone number Mank had given me was no longer in use. Thanks, Verizon. Now on phone call number five, I was in my office, with the door closed, talking to Philip Monroe, the retired detective who had 'investigated' Helen Hawley's murder in Kearny.

'The husband did it,' he said, calling on his mobile phone from the assisted living center that was now his home. 'There wasn't anybody else who would have. He found out she was cheating on him, and he bashed her in the head with a tire iron, or something.'

'A dumbbell,' I corrected. 'An eight-pound dumbbell.' Mr Monroe was now seventy-nine years old and agile mentally, but some details did elude him. So far he had been almost entirely on point. He had broken an ankle, moved to this assisted living facility and spent most of his time playing pinochle with anyone he could teach to play pinochle.

'That's right, an eight-pound hand weight. Big weight to swing back and forth.'

This was where I'd decided to employ a somewhat unorthodox strategy, which involved a lot of guessing and a little lying. 'But I'm not calling about the murder itself, Mr Monroe,' I said. 'It's about the human trafficking operation that was going on around it.'

That seemed to throw former Detective Monroe; he sputtered a bit and there was the sound of some movement around him. 'I'm walking to the garden and I don't walk as fast as I used to,' he said. 'What are you talking about, human trafficking? You think Marc Hawley was importing young girls for prostitution? That's crazy.'

He was right; that would have been an insane leap of logic. 'No, sir,' I said. 'I don't believe that at all. I think that someone – and probably not Mr Hawley – had found a supply of young children and was essentially selling them to adoption agencies.'

Well, think about it. It fit all the facts I had and wasn't contradicted by any of them. Janet Hawley had been 'fostering' a revolving door of boys when he was a child, Bill Hawley had said. Roberta Newman had said that the Roosevelts brought in children, but only for short periods of time, and then sent them to another family, in Austin Cobb's case, remarkably, the Hawleys (but *which* Hawleys?). And then out of the blue the birth mother had a change of heart, as Roberta had said happened occasionally, and took Austin back from the Friendly Family service, only to return him just weeks later, from which he was adopted by the Cobbs, who were, from all reports, lovely people and good parents. So win-win, right?

Except there were discrepancies, and that was why I was calling Philip Monroe.

'A *supply* of young children?' he said, with the noise behind him indicating he was now outdoors. 'What does that mean?'

'That's a good question,' I said. 'You were a detective on the police force there at that time. Were there reports of children going missing? Maybe from pediatric wards in hospitals? Particularly children who might otherwise have been abandoned? There was a baby boy left next to a dumpster at a Dunkin' Donuts. Do you remember him?'

There were no other voices on Monroe's end. He had sought out a place in the garden of his assisted living facility where he could speak without being heard by anyone but me. I heard the occasional bird chirp and some wind, not like a hurricane but just like you hear when anyone with a mobile phone is talking to you from outside. 'I don't remember that,' he said. 'Well, maybe vaguely, but a detective wouldn't have been assigned to a case like that. It would have gone to DYFS and a social worker, in all likelihood.'

He had fallen into my brilliant trap. 'That's exactly what happened, sir,' I said. 'A social worker at DYFS did end up sending the child to a foster family, and then he bounced around from one family to his birth mother, who appeared out of nowhere, then to another foster family then to an adoption agency who led him to a family who thankfully raised him. But

I'm wondering how that could have happened. It seems awfully haphazard.'

'I would say so, but it had nothing to do with the Hawley murder, and it certainly didn't indicate that any human trafficking was going on,' Monroe said. 'I don't know what you're talking about or why you're talking to me about it. This was all a long time ago.'

'Yes, it was,' I agreed. 'But the family that fostered that child was Howard and Janet Hawley. Were you aware of that?'

Monroe sounded less annoyed and more befuddled than he had before. 'The brother and sister-in-law, right? I didn't know anything about a foster child in the house,' he said. 'Was he there when Helen was murdered? It would have been in my report.'

'No, sir,' I answered. 'He would have been in his forever home by then and away from the Hawleys. But are you certain that Bill Hawley was the only child in the house when the murder occurred? Because I'm told that his aunt and uncle, the ones who ended up raising him, have been fostering children, almost exclusively boys, very close to constantly, maybe even until now.' That closet full of boys' clothes wasn't an accident.

I heard a voice say, 'Time to go in for lunch, Phil,' and then Monroe answer impatiently, 'I'll come in a minute. And call me Philip!' Then he waited a short while, presumably for the staff worker to leave him alone, and said into his phone in a confidential voice, 'I don't know anything about that. I only know about the murder.'

'Of course that's true,' I said. 'You wouldn't have investigated anything else. Why would you?' Unless people were looking for their missing kids who weren't being reported officially on any form.

'Exactly,' he said. 'So I'll ask you again, Ms Stein: Why did you call me?'

'Who was the man named Jack – not Marc – who was involved in that family when Helen was killed?' I asked. This had been the whole point of the call to begin with because I was certain Monroe would know, and that he'd be flustered when I asked.

'Who? Marc Hawley?'

He hadn't cultivated the doddering old man persona enough for me to buy it now. 'No, Mr Monroe. Jack. I don't have a last name, but I believe he was at the very least a business partner with Helen Hawley or Janet Hawley, or both. And I think you know about him because the report you filed is the work of a scam artist or an amateur and I don't believe you're either of those things. Who are you covering for? What's Jack's last name?'

'I don't have to talk to you,' Monroe said. His voice was shaky, and it was not due to age. 'Goodbye.'

I had less than a second to get his attention. 'I'd hate for your reputation to be destroyed because of a guy like Jack,' I said.

He didn't hang up, which was a definite plus. 'What reputation? Nobody remembers me.' Aha! The Achilles heel.

'People you worked with remember you,' I said. 'I spoke to two of them today. People you helped remember you. You served your community for a long time. It would be a shame if your obituary said that you'd been discovered to have covered up a crime this serious. I can't imagine it was for money. Were you being blackmailed?'

If I stretched any more on this conversation, I'd be that guy in the Fantastic Four that stretches all the time. I saw the movie on TV once. But I didn't think Monroe was a dirty cop. From what I'd been able to read about him, this was the only questionable case in his career, and no one had questioned it because he'd insisted Marc Hawley had killed his wife. And nobody could find Marc Hawley to prove otherwise. The fact that I sort of had his phone number was not something I was eager to divulge.

'You have no proof,' Monroe said. No innocent person has ever said that.

'I've researched your career,' I told him. 'This case stands out like a sore thumb. Why did you cover it up? What was going on? I have a client who's felt like an inferior human being all his life because of this. Help me show him it's not true.' I'm pretty sure Austin had never felt inferior in his life, except maybe at basketball. But Monroe didn't know that.

'Jack Powell was ruining my life,' he said in a low, weak voice. 'He was telling people things about me that weren't true. He told my wife things that *weren't true*. And he said it would all stop if I just forgot about the boys, let them live their new lives, and said Marc Hawley had killed his wife, which I believed he did.'

So now I had a last name! I immediately texted Ken: **Get all you can on Jack Powell.**

'How did you know Jack?' I asked Monroe. 'How did everybody know Jack?' That was an exaggeration. A lot of people don't know Jack.

'He was Helen Hawley's personal trainer.'

Oh, he had to be kidding. 'Helen had a personal trainer, she was killed with an eight-pound dumbbell that had been brought in from outside, and nobody thought that Jack might have murdered her?'

Monroe sounded positively defeated, like he was turning himself in to the intrepid cop at the end of the movie. 'That's why he was telling lies about me to my wife,' he said, barely audibly. 'She was going to divorce me. I could have lost my job. I figured Helen wouldn't have been any less dead no matter who got caught, and if they found Marc, he'd be able to prove he didn't kill her.'

I've dealt with a few cops in my time, but this was the least cop-like behavior I'd known about. 'So Jack Powell got away with murder for all these years.'

'And he's gonna keep on getting away with it,' Monroe said. 'If you tell anyone about this conversation, I'll deny it.' I could have kicked myself for not recording the call.

'What about your reputation, Detective Monroe?' It was worth another shot.

'A reputation isn't worth much to you if you're dead,' he said.

And then he did hang up. It was getting to be a regular part of my day.

THIRTY-SIX

Ken hadn't gotten back to me, which indicated that he was either hard at work doing the research on Jack Powell or taking a long lunch. You can't be sure.

I strode into the precinct past Bendix and toward Mank, but had to wait because he was talking to a woman in the chair at his desk. She wasn't a superhuman, so I didn't feel threatened. Besides, Mank was taking notes on his iPad. This was business.

It took at least six or seven minutes, and Bendix felt that gave him license to come over and make my life just a little less OK. He sidled up to me, looked up into my face, because that was the only direction that worked, and said, 'I understand why you don't want to go to the wedding with me, Gargantua.'

I shut my eyes for a second or two and tried to think of a peaceful place in a park with a meadow. Then I focused on Bendix. 'Is part of it that you always call me "Gargantua?"' I asked.

'Nah. It's because I'm short and fat and older than you.' All those things were true, but none of them were relevant.

'You don't get it,' I told him. 'It doesn't have anything to do with how you look. It's complicated, but it's mostly about how you treat me and every other woman who walks into this room.'

Bendix, being Bendix, had – I won't say the nerve, but the incredulousness – to look surprised. 'What? What's wrong with the way I treat women? I love women!'

'You talk about women's appearances and ignore literally everything else about us,' I said. I didn't know if any of this was getting through to Bendix, but it was making me feel better. 'You don't see us as people the way you see men. You see us as collections of body parts.'

'You saying I'm sexist?' That's what I was dealing with, ladies and gentlemen.

'Let's say a little more respect and a little less ogling would go a long way. Also, I don't want to go to *anybody's* sister-in-law's cousin's wedding. Now if you don't mind, I have business with Mank.'

'I'll bet you do.' Never believe that there's no such thing as a lost cause.

Mank was thanking the woman, in her late thirties and average in every way, for her help in whatever it was they'd been talking about. He shook her hand and she walked away as I approached. When he saw me he did not roll his eyes, which I took as a positive sign.

'I know who killed Helen Hawley,' I said.

That smug jerk. He didn't even look surprised. 'Really,' Mank said. 'Sit down and tell me.'

So I sat down. 'She was murdered by her personal trainer, a guy named—'

'Jack Powell,' Mank said. He was determined not to let me have any fun. 'Your pal Jack.'

'You know about this? Why am I telling you?'

Mank put his hands out flat and lowered them, telling me to calm down. Women are so hysterical. 'No, I didn't know he was involved in the murder, but I did know he was Helen's personal trainer, and a lot of other women in the area, too. So naturally with the murder weapon being a piece of exercise equipment, you put two and two together. What's your resource?'

I sort of slumped in the visitor's chair. 'A guy who knows it for sure but will deny he ever talked to me if he's asked. Powell was blackmailing him at the time of the murder.'

Mank nodded with recognition. 'Detective Monroe, eh?'

I rubbed my eyes with my thumb and forefinger. 'Stop knowing everything,' I said.

'The last time you were here you asked me for his telephone number,' he reminded me. Oh, yeah.

I waved a hand to declare it insignificant. 'Anyway, apparently Jack Powell killed Helen Hawley. Except I don't think he did. I can't put my finger on it, but I think it was either her husband Marc or someone we haven't thought of yet. Marc because he ran away. Jack because he's creepy and had dumbbells. And I think it had something to do with children being sold to people who couldn't adopt.'

'Where were they getting the kids?' Mank asked. 'Was it illegal?'

I tilted my head to the right to indicate I didn't know. Seriously, try it; it works. 'My *source* mumbled a few things about not telling anyone about "the boys," but I got the feeling he really didn't know, or had forgotten. He was in an assisted living facility.'

Mank looked a little surprised. 'I didn't think he was *really* old,' he said.

'He's not. I'm not sure why he's still there, but I get the feeling it's been a while. He had an ankle injury and just stayed, I guess.'

He gave me a significant look. 'Memory issues?'

'Strikingly, I flunked that class in neurology school, so I'm not sure, but I got the impression he remembered Helen and Marc Hawley and the personal trainer just fine. If Jack Powell really is Austin's birth father, that's a hell of a coincidence, isn't it?'

Mank leaned forward, elbows on his desk. 'So you want some advice?'

'No. I want the NYPD to solve this for me so I can find out why Austin was put up for adoption and then my job will be done. Finding Barry Polk wouldn't be an awful thing, either. I pay taxes. Go out there and do your job.'

Mank knew I was kidding, so he didn't tell me to go away and never come back. He couldn't let it go by, though, so he said, 'You are aware that any crimes that were committed took place in New Jersey, which thankfully is not in my jurisdiction.'

'I'm just tired.' Yeah, a nice charge wouldn't be an awful thing. When I got home.

My phone buzzed a text from Ken: **A Google search of Jack Powell gives me a car dealership, two UK footballers, a baseball player from 1906 and five investment bankers. Anything else, BOSS?**

I didn't answer him.

'Yeah, so am I. So is there a reason you came to see me?' Mank was probably still smarting from my (lack of) reaction when he said he loved me. And I didn't blame him.

'About what you said,' I began.

'Not now.' His voice almost gave me frostbite.

'When?'

'I don't know.'

OK. I stood up. After all, he wanted me to leave. 'Suppose I ask you out to dinner.'

'Suppose you do.' Wow. Nothing was going to be easy with this guy.

'Would you say yes?' I asked.

'Dinner with no shop talk?' Mank said.

'Yes. Completely devoid of shop talk. I'll bone up on baseball or something so it won't be awkward.'

'Basketball,' he said. 'It's harder to understand. When?'

When, what? 'Dinner?'

'I'd love to. When?' If this sophisticated banter went on much longer, I'd have to head over to the Algonquin Hotel just to soak in the wit.

'Um . . . tomorrow night.'

'Where?'

I guessed we were going, then. 'I'll pick you up here.'

Mank shook his head almost violently. 'Not here. With the carcasses of men you've left in your wake?' He looked at Bendix. 'Besides, I'm off tomorrow.'

'All right, I'll pick you up at your apartment.' I'd been there once before.

'It's a date,' I said.

'Is it?'

It was necessary for me to go home and lie down. First I texted Barry the standard message. Did not immediately get back an answer. I was trying to balance being worried about Barry and being annoyed with him, but worried was still winning.

I did make it to the apartment and I did plug in and lie down on my bed. And that was as far as it got. My phone, which could have used a charge itself but would have to wait its turn, buzzed. I hadn't been this popular before in my entire life.

The number was the one Jack Powell had used to contact me before I'd been told he was a murderer, and he had threatened my life *then*. I was a little more on edge this time. Knowledge is power.

'What do you want, Jack?' I still observe the niceties of polite existence.

'I want you to come to Janet Hawley's house,' he said.

I didn't have a clue why he'd want that, but if he wanted it, I certainly wasn't going. 'By the way,' I said, 'I understand you murdered Janet's sister-in-law Helen Hawley. Why'd you do that?'

'There's a little boy here named David,' Jack went on, ignoring what I'd said. 'If you don't get here within two hours, he might not be here anymore.' There was the far-too-familiar click and the conversation was over.

There was no question about it; I was spending way too much time with men.

THIRTY-SEVEN

'What's our goal?' Ken asked.

'Our goal is to get the boy away from Jack Powell, to get Jack arrested for murdering Helen Hawley, actually finding out whether he really did murder her, and to find out who Austin's birth mother was, and why they put him up for adoption,' I told him. 'I thought that was obvious.'

'That's five goals,' my ever-helpful brother pointed out.

'It's good to be ambitious. Now shut up while I'm listening to Fleetwood Mac.'

We drove silently for the duration of *Landslide*, which is perhaps the finest song ever written, but I could see Ken was just bursting with something he wanted to say but was wary I would yell at him, and he was right. So I chose to let him off the hook.

'What?' I said.

'What, what?'

We were through the Lincoln Tunnel and heading toward Janet Hawley's house, where presumably Jack Powell was holding the boy who must have been Janet's latest product for an unauthorized adopter.

'What is it you're desperate to say?'

'OK, I'll say it. We don't know that Jack killed Helen. We know that this ex-cop *says* he did, but we have no proof. The cop won't talk to other cops or anyone else. So you can call the police all you like, but you have nothing to stand on to demand an arrest.'

'I just want to let Austin know about his parents and get the case closed so I can start sleeping again, and I want to find Barry Polk.'

'That's another goal,' Ken said. 'That makes six.' I wondered why I'd asked him to come along. It was just New Jersey, for crying out loud.

We drove for another ten minutes, each of us stewing in our

complete lack of a cohesive plan. Or maybe that was just me, because Ken said, 'About those VHS tapes we stole from Janet's place.'

How had I forgotten about those? 'You watched them.' It's best to sound authoritative when you've just remembered something you should have been thinking about for days.

'Not all of them; that would take days.' Ken adjusted himself in his seat. His hair was almost scraping the car's ceiling. This is what happens when you take the economy model and you're way too tall. 'But I haven't seen any little kid who might be Austin Cobb in any of them.'

Well, that was disappointing. I uttered a word that would communicate exactly that thought to my brother, and he nodded his agreement. 'But these videos have been edited pretty heavily. I'd bet on it.' Ken would bet on which cockroach would make it across the floor faster, so that wasn't saying much. 'I have seen a video in there that was taken at Marc and Helen's place and I've seen the workout area. There was no second eight-pound weight. I think someone brought it with them. There's got to be missing footage, maybe including Austin. Maybe even in cassettes I haven't looked at yet.'

It made sense; Janet had a *lot* of VHS cassettes in that storage closet/mudroom in her house. If the tapes in some of them had really been seriously edited to excise incriminating footage, she was just the kind of anal-retentive maniac who would keep the original as well as the less dangerous copy. But they might still be somewhere else in the house, somewhere less conspicuous.

'How many do you have left?' I asked Ken.

'Maybe twelve. She recorded on the slow speed. That's six hours a tape.'

My throat caught just thinking about watching that much home video footage of someone else's family. Which reminded me. 'Have you heard from Mom lately?'

I was looking at the road, not my brother, but I could tell he was giving me one of his patented sarcastic glances. 'Yeah, Mom got in touch and I just forgot to mention it,' he said. 'Not that it's never happened before.' He was still pissed at me for not telling him I'd heard from her for at least three months because she had advised me not to say anything. Sort of.

'Glad to see you've gotten over it,' I said. 'But you've never met Jack, so you might want a quick explanation of why he's so seriously weird.'

Ken folded his hands across his chest. 'Because he dresses like a villain from a bad 1940s western and he talks like Lex Luthor?' he said. 'You mentioned that already. After you didn't tell me he'd kidnapped you in front of a coffeehouse.'

I was starting to get the message that I was not quite forthcoming enough to my brother and partner. 'I promise I'll stop keeping secrets,' I said, sounding like the fourth grader I once was. 'But what you need to know about Jack is that he's not afraid of hurting people and he doesn't seem to care about what he has to do to get what he wants.'

Ken grunted. He can't help it; he looks like a guy who would grunt. 'So what does he want today?' he asked. 'Why did he go so far out of his way to make himself visible to us and get you to go to Janet's house?'

'If I could think of a reason he'd want us out of our office, I'd say that, but there's nothing he can find there that . . .'

Ken waited, then waited some more. 'Find there that . . . what?'

'Ken, is it possible that Jack doesn't know his son became Austin Cobb? Does he want us out of the office so he can find our client's name?'

My brother had already reached into his pocket for his phone. 'Igavda,' he said. He pushed the button for the office number. 'How can he not know the son he put up for adoption?' he asked. Then someone on the line picked up. 'Igavda?' Even from the driver's seat I could hear the call disconnect.

'He sent someone to our office.' Like I hadn't figured that one out already.

'Is Igavda OK?' I asked.

'Igavda is almost as strong as us.'

Nonetheless I texted Mank: **Someone broke into my office. Can you send cops over to see if Igavda is OK? Please?**

We were approaching Janet's street and I looked sideways at my brother briefly. 'Do you have your gun with you?' I said. 'If he already sent someone to the office, he might not even need us here. Maybe we shouldn't go in.'

There was a minute or so of silence. I guess Ken was thinking, but I didn't smell any wood burning, so it was hard to tell. Finally he breathed audibly and then looked at me. 'We're going in,' he said, I guess assuming I'd left it up to him when I was just thinking out loud. 'But we're going in my way.'

That didn't sound good. 'I don't think we're doing *anything* your way unless I hear why it's a good way,' I said.

I parked a block away from Janet's house in case Jack was looking out the front window. 'He knows we're coming,' Ken said. 'What does hiding do for us?'

'It buys us time and adds the element of surprise. So what's *your* way?'

'I kick in the front door and hold a gun on Jack.'

Much as expected. 'OK. I think we'll stick with my way, just because I'm an egotist.'

'Admitting you have a problem is the first step, Frannie.'

We got out of the rental car and walked toward Janet's house, trying to look casual. There was nothing appropriate we could hide behind when we got to the house, so I motioned Ken to the back door and I decided to take the side, seeing as how we'd (Ken had) already pushed that one in. Maybe no one had noticed.

The driveway was done in asphalt, which isn't the least bit unusual. All the houses on this side of the street looked to have been done at the same time; they probably got a 'group rate' that was the usual rate for anyone wanting an asphalt driveway. The important asset of asphalt at the moment was that it's generally pretty quiet, and I was wearing sneakers.

When I got to the side door, it became clear that someone (probably a handyman Janet would have hired, because she wouldn't have been able to do it) had noticed the damage Ken had caused to the jamb, and had repaired it on what I could only assume was an interim basis. They had not replaced the broken piece of door jamb and they had not changed the lock. They'd basically put up a small block of wood over the bolt. I could have opened it easily enough by breathing on it. Not even hard.

The first step was to remove the block of wood, which I figured would be easy enough to do by hand. But when I reached for the door, it opened into the stairwell.

'Come on in,' Jack Powell said. 'We've been expecting you, Ms Stein.'

He was standing at the landing, wearing the same bizarre outfit he'd had on by the 6 train. There was no child with him; 'David' must have been inside.

Jack was holding a handgun and gestured with it toward the stairs. 'No fair stalling. We have business to do.'

'Where's David?' I said. 'I don't move from this spot until I see him.'

Jack's smile was crooked; it must have taken him years to perfect it. 'I'm afraid David was a figment of my imagination, Ms Stein. But here you are anyway.' There wasn't even any sign of Janet.

At least there was no sign of her until she appeared in the kitchen, holding a gun on my brother, who looked downright mortified at the humiliation. His hands were held up and the elbows were close to his sides to ensure he wouldn't be able to reach out for anything, or anyone.

'We should have done it my way,' Ken said.

THIRTY-EIGHT

I don't care much for being tied up, and get your mind out of the gutter. But now Jack, minus his somewhat brawnier goons from the other day, and Janet, who appeared to be tougher than I had given her credit for, were discussing whether it was better to tie me to a kitchen chair or a dining room chair. I personally had no preference.

'The kitchen chair is smaller and less sturdy,' Jack, who was still aiming his gun at me, told Janet. 'She's too strong for the kitchen chair.'

Janet had a sort of hangdog look on her face, and studied the dining chair Jack had brought into the living room. 'But the dining room chair was a wedding present from my mother,' she said with a little whine in her inflection, real or forced. I was going for forced. Janet wasn't a natural whiner.

'Your mother is dead,' Jack said.

Janet, who was watching Ken, didn't look back at him. 'That was cruel. Use the kitchen chair, Jack.' There would be no argument. Ken, sitting in an easy chair and looking quite comfortable, smiled the kind of smile I associate with smug Wall Street traders who haven't figured out the next crash is always just a matter of time. I'd have to give him a strong talking-to when we got out of this. And we would get out of it. All they had was guns.

Jack seemed miffed but unwilling (or too weak?) to tangle with Janet. He lugged the dining chair – which indicated Janet's mother had awful taste in furniture – away and carried in the kitchen chair, a standard white wood model with a scalloped back, into the room, placing it right in front of me. He'd somehow managed to keep the gun pointed at me the whole time. He was used to guns.

'What's the point of all this, Jack?' I said. 'You killed Helen Hawley twenty-five years ago and you got away with it. Now you're holding my brother and me here when you already had our offices searched so you could find the name of our client. What's your game here? I don't get what you're trying to achieve.'

They must have scoured the shed in the backyard looking for something they could use to bind Ken and me to chairs. Because they clearly had not planned this well ahead of time. For Ken, as was evident from the pile by his feet, they had decided to use a thirty-foot extension cord. He'd be out of that in seconds, if it took him that long.

For me, they were using – and I swear I'm not making this up – a collection of bungee cords. Seriously. With the metal hooks just dying to be twisted straight by applied pressure, which wouldn't be necessary because bungee cords stretch. Jack had gotten the jump on us by claiming to be holding a fictional little boy hostage and then hadn't really thought through what he'd do once we got here.

'That's the second time you've said that,' Jack said, gun still level at my chest. 'What makes you think I killed Helen? I didn't kill Helen; Marc did.'

'Come on,' Ken said. Ken had decided, it seemed, that this was going to require a macho touch. It's not that he's bad at doing that; it's more that he never knows when it's needed versus the other ninety-five percent of the time. 'You were her personal trainer. You had access to her home. You brought your own eight-pound dumbbell. You were blackmailing a cop to lie about it. Why *wouldn't* we think you killed her, Jack? You left a trail of breadcrumbs so thick I'm surprised birds aren't lined up outside the house, pecking away all these years later.'

Wrong house, I thought immediately.

'I was her personal trainer,' Jack admitted. 'I was also her lover.'

Janet winced a little. 'Jack,' she said.

'It's true.' He was wrapping the bungee cords around me at the biceps level, a mistake a lot of amateurs make, and starting to realize they would just keep stretching. Think about people jumping off a bridge with one of these tied to their legs. They stretch a bit. Jack looked at the cords holding my shoulders and pulled. It got uncomfortably tight, then loosened because bungee cords. He frowned. 'I was Helen's lover and we had a child together.'

'So you're my client's father,' I said. 'His birth father, not the man who actually raised him.' That last part was meant as a dig. When a guy is tying you up with bungee cords, the least you can do is be impolite. I had a few other tactics in mind, but they'd have to wait.

'Yes,' Jack said. 'I am Austin's father. His *real* father.' That was it; I'd never killed anyone, but for Jack I might make an exception.

I wasn't crazy about him knowing Austin's name. 'And yet you and Helen, who was how old when he was born? You decided to dump him at a Dunkin' Donuts, then get him back from his foster family, then put him up for adoption? What was that about? Was it because he has autism?'

Jack stopped looping bungee cords around me (he appeared to have decided that quantity in binding would have to substitute for quality) and looked surprised. 'Of course not,' he said. 'It was that Helen was married to Marc and I was . . . involved in things that didn't lend themselves to being a full-time parent.' Jack Powell, Responsible Dad.

OK, so I knew who Austin's birth parents were and why they'd dealt with Friendly Family to see him be adopted. My work was done; the case was closed.

Ken, however, doesn't have a business mind. 'So why all the secrecy?' he asked. 'How come the files on his adoption are all closed and nobody will even discuss them with us? What are you leaving out, Jack? For that matter, why are we being tied up?'

'Yeah,' I added. 'Now that you've told us what we need to know – which, by the way, you could have done any time after I started asking – our work is done. There's no need to hold us here, or whatever it is you think you're about to do. And how come you've been fostering all these boys for all these years, Janet? And the little suits and ties: You grooming the next generation of traders in mutual funds?'

'I don't have to say anything,' Janet said, which was interesting in that it was the first thing she'd said in quite a while. It wasn't interesting in any other way.

Jack stood back like a hair stylist who has just completed the best haircut he'd ever given. His hands went straight up, bent at the elbows. 'There!' he shouted.

I shrugged, and the bungee cords fell off. 'Where?' I said.

I stood up and reached for the gun before Jack could think of it. I grabbed it out of his hand because, let's face it, I was stronger than him by quite a margin. Quickly I pointed the gun at Janet, who was fiddling in her belt for the one she was carrying. 'Don't!' I barked.

Ken stood up and looked at me. 'Bungee cords?'

'They weren't especially well equipped.'

Ken took the gun from Janet's belt and slipped it into his pocket. 'So there's no kid waiting to get sold at adoption now?' he asked.

Janet seemed stricken. 'No. No one is selling children.' Her voice was reedy and shaking, and it hadn't been a minute ago, before Ken took her firearm away.

'Because if there was a boy here, we'd need to save him from *you* and get him back to his parents.' I looked at Jack. 'His *real* parents.'

Jack, for the first time since I'd seen him, looked angry. He took a step toward me, but I turned to face him head on and he rethought the strategy. He folded his arms in front of him and pulled down on the brim of his hat, best to shadow his face even more. Maybe he thought it looked like The Shadow. I wouldn't know.

'There's no one to save,' he said through clenched teeth.

Ken looked amused. He picked up the extension cord they were going to use to tie him up with and gestured to Janet for her to make herself comfortable in the kitchen chair. Her spine stiffened, but Ken took one step closer and she had to look up at him. She sat down and my brother began coiling the cord around her, starting at the legs, which is how it should be done, if you're taking notes at home. Nobody's going anywhere with their legs tied up.

'Their parents abandoned them,' Jack hissed. 'They were *ours*.'

'Yours?' Ken said to Jack. 'You and Janet had children together too? That's a little kinky.'

Janet and Jack exchanged a glance. She was almost completely bound to the kitchen chair now. Ken was tying off the extension cord. 'No rope in the house,' he mumbled to himself. You wouldn't have heard it. Then he looked at me. 'Respiration and heart rate up,' he said. He can hear those things in people.

'Which one of them?' I asked. I can too, but I have to be closer to the subject.

'Both of them.' We'd hit a nerve. But I didn't think Jack and Janet had children together, certainly not within the past fifteen years.

'Where do you get the children, Jack?' I said. I gave him a very light tap and he fell back onto the chair where Ken had been sitting. 'You sell them to people who can't get a reputable adoption agency to give them a child, don't you?'

'The system is rigged!' Jack's face was flushed. Yep, respiration and heart rate were up, OK. 'People who aren't in the upper echelons don't have a chance if they have a slight blemish on their records! We're providing a public service!'

'We make people happy,' Janet chimed in. 'What's wrong with that?' About seventeen federal laws and any number in the state, but I'm not up on New Jersey legislation.

Wait. New Jersey legislation. Maybe I didn't need New Jersey. I mean, who does, really? I got out my phone and got a response from Mank.

She's fine. Place is largely undamaged.

I sent back, **I'm at Janet's house and Jack Powell is here.**

Almost immediately I got Mank's reply. **Does Jack need an ambulance?**

No. I'm tying him to a chair in New Jersey, but I'm not using bungee cords.

Of course.

Mank was on the job. That was going to make a difference.

'You want to know what's wrong with making people happy by convincing people who got pregnant by accident to give up their children to you and then selling them to others who can't adopt because they might have a prison record or a history of domestic violence?' I looked at Janet. 'Aside from all the legal issues – and there are plenty – do you ever think about who you're making happy? Is it ever the kids?'

Janet sucked in her lips like she wanted to say something to the giant woman in front of her but felt, let's say, intimidated. She remained silent.

Just as well. The giant woman was pretty seriously pissed off. I turned my attention to Jack, who was not yet tied up, so I said to Ken, 'Can you find something better than bungee cords?'

'Almost anyone could,' he said. He walked out through the kitchen, I assumed toward the backyard shed. Janet wasn't going anywhere and I could certainly handle Jack if he decided to get feisty.

'Now.' I spoke in a low tone in terms of volume and pitch. I wanted him to listen, but I didn't want him to be overly excited because then he'd lie and I wouldn't get what I wanted. 'You tell me exactly how you know Malcolm Mitchell and what you two have going in Atlantic City.'

Jack seemed surprised by the question, as if I should have known. 'Malcolm?' he said. 'Malcolm is my son.'

Everybody was Jack's son today.

THIRTY-NINE

Ken came back from the shed with a coil of rope that he said he'd found in a cubbyhole under the tool box. He looked at Janet. 'Bungee cords?' he said. 'Did you even *look* around in there?' My brother hates it when people don't respect us enough to challenge us properly. Not that the rope would have done much against me, but it worked just fine tying up Jack.

'How the hell is Malcolm Mitchell your son?' I hissed at him. We didn't gag him because there was no need to, and we needed Jack to talk. 'I thought my client was your son.'

'People can have more than one child.' Jack was going to play this as if I was the idiot and he had all the knowledge.

'Are you the father of everyone I've met in the past six months?' I asked.

'I have two sons. You appear to be in touch with both of them.' I have a low tolerance of smug. I clenched my fists.

To the side I heard Janet mumble, 'He's not your *son*.'

Ken, a determined expression on his face, leaned in toward Jack. Their faces were inches apart. 'What lies did your *son* tell you about us?' he demanded.

'About the charging units under your left arms?' Jack said. 'About your abilities to throw grown men around?' He looked at me. 'I've seen that for myself.'

But my brother was not playing it for laughs. 'Awfully big coincidence that Malcolm's dad is involved in our latest adoption case, isn't it?'

Jack, settling into his role as the jolly megalomaniac villain, shrugged. 'Coincidences happen.'

Ken put his hands on Jack's upper arms, which were bound to the chair. 'Usually they happen when they've been arranged,' he said. I knew he wasn't going to injure Jack seriously. But Jack didn't know that.

'You're hurting my arms,' he said.

My brother, intense glare uninterrupted, said very quietly, 'Tell me how this one happened.' Then he lifted Jack – and by extension, the chair – by the arms to look him eye-to-eye. 'Now.'

One thing you have to say for stupid macho gestures: occasionally they're effective.

Jack let the look happen for a long moment and said, 'Put me down and I'll explain as well as I can. I don't know all the details.'

Ken looked at me and I nodded. He lowered Jack and his seat to the floor again, leading Jack to breathe out for an extended time. Five seconds. Try it sometime.

'Let's hear it,' Ken said.

'OK. OK.' Jack was still catching his breath, but now I felt like it was forced. I almost looked over at Ken to lift him up again.

'Lie to us and you'll be back up near the ceiling,' I told him. It's so easy to lose your focus when the danger has passed.

Jack opened his eyes wide and shook his head. 'No. I'll tell you what I know because there's no harm in it for me.' That was consistent with what I knew about Jack, so I relaxed a tad. But I kept an eye on Janet, who certainly wasn't going anywhere, but might try to talk him out of giving us any useful information.

'Tell,' Ken said in a calm voice. Ken can do a scary calm voice better than anyone I know.

'Yeah. Malcolm is my son, but he was put up for adoption when he was less than a year old.'

'Wait. I've heard this story before,' I told him. 'Are you in the business of fathering children and then deciding they're too much trouble for you?' Before you start emailing me, keep in mind that I'm aware the vast majority of parents who put their children up for adoption do it for very important reasons and it's a heartrending decision. But this was Jack Powell, and he'd pretty much worked my last nerve.

'The circumstances aren't relevant to what you asked,' he said. 'Malcolm and I were not in touch for more than thirty years. His mother never even told me who had adopted him.'

'Not even how much you got for it?' Ken asked. 'Didn't you want your cut?'

'It didn't work like that.' The voice, surprisingly, was Janet's. But she didn't say anything more. Jack didn't even have to shoot her a look.

'Malcolm. You. How did our paths all cross at once?' Sometimes the tangents lead away from what I need to know, and what I need to know is clearly what's vital. It's amazing how the people I deal with lose sight of that.

'Yes.' I hadn't asked Jack a yes/no question, but he was answering one. 'I got in touch with Malcolm accidentally about two years ago, in connection to an adoption . . .' He gave me a significant glance. '. . . of a child who was not my own. Malcolm was involved only peripherally, as a technical consultant to one of the birth parents who wanted to be certain that the online services they were using were secure. They gave me his contact information to coordinate communications that would not be traced.'

There was no point in going deep into the legality – or lack thereof – of the transaction (and it was nothing but that) being discussed. I had to focus on Malcolm Mitchell and Jack Powell, not to mention my actual client Austin Cobb, whom I'd decided to take to a place with a lot of alcohol for his post-investigation meeting. This one was a corker. I didn't say anything and gave Ken a look when it seemed to me he was about to. We weren't the police. Mank was the police, but he was in New York. I quickly got out my phone and texted him: **Know anybody at the FBI or the NJ State Police?**

'How did you determine that Malcolm was your son?' I asked Jack while still letting my thumbs do the talking to Mank.

'We didn't right away,' Jack said, suddenly seeming downright eloquent on the subject. He was turning into a raconteur, eager to enthrall us with his tale. I wasn't enthralled so much as disgusted, but I let him believe what he wanted to believe. You'd be amazed how often that works with men. Unless you're a woman. Then you won't be amazed at all. 'But because we were dealing with an adoption, Malcolm made reference to his own experience, and eventually we put two and two together.' And got twenty-five-to-life, as in the years they'd spend in jail if Ken and I (and Mank) had any influence in the matter.

'So you had a touching, sentimental reunion over an illegal adoption?' My brother is the very soul of tact. Sometimes.

I could have told him that would tick off Jack. 'Illegal,' he said. He would have spat if he thought he could get away with it, but Janet probably would have broken her bonds and hit him with a baseball bat if he'd tried. 'The state wants to restrict the happiness of children and parents.' And the income of those who steal children to sell them to parents. To Jack it wasn't even a moral gray area. It was about staying in the black and avoiding the red.

'How did that lead to me tracking down Austin's birth parents and stumbling over you and your charming tactic of threatening first and talking later, but only when you're tied to a chair?' I said. Well, Ken had already jettisoned tact.

Jack looked like he wanted to get mad, but there was Ken only inches from him. He resumed the storyteller persona he'd momentarily abandoned. 'Well, Malcolm was keeping an eye on your office because there were things about you he wanted to understand better,' he said. Seriously, if he hadn't been talking about someone staking out my office and keeping tabs on my clients and me, I'd have been absolutely fascinated with his tale. 'So he saw Austin leaving your building and, as we'd arranged, he sent me a picture. I was wondering if we'd run into one of our own clients who had become one of yours. I never dreamed I'd find my own son through my own son.'

This story had holes in it you could pilot the Starship Enterprise through. 'That's two major coincidences in the past five minutes,' I told him. 'I don't see any reason I should believe this, except that you and Malcolm are in fact slimy enough to stake out our office and take pictures of our clients. What is it Malcolm needs to know so badly?'

Jack smiled, like he had hooked me in at last. 'About the technology that created you and keeps you alive,' he said. 'We believe that it could lead to the development of eternal life.'

Of course they did.

'So you followed Austin to me and then Barry followed Malcolm and it all came down to you taking us hostage,' Ken said. 'That didn't work out so great for you.'

'You'll let us go,' Jack said confidently. 'Because Malcolm

is about to pick up Austin from the bus in Atlantic City. They're having dinner tonight.'

Austin was the next hostage and he wouldn't be able to break out of ropes or chains or even bungee cords. That led me to the last question I didn't want to ask.

'What have you done with Barry Polk?' I snarled at Jack.

'He'll be the third person at their dinner table.' He grinned, thinking he'd just snapped the trap shut.

I stood up and looked at Ken. 'Let's go,' I said.

'What about them?' Ken gestured at our two guests.

'Bring them with us. We'll get a bigger table for dinner.'

FORTY

Mank texted me when we were at Exit 117 of the Garden State Parkway on the way to Atlantic City, which was still at least an hour away.

FBI alerted, not exactly rushing to you. NJ State Police R skeptical.

Of course they were. We had virtually nothing of use to tell them.

Did they sell any kids to people in NYC? I could help you.

There was no sense in asking Jack whether he'd done anything illegal in New York. He didn't think what he'd done should be illegal anywhere, but he'd been more than happy to tell us all about how the 'service,' as he called it, had worked.

The young woman who was Austin's birth mother was not Helen, which made perfect sense. We'd had to scream at Jack to get him off his original claim about fathering Austin with Helen, which made no sense given Austin's race. The birth mother had been a Black teenager who knew she couldn't handle raising a child and didn't know what to do.

But when Helen and Jack – who were, in fact, having an affair – had found out about the baby through the Roosevelts, whom they knew peripherally, they hit upon a scheme: Helen would go to the authorities, claim to be the baby's mother and, after a short period of time when she'd been granted custody, would tell DYFS she couldn't raise Austin and put him up for adoption through Friendly Family. He was the test case. In his trial adoption, no money would change hands. That's why they used the agency.

Jack made contacts, 'close friends,' he said, with some of the nurses in local maternity wards in hospitals who would know about abandoned babies that needed families. They never stole any children, so the FBI might not be interested in kidnapping charges. But they would convince the birth parents of these poor children, who were usually children themselves, that they could help find better, more stable homes than the ones found through adoption services or state agencies. Then they would scour records at adoption agencies, public and private, for applicants who had been denied adoption rights. Those people were often open to the idea of paying a pretty significant fee to get a baby with no questions asked. The birth parents would not be cut in on the profit; that went to Jack and Helen, until Helen was killed, according to Jack by her husband Marc. I thought that unlikely but not out of the question. The killing part. The fact that Jack and Helen kept all the money was completely in character. For Jack. I knew nothing about Helen.

Once Helen was dead and Marc on the run, Jack had a choice, and naturally he decided to keep the enterprise going and keep all the money. It got easier, in fact, because now he didn't have to run every decision through his partner. He took every abandoned child he heard about and basically sold them to waiting adoptive parents, some of whom were perfectly nice people and many who were the other kind. He kept no records. He didn't take credit cards or checks. It was a cash-only business, and business was good.

Until my brother and I had been disruptive enough to search for Austin Cobb's birth parents, and despite Austin's adoption being legitimate, Jack got antsy. He had to do something about us, but he'd been having trouble with that because we were us. In true Jack Powell fashion, his ultimate solution was to offer us part of his business. A small part. Somewhere around Long Branch he made his pitch.

'Think of it,' he said while Ken drove and I checked my emails. 'You have connections in adoption areas I've never even dreamed of. We could make a lot of money together.' Jack was not an especially good salesman, which led me to believe that those birth parents had really not wanted to raise the newborns they found themselves with.

'I don't think so,' Ken told him. 'You seem to be all tied up at the moment.' Jack strained at his bonds and made an annoyed face, which was something Ken was probably used to from me.

But then my attention was refocused. There was an email in my file that was clearly from our mother. Did I dare open it with Jack, who was allied with Malcolm (in some weird way), in the back seat? Would he be able to see? Defying every urge in my body, I closed my emails until I could take a better look. I didn't even look at Ken and mouth *Mom*. Too easy to read.

I had texted Austin to try to warn him off, but like Barry, he was suddenly not answering his messages. Just for the record, I sent Barry a vague text too, but was not terribly optimistic I'd be hearing back soon. Malcolm probably still had his phone.

Janet, for her part, had fallen asleep, and was snoring prodigiously. Everyone responds to stress differently.

We sat in silence, with that email burning a hole in the back of my brain, for half an hour. Towns went by. If New Jerseyans really do define themselves by the Parkway exit they live closest to, and friends from the state say they don't, we left a lot of people's identities behind. I decided to get in touch again with Esme Rodriguez-Cohen, my non-Jewish non-mother at the agency whose name is none of your business.

Important: You ever hear of a guy named Jack Powell?

Esme, without question, would get back to me, even if she had nothing of substance to relate. I just hoped she would text instead of calling because I couldn't have that conversation with Jack in the back seat.

He, as if he'd been in a trance for thirty minutes, said, 'Don't you see? You can be very wealthy, well, wealthy, anyway, and you'll be helping children and people who want to be parents. Isn't that what you set out to do yourselves?'

'I have an idea, Jack,' Ken said without taking his eyes off the road. 'Shut up or I'll make my sister beat you up. Again.'

'It's the best deal you'll ever make!' Jack protested. 'Fran, listen to me!' Now we were on a first-name basis?

Esme, reliable, wonderful Esme, texted me back.

I've heard of him. Supposedly was in the adoption-for-profit business a while back. I never dealt with him, but others did.

That was all I needed to know to get my Plan B in place. I texted her back with a phone number and told her to expect a call from it.

'You're going to have to fuel up,' I told Ken after looking at the gauge. 'There's a rest stop coming up. Do you see any upside to us keeping these two with us?'

Jack's jaw went down a couple of inches. Janet continued to snore.

'Well, if we cut them loose, they could warn Malcolm we're on the way.' We were about thirty-five minutes from Atlantic City.

'We could take their phones,' I suggested.

'Fran,' Jack began. I gave him a look and he didn't finish the sentence.

'Yeah, we could. That would be kind of fun,' Ken said. 'But the Garden State Parkway rest stops are probably the kind of places that still have pay phones.'

Jack's eyes took on a desperate quality. For a guy whose office was maybe twenty feet from the 6 train, you'd think a nice highway rest stop would be like going to the country. He was sweating around the hairline and off his nose. Gross.

'We'd probably have enough time,' I said. 'Besides, the element of surprise isn't our greatest weapon.'

'No,' my stupid brother agreed. 'I am.'

We got off at the Frank Sinatra rest stop, celebrating Hoboken, New Jersey's, favorite son about 110 miles from Hoboken. But it still had a Dunkin' Donuts, an Auntie Anne's and a convenience store type of area, as well as the ever-popular restrooms. But we were here to fill up the tank and empty the back seat.

Janet woke up when Ken parked the car and protested when I started going through her pockets for her phone, which I found immediately. Ken frisked Jack, whose phone was in a pocket on the inside of that ridiculous duster he was wearing. He checked the other 973 pockets just to make sure Jack had only one phone. We took that and Janet's, untied the two of them (although Ken had wanted us to sit them on the curb with a sign that read, 'Don't Feed the Animals') and left them at the entrance to the pavilion. Then Ken drove over to the gas station and filled up and we were gone.

I had just texted Mank when we were back on the highway and Ken said, 'I thought they'd never leave.'

But I had no time for his silly banter. I had to read an email from my mother.

Dearest daughter,
I'm sorry to hear that things are getting difficult for you. Your father and I are doing everything we can to ease the burden. Malcolm Mitchell is a danger. Stay away at all costs. I promise I will get back to you with more details as soon as I possibly can.
All our love. Mom.

We were doing exactly what she was telling us not to do, but Austin and Barry were somehow being held by Malcolm and we needed to stop that. We had no choice.

'Mom's saying we have to stay away from Malcolm at all costs,' I told Ken.

He took a moment, nodded once and said, 'I'll drive faster.'

We did 85 mph the rest of the way and we were passed on the left at least seven times.

FORTY-ONE

Atlantic City was like Las Vegas's budget-friendly cousin. It was smaller than the gambling center in the Southwest and was actually situated on the Atlantic Ocean, so there was a boardwalk and the usual games, arcades, Ferris wheel and salt water taffy stands that go with one. But you got the impression it would be better to stay inside at night, which is exactly what the casinos wanted you to do anyway.

We knew that Malcolm had, close to a week ago now, set up shop at the Borgata casino, or at least that was what Malcolm had wanted me to think when he was pretending to call as Barry.

I reminded myself that the mission today was to bring back Austin and Barry. And, if possible, to convince Malcolm and Jack to leave us alone forever. But the first part was the most important.

We had no guarantee that Malcolm had been telling the truth when he said the Borgata was his base of operations, although Ken knew from his first visit to AC that Malcolm had been there, and so had a couple of Jack's burlier assistants. So we felt it was probably best to stake out that hotel and see who showed up.

Ken parked the car in the Borgata's lot, which was going to be expensive but from which we could see who came and went. The building itself was all glass and gave the impression that the monolith from *2001: A Space Odyssey* had landed here and had many, many children, all of whom were now standing on each other's shoulders. If you ever find yourself needing a mirror, go to the Borgata and look at yourself from outside.

As we'd expected, the wait didn't last terribly long, only about forty minutes. Then sure enough, a hired car pulled up and out stepped Jack, followed by a particularly prickly-looking Janet.

'We gave them just enough time,' I said to my brother.

'They're nothing if not predictable.'

We got out of the car and started to casually walk toward the hotel. It would be a question of following our two close pals, who would almost certainly lead us to Malcolm, who allegedly had Austin and Barry with him, for reasons as yet unknown. But they weren't going to be good reasons.

It was windy near the shore but not very cold, so the walk wasn't unpleasant. We kept Jack and Janet in sight as long as we could, but once they were inside the building we picked up the pace of our walking to avoid letting them get too far ahead of us. Ken had to walk faster than me, of course, because he's incredibly competitive and I didn't need the pressure and . . . anyway, he got to the door first.

Once inside all was chaos, but that's normal at a casino hotel. People were checking in, checking out, passing through and generally asking which way to the casino. There were signs, but why read those when you can bother someone in the course of their work? I looked around immediately for a glimpse of our quarry (quarries?) but didn't see them.

'We lost them,' I told Ken.

'No, we didn't.' He started walking across the lobby. 'They're not headed to the casino. They want to meet Malcolm in a suite, I'll bet you.'

There was an older couple, I'd say early sixties, dressed in summer casual for people of a certain age. The man was in cargo shorts and the woman was wearing a sundress. They looked at us with some concern, as if wondering if they should approach, and then they did.

'Are you looking for the elevators?' the woman asked. 'You looked lost.'

I gave Ken a derisive look. 'No, thank you,' I told her. 'We know where they are.'

'Oh, good. Well, you enjoy your visit.' Did they work for the casino? No way to know. They walked away, and Ken was already off, making me trail behind him.

The pace wasn't killing me, but it wasn't making me feel great about myself either as I struggled to keep up with my competitive brother (I mentioned that, right?). We turned the corner to face the elevators and I still didn't see Jack or Janet.

'Now what, Toby?' I said. Toby was the name of a

bloodhound in the Sherlock Holmes story. It was also the name we gave an imaginary dog we never owned when we were children. Aunt Margie wasn't going to be expected to walk a dog on a cold, windy night in February on Manhattan streets. Only now was I beginning to see her point.

'Watch the lights. It's not going to be a low floor.' Ken pointed above the elevators to the red LED lights showing the position of each elevator in the hotel.

'We don't know which elevator it is, or even if they came this way,' I pointed out.

'Watch.' Ken likes to think he's Zen. He's not.

He studied the indicators for at least a full minute while I considered texting Jack and asking him what floor he was on; it'd be quicker. Instead, my phone buzzed and I saw an email had come in from the account my mother had been using earlier. I leapt on it.

Dearest daughter. Under no circumstances should you go to the seventh floor. Suite 7G.

Now my mother was being funny. The laws of the universe no longer applied. I turned toward Ken, but he was already pushing the button for the elevator.

'Fifteenth floor,' he said. 'That's where they went.'

I didn't contradict him. There would be no point. We waited until the elevator doors opened, which wasn't long at all, and stepped inside. But I beat my brother to the buttons and pushed the one marked 7.

He tried to reach over my shoulder. 'I said fifteen.'

'Your mother says seven,' I countered. I showed him the email on my phone.

'How can Mom know what floor they're on?' It was a very reasonable question.

'Next time I see her I'll ask,' I said.

The doors opened at the seventh floor and Ken and I stepped out. We stood in the corridor for a bit, studied the sign and headed toward suite 7G. But I stopped Ken when we were two doors away. 'How do we want to play this?' I asked. Might as well get his input before we did it the way I wanted to; it made him feel good.

I figured that, as usual, Ken would want to kick in the door and take no prisoners. 'Maybe pretend to be room service, but what if they haven't ordered anything?' he said. People can surprise you if you give them a chance. 'Then we throw them around and grab Austin and Barry.' Not my brother, but people. They can surprise you.

Avoiding conflict – with Ken – was the point here. 'Maybe we should try just me going in first,' I said. 'You can be parking the car or something. Let me see what the situation is, who's actually there, and I'll keep my phone on speaker so you can hear. If I get into trouble, you can kick the door in.'

His eyes lit up. 'I like that plan.'

We moved one suite farther from the targeted one and I called Ken's phone. He picked up and then I put my phone on speaker, and he put his on mute. He could hear; no one in the suite would be able to hear him.

I walked down the three doors to suite 7G. I wasn't nervous, but I wanted to mentally go through my steps before I entered the room. I had a plan of action and a backup plan if the inhabitants of the suite didn't respond as I anticipated they would. OK. I raised my hand to knock.

And the door opened.

Grinning behind it was the man I knew as Malcolm X. Mitchell. I was having a bad day opening doors. Malcolm's grin was, let's say, not ingratiating. I almost reached for his throat right there and then. I couldn't see behind him into the suite to take an assessment of who and/or what I'd be dealing with in there. Malcolm leaned in the doorway against the jamb, unarmed from what I could see, and held up his hands in a gesture that was not a surrender, as I might have hoped. It was more like delight at the lovely surprise he'd discovered outside his hotel room.

'Why, Fran!' If he camped it up any more, this would be an awful French farce as played in a summer camp talent show. 'How nice of you to drop by. Where's your brother?'

Of course. Jack and Janet would have mentioned Ken for sure. 'Parking the car,' I said. 'He'll be up to beat you senseless any minute now.'

'No need,' Malcolm said. 'Come on in and join the group. We've been waiting for you.'

I could bet. I was sticking with the plan. But I did some revising when I got inside.

It was a fairly large suite, so somebody was getting comped or was buying. Either way, they had some serious bucks. It had a small kitchenette at the far end, two bedrooms based on the closed doors I saw, and a fairly expansive living area with a wet bar, a sectional sofa and a flatscreen TV. There was a coffee table, a very large one, in front of the sofa, and it held a rather heavy-looking circular platter showcasing hors d'oeuvres. Frank Sinatra would have loved it here.

Occupying the room was a rogue's gallery of the Austin Cobb case. Austin himself was there, looking uncomfortable and almost curled into a fetal position on the floor next to the sectional. But he appeared to be uninjured; he was probably panicking due to the situation and the crowd around him. Jack was there, of course, no weapon in hand, but I had the feeling there was one quite close by, probably in one of his pockets. We'd relieved him of the gun he'd had at Janet's house, but it's just too easy to find another firearm in this country. The duster was hanging a little lower on the right side and Jack was righthanded. Do the math.

Janet, staring daggers, followed me into the room with her eyes and I really thought she might start to hiss and spit before Malcolm managed to close the suite door, but she held herself back. There was a weird grinding sound in the suite, but that might have been the air conditioning.

Two of Jack's merry band loomed up behind me as I walked in. If they thought they were surprising me, they were even stupider than they looked, which would have been quite the achievement. They decided to escort me like I was a recipient at an awards dinner, so I put out my hands and touched each of them on the forearm, on either side. Having dealt with me before, they both flinched.

There were three people near the wet bar I hadn't met before, two women and a man. They appeared to be completely uninterested in what was going on, and I figured there were no weapons of any kind being brandished because those three would have been upset by it. I decided to head for them.

Barry did not appear to be in the room, despite the promise I'd been made. It was not a shock.

'Nice place you got here,' I told Malcolm. 'You having a convention, or are all these people your birth parents?'

It was a low blow, but he deserved it, trying to get to my parents through me and running around kidnapping people. I mean, do civilized people behave that way? Have you ever met any civilized people, and if so, can I have their numbers?

'You have a great opportunity here,' Malcolm answered. Sort of. 'You can help advance medical science, biology and technology by unprecedented leaps, Fran. You can make the human race stronger and more durable. Why wouldn't you want to do that?'

The two human bison to my sides decided to step in front of me when I reached the sofa and block the route to the three unidentified attendees. 'Largely because it's what you want,' I told Malcolm. 'But also because I don't trust you – or anyone besides my parents – with whatever data you're trying to gather. I imagine the gathering itself wouldn't be tons of fun for me, either.'

My escorts, doing the work of two apartment buildings, were not about to budge and I didn't want to start throwing people through walls just yet. I sat down on the sectional at Austin's end to see if he was in fact all right. And 'all right' would probably be an overstatement. He was uninjured and healthy, but also appeared to be terrified. He looked up at me and, in a gesture that was as clichéd as it was effective, I winked at him. Austin's eyes narrowed as if he were trying to understand something said in an unfamiliar language. He mumbled, 'I'm sorry.'

'Nonsense.' Malcolm thought I was afraid of his medical, let's say, tests. And he was right, but that wasn't the point. I was considerably more afraid that he and/or Jack would find out about Mom and Dad's research and do irreparable harm to the human race for profit. And other little details like that.

'We don't need anything from you, although a DNA test would be fascinating,' Malcolm went on. He was an even worse salesman than Jack. 'You would probably break 23andMe all by yourself. But your parents can cure cancer, and we certainly could do something with *that*, couldn't we?'

Malcolm was one of those guys who thinks he can convince

you to do something completely against your whole makeup by telling you how well *he* could do if you just agreed. 'What's in it for me?' I asked. It hadn't occurred to me until this moment, but it was a way to keep him talking, keep Ken listening and give Plan B a chance to pick up some much-needed time.

Malcolm, who had been walking a little between the sofa and the three unidentified guests, but not enough to let me get by, stopped and regarded me. 'You? Wow. It didn't occur to me. How does ten percent of an unbelievable fortune sound?' He gave me what I'm sure he thought of as his winning grin again.

I grinned back. 'Ten percent? I have everything you need, and I only get a tenth of what you're going to recoup? How does that work?'

The two supposed musclemen stood now behind Malcolm like he was Taylor Swift and they were her backup dancers. I expected someone to throw Malcolm a microphone from offstage.

'I make the fortune,' he said, pretending to be reasonable. 'You just supply an address or phone number, and I use my connections and my expertise to turn it into the largest pile of money the world has ever known.' It was good he wasn't indulging in hyperbole.

Jack, who had been standing near the three unknowns, put a hand in his jacket pocket (uh-oh!) and ambled casually over toward me. 'We are holding your client and we have your investigator friend,' he said. 'Surely their return will be compensation enough.' The man had certainly graduated from Marvel University after majoring in Advanced Villainy.

Enough of this couch business; I stood up and walked over to face him. I looked at the three people I did not know and then back at Jack. 'Why don't you introduce me to your three new friends?' I said loudly enough for them to hear. 'I don't believe I've had the pleasure.'

'In fact, they are three of our many potential investors,' Malcolm, who had not been asked, answered.

'Malcolm.' Jack's tone was not fatherly. He sounded like a displeased CEO who had been told his son-in-law had botched the Fenneman merger. Malcolm, giving his father (if that was true, which I doubted) a frightened look, dropped his shoulders from proud to timid and took three steps back. All that from hearing his name spoken.

Jack Powell looked at Janet, who was returning from the bar holding a glass of amber fluid. Not her first. 'Perhaps you can do the introductions,' he said to her.

Janet did *not* look frightened at all. She looked like a glass-ceiling-busting CEO who had just engineered the Fenneman takeover. 'Do it yourself, Jack.' She sat down with her drink, which she looked at like it was her best friend. And it might have been.

Jack hiked his shoulders as if this was what he'd intended all along and indicated the first woman in the little cluster, a silver-haired type who probably had her hair treated with real silver. Not a wrinkle on her face, which had none of the features her mother had given her. 'This is Isabella Concetta Fabrini,' he said. 'She flew in from Milan this very morning.'

'She left Milan to come to Atlantic City?' I said. I nodded to her. 'You show poor judgment.' She puckered her lips like I'd thrown her a lemon for sucking. She said nothing. She was a world-class wit.

Jack chose to ignore my rudeness because . . . reasons, I guess, and indicated the man standing between the two women. 'This is Mr Raoul Patel-Rabinowitz of Istanbul, Turkey,' he continued, as if I'd said nothing. 'We have had the pleasure of his company for three days now.' For some reason he felt it necessary to tell me how long everyone had been in New Jersey. To each one's own.

'One question,' I said to the man who was wearing – I'm not kidding – a black tuxedo, probably gearing up for a game of baccarat with a mysterious Mr Bond. 'What's your *real* name?' The guy in the tux looked up and to the right, as if trying to retrieve information, but did not answer. Maybe he couldn't remember.

'And *this*,' Jack went on, trying to move through quickly, 'is Frances Goodwin Beckett, of Beckett Investments.'

I nodded toward her. 'Nice to meet you,' I said. 'I've never met a collection of investments before.'

'And I've never spoken with an oak tree,' Frances responded. I was starting to like Frances. The other two could get back on their private jets and head for wherever they were really from, for all I cared.

'I just worry about my acorns,' I told Frances, and she gave a very polite light chuckle. She was probably compounding interest in her head.

Jack, who hadn't had the spotlight on him for close to a minute, made a sound in his throat and watched as some, not all, of the eyes in the room shifted toward him. He casually put his hand into that right pocket and I noticed the weight at the bottom of the coat ease up. He was reaching for the gun. I assumed it was a gun. He glanced toward the door, then at me.

'So you've met our investors,' he said.

'*Potential* investors,' Frances corrected. 'No funds have exchanged hands yet.' She turned her attention toward me. 'Is it true what they say about you and your brother?'

'No. We're just good friends.' I was talking to Frances but watching Jack closely. Malcolm, who had backed off, stayed backed off. He was, in fact, doing something on his phone.

Frances didn't care for my wit anymore, and could you blame her? 'I meant, is it true about you having special abilities?' She emphasized the word *abilities*.

I shrugged. 'I dunno. We're big and strong, but we can't fly or anything.' There was no use in denying it.

'And that's because you were built, and not born?' she asked.

Now, don't get me wrong: I was already in a fairly stressful situation and wondering what my brother might be thinking about in the hallway, or wherever he'd relocated to. But I don't care for the idea that Ken and I are anything but human, and I especially don't like the idea that we were constructed, as if in a factory. We're people with a few changes, created because our parents wanted us and happened to be brilliant. So I get a little testy when that kind of terminology is used, which isn't often because almost nobody knows about us.

What I'm saying is that I'm hoping you won't think less of me because I stuck my arms out in front of me, lunged in Frances's general direction, and, yes, growled. It was reflexive, not cognitive. I got mad and I reacted. I apologize.

As you might expect, she flinched and leaned back where she was standing, apparently thinking – and again, I can understand it – that I meant her some harm. I just wanted to shake her up a little. I think. Frances pushed back, hands held up as if she thought she could hold me back, and skidded a little on one foot. Momentum carried her backwards and she landed on her rump in front of the bar. I'm pretty sure I saw Isabella stifle a chuckle.

I, on the other hand, was mortified. 'Oh, I'm so sorry,' I said, but it was too late. The two large beings Jack had brought for security purposes, living up to their natural expressions, hesitated in some effort to figure out what they should do next. Luckily for them, Jack was still holding what he thought was center stage.

'Get her, and bring her here,' he instructed them. Again it took them a good long moment to comprehend both the command and the situation, and they moved toward me. But I'd seen what I needed to see. I reached down and pulled Austin up off the rug, still curled around himself and shaking a little. His right hand shook back and forth as if he were waving at someone on the rug because he was still facing down. I held him in one hand and turned toward the door.

Jack's hand came out of his ridiculous coat holding a very intimidating gun and he had just cleared it. With my free hand I reached down and grabbed the big platter of hors d'oeuvres, yanked it off the table and flung it, discus style, in Jack's direction. He probably had card table flashbacks from the subway station.

He did fire the weapon, though, hitting the wall behind me and damaging a plaster (I hope) statue of Rodin's *The Thinker* on a shelf to my back and right. But the platter hit his hand immediately after and he dropped the gun. Which I saw as a plus.

I leapt over the coffee table, dropping Austin on the sofa this time, and grabbed Jack by the lapels of his duster. 'You monster,' I said, with my voice perhaps a trifle more agitated than usual. You know, like I was spitting adrenaline and had flames shooting out of my eyes. Just a little on edge. 'You've destroyed how many lives, and now you want to extort my parents into giving you their research while you're selling my DNA?' I held him up two feet above the floor and heard his throat gurgle. I didn't care. 'Tell me why I shouldn't drop you out the seventh-floor window, and use small words because you don't have a lot of time!' With that, I started toward the windows, which it should be noted would not open. He'd have to go through glass.

The rest of the gathered crowd was scattering, some in horror, some to get a better view. The three 'investors' were clearly heading for the exit, so I felt Jack would need to go elsewhere for funding, but that wasn't going to be his most pressing issue in a few seconds. Because I really and truly did intend to send him downstairs quickly without an elevator. I couldn't think beyond my own rage.

'I . . . know . . . where your parents are,' Jack managed.

I almost didn't stop; I'll admit it. I was so committed to ending Jack that even this wouldn't have stopped me. If he knew where Mom and Dad were, there was no point in threatening me to get that information. He was lying. I took another couple of steps toward the windows, now showing the Atlantic City boardwalk just as the sun was going down. Frankly, it wasn't that great.

'Please,' Jack said.

The next thing I heard was my brother's voice, sounding absolutely livid. 'Don't do it, Malcolm!' he shouted and even I was a little scared.

Malcolm had moved to the sofa and was holding a very efficient-looking carving knife to Austin's throat. But my brother Ken had his gun, which he calls his 'service weapon' despite the fact that it's not, in his hands and was leveling it at Malcolm. The situation had, you might have noticed, gotten a bit more complicated.

FORTY-TWO

'She has to put him down,' Malcolm said, the usual swagger no longer in his voice. He sounded like a frightened fourteen-year-old. 'I'll cut this one's throat if she doesn't put him down.'

Ken nodded once, like he was in charge. 'Put Jack down, Fran.' He never calls me 'Frannie' in front of clients or people with knives. 'You don't want to throw him out the window.'

'Don't I?' It had seemed like such a good idea a minute ago. 'I really think I do.'

'No. You don't.' Ken took his left hand off the gun and gestured for me to calm down, palm toward the floor. 'We're the good guys.'

From over by the door I heard Frances mutter, 'Some good guys.' I had lost Frances. So had Jack; she and the other investors left.

Of course I knew Ken was right, but I wanted Jack to be as terrified as possible, partly because it makes people talk more freely and partly because I really hated Jack by now. 'I dunno,' I said and took one more step toward the window.

I heard Jack whimper and that was all I needed. I put him down and he sat heavily on the well-vacuumed carpet. I'm not certain he was weeping, but I can't say definitively that he wasn't. Good.

Out of nowhere the door to the suite opened and the couple who had directed us to the lobby elevators walked in. I looked quickly to Malcolm, who put the knife down as Ken pocketed his gun. I looked at the older woman, who seemed to be timid, walking in with her eyes more toward Jack on the floor than anywhere else. The gentleman strode in like it was his suite, which for all I knew it was.

He looked directly at me. 'Young lady,' he said. Nobody had called me that since Aunt Margie had caught me using her makeup when I was nine. 'I believe we have some business.'

Business? The couple had pointed us toward elevators when we already knew their location. Did he expect a tip?

He walked over to me, not at all slowly, but in a very average gait. 'I believe you dropped this in the lobby,' he said. He reached into his pocket and pulled out . . . my wallet? 'I assume you need it.'

How was that possible? I hadn't taken the wallet out in the lobby. I reached over and took it from the older gentleman. 'Thank you, sir,' I said.

He smiled. 'No charge. But it looks like we're interrupting.' He gestured toward the slightly less crowded gathering. 'We'll be on our way.'

There was something about 'no charge.' I took his hand and held it. 'No, please,' I said. 'Stay for a few minutes. We were just completing our business here.'

Jack, head no longer in his hands, stood up and glared at me. 'I don't think we are, Fran.' He put up his arms to try to grab me around the upper arms. I responded by knocking his hands away and reaching for his collar again.

'Oh my goodness,' I heard the older lady say, but I couldn't let that stop me.

Jack, on the other hand, had learned from his experience and dived behind the sofa as soon as I touched him. From down on the floor, I heard his voice hiss, 'Damien! Lucius! Take them and show no mercy!' He really had read too many comic books, to the point that he'd only hire henchmen named Damien and Lucius.

I mean, 'Show no mercy?' I suppose that was supposed to curdle our blood, but I didn't feel very curdled. Mostly I was ticked off.

My brother, on the other hand, seemed downright tickled. He smiled at the two men. 'Damien! Lucius!' he said, like they were old frat brothers, which for all I knew, they were. 'You guys healed up pretty well considering I tossed you around only recently.' So they were two of the three Jack had sent after Ken when I asked him to find Barry. (Where was Barry?)

'Yeah,' I said to Jack. 'How come they followed him on the bus to Atlantic City? How did you know Ken was coming to find Malcolm?'

Malcolm and Jack exchanged what appeared to be a genuine confused look. 'What are you talking about?'

'You sent these guys and their other friend, who I'm assuming is in the hospital, to follow me from Manhattan,' Ken said. 'How did you know I was coming?'

'We didn't,' Malcolm said. 'I don't know what you're talking about. We sent them after him once he was here already. I mean, you can't miss him.'

I gave Ken a look that indicated he should have been less conspicuous, but he's Ken.

'Oh, just kill her,' Jack said to his two henchmen. He meant me.

I saw the older lady flinch a bit and tried to think of a way to get her and her husband (?) out of the suite quickly. But there was no time to think because Damien and Lucius – or Lucius and Damien – were headed my way. Oddly, no one was approaching Ken, which probably bruised his ego.

First thing to do was establish the order of things. 'Now, look,' I said. 'I don't want to hurt the two of you, but you're outmatched and you know it. So why not just back off and nobody has to get *severely injured or killed*.' I thought that was reasonable.

So did the older lady. Behind me I heard her say, 'You go.' She probably thought that was still a hip, current saying. I'd have to clue her in later.

Whichever bruiser was on the left growled in his throat like a Doberman. Again, no curdling was invoked. 'We need pieces of you,' he said. 'It doesn't matter if they're attached.' Gross, but not curdling.

I probably sighed out of the tiresomeness of his approach. 'OK, Hercules, come get me,' I said. Out of the corner of my eye I saw Ken put an elbow into Malcolm's forehead and drop his unconscious body onto the floor. He bypassed the cushy sofa. Malcolm had probably made a snarky comment. Ken hates it when someone does that who isn't him.

The guy pulled an object out of his pocket and when he gestured with it, I saw it was a straight razor. I didn't even know they made those anymore. But it did push a little adrenaline in me because I'd have to be careful about tossing him around to make sure nobody (including me) got slashed, even by accident.

He lunged and I grabbed at his hand and missed. But the razor didn't touch me. Behind 'my' henchman I saw the other one – finally – rush over toward Ken, reaching in his pocket for something, probably another razor. Maybe they got a discount for buying in bulk.

I grabbed my guy's other hand at the wrist and twisted. Unsurprisingly, he found this somewhat uncomfortable and tried to twist it back. But I was stronger than he was (again, not a shock) and held firm. Unfortunately, his right hand still held the razor and he wasn't timid about using it. He swung it at my midsection and just missed when I jackknifed to avoid it. But I lost my grip on his left hand doing so. You gain, you lose.

Ken, master of subtlety that he is, picked up the guy coming after him and threw him against the bar, making a number of bottles fall over and leaving his attacker seated on the suite floor looking dazed. Whatever he was holding in his hand had fallen out mid-toss. So Ken picked it up and headed in my direction.

Jack, sleazeball that he'd always been and always would be, was trying to crawl to the door unnoticed, except that everyone saw him. My best plan was to finish with the razor guy ASAP and then block Jack at the door, assuming it would take him about twenty minutes to get there at this rate.

Malcolm seemed to rouse himself from whatever stupor Ken had induced and came shakily to his feet next to the sofa, where Austin was still frozen in fear, and I didn't blame him. Many people with autism are averse to large groups of people, and disorganized action (you wouldn't be able to find anything less organized than this suite) is extremely troubling. Austin had a pillow up to his chin, looking over it. He was holding it together, but not by much.

Problem One: Razor Guy. When you don't want to get too close to your adversary and you're built like me (which you're not), the best weapons you have are your legs. Most men especially don't expect you to use them, but they're very powerful and have a long reach that, when carefully deployed, can keep you away from things like razor blades.

Aunt Margie had insisted on martial arts training when I was young, largely because I had nagged her to get me out of piano lessons and wanted to learn to beat people up, but in a civilized way. And now it was coming into play, as it had a few times before in my life when men (it's always men) decided to test the big girl. Some men are delightful, and then there's all the other ones.

Jack had made it roughly halfway to the exit, still crawling on his belly and pretending he was being inconspicuous. This would have to be fairly quick, which was fine with me.

I pivoted on my left leg and kicked my right one out to catch Razor Guy in the belly, which – and I'm not making this up – caused him to say 'Oof' and double over. Having anticipated that reaction, my left leg was now free to come up with a knee to his forehead, and the razor hit the floor. I picked it up as a safety measure. Wouldn't want someone playing with that thing. The guy just sat there. I'm not sure if he was conscious or not, but he sure didn't look like he'd be coming after me anytime soon.

Austin put a determined look on his face, picked up Jack's gun from the floor and held it on the dazed henchman. I gave him a look that indicated he shouldn't pull the trigger, brows down and head slightly shaking. He nodded. And they say people with autism can't read body language. Another mistaken assumption.

That made stopping Jack Problem One, in the revised agenda. That probably wasn't going to be a speed issue. Ken and I headed to the door at normal speed, well in advance of him reaching it. He stopped and looked up. 'I was just leaving,' he said.

But there came a sound from across the room that chilled even my blood. Janet, forgotten Janet, howled with such ferocity and anger that I wondered if something awful had just happened to her, like hearing that someone had soiled the carpet in her living room. But her wrath appeared to be directed not at Ken and me but at Jack, who was still in belly-flop position a few feet from the door.

'You did this!' she screamed, picking up a small marble bust from a shelf behind her. 'We had a perfectly good business going and *you* had to screw it up!' And the last thing I would have anticipated: she dived across the room at Jack and raised the statue above her head.

Jack squealed like a piglet and put his hands over his eyes because that was the only defense he had left. 'No.' It was almost inaudible. But it was just a split second.

Ken, looking slightly amused, watched Janet fly through the air and caught the hand with the statue as it went by. Reflexively, Janet let go of the bust and simply landed, face down, on Jack's back. He screamed in terror, waited, didn't feel a heavy object smashing his head, and looked confused.

'You kind of want to let them kill each other,' my brother said.

The older couple we'd met earlier looked understandably shaken and lowered themselves into seats, the man in an armchair and the woman into a sturdier seat that didn't look all that comfortable, but she didn't seem to mind. She just kept looking at me, then at Ken, and shaking her head in disbelief. I didn't see how you could blame her. I didn't recognize her, but her face was somewhat familiar, maybe from a photograph I'd seen.

'Yeah,' I told my brother, 'but the paperwork wouldn't be worth it.' I walked over to the woman in the lower chair and put my arms around her. 'Mom,' I said.

'Darling daughter.'

And that was when the door opened and Mank walked in.

FORTY-THREE

'Your friend Esme called and said she'd found a twelve-year-old adoption linked to Jack Powell that looked fishy,' Mank was saying. We were back at our apartment after a good deal of questioning, some arrests (none of me or my brother) and a long trip back to Manhattan. Many of our fellow inmates from suite 7G were under arrest by the New Jersey State Police, but Mank would get his shot soon, and the FBI would probably join in just to take a victory lap. 'It took a little digging, but there was definitely an exchange of cash, and it took place in New York City, so that gave me enough to come down to where you were and see the grand pageant that was your situation at the time. You guys know how to mess up a suite, Fran.'

Our apartment isn't incredibly small, like many are in our neighborhood, but the current crowd of Ken, me, Mank, Aunt Margie and the people we now knew were our parents in our living room was a bit of a crowd. Luckily Jack, Janet and the two 'bodyguards' were in custody awaiting arraignment, the three investors were probably already on planes to their respective homes, Malcolm was being held on weapons charges, extortion and suspicion of kidnapping, and Austin, spent, had gone back to his apartment. The poor guy probably wouldn't come out for at least a week.

I'd used Uber Eats for some delivery of various cuisines because I had no idea what kind of food my parents enjoyed. It was still taking some getting used to, the idea that they were here, in this room, with us after all these years. I don't think Mank was entirely clear (although he'd been told the story) of how momentous this event was, or why I was staring at Mom like she was Taylor Swift.

Aunt Margie, reunited with her friends after decades, was almost silent. I'd never heard her go this long without speaking. But her eyes kept darting back from Mom to Dad and back again as if she were afraid they were mirages and would dissolve if she didn't keep looking at them.

'We take pride in our work,' Ken said, and everyone laughed but me. 'Do we understand how the adoption racket operated?'

Mank opened his mouth to answer, but Dad was quicker to the punch. 'From what we can tell, it wasn't just abandoned babies they were brokering,' he said. 'That was a small percentage. Mostly there were some children whose parents simply didn't want them, and it would have been great to get them to loving homes if they hadn't been bypassing the sanctioned pipelines. Jack and Janet were preying on young people who had children they couldn't raise and adoptive parents who were generally right out of jail or rehab and didn't have any intention of changing their ways. It was a truly evil operation, and I'm glad you could help break it, Rich.' (Mom and Dad had taken to Mank immediately, which was a little unnerving, if you want to know the truth.)

It took me a moment to absorb all that. 'You're a couple of scientists,' I reminded my parents, who appeared to have forgotten. 'When did you assemble an international network of criminal justice operatives?'

Mom smiled, a lovely smile I can't say for sure I remember from when I was three. 'It's been such a long time since we saw you,' she said. 'We've learned a lot along the way and, clearly, so have you. We made a lot of . . . friends.'

There had been no way to talk in the car on the way home. Mom and Dad had taken their own rental from the casino, and I'd almost insisted on riding with them just to ensure that they wouldn't vanish into the mists again, but Austin was coming with us and I felt he needed me in the car to stabilize him; he'd barely spoken since the whole scene in the suite. Mom had assured me they'd see us at the apartment, and as far as I knew, she'd never lied to me, so I trusted her against my instincts, and she had come through.

But I wanted to talk to Mank, who had driven home on his own.

'It was almost all Ken and Fran, Brad.' Mank wasn't being modest; we really had done most of the work. And Dad had insisted on using Brandon Wilder, the name Aunt Margie knew him under. Mom was Olivia Grey. Right now. 'You saw, they had the situation well in hand by the time I got there.' He gave me a look. 'Well, mostly in hand, anyway.'

Mank stood up. 'But you have a family reunion to get to, and I'm just in the way.' Mom, Dad and Aunt Margie tried to protest, but he held up a hand. 'I hope you'll stay in town long enough for me to see you again when we can talk more.' And he walked toward the kitchen, where the apartment door could be found.

I followed him there and stopped him at the fridge. 'I want to talk to you,' I said. 'I've been rough on you lately and I'm sorry.'

He looked surprised, the swine. 'I thought that was just how you felt.'

'It's how I *thought* I felt, but I miss how we used to be, and I think you do, too.' I stood in front of the door. 'So you're going to have to kiss me if you want to leave.'

Mank raised an eyebrow. 'Well, if that's the toll charge . . .' He leaned back, behind the fridge so as not to be visible to the others, but he was too short to reach me. So I held his upper arms and gently raised him off the floor. Suddenly we were face-to-face. Mank kissed me very skillfully. Eventually, as with all kisses, it had to end, and that was too bad.

'You may pass,' I said when I could talk again. I stepped aside and Mank opened the apartment door. 'But let's talk soon.'

'Dinner? Tomorrow night?'

I tilted my head toward the living room. 'Let me find out how long they'll be here.'

'Bring them along. We could use chaperones.' Before I could answer, he was gone and the door shut behind him.

I sat down and looked at my parents. 'OK, fess up. How did you know where we were and why did you come back after all this time?'

Ken laughed. 'Do you think we haven't been talking about that while you were in the kitchen making out with Mank?'

'We weren't *making out*.' Is one kiss making out? The lines are so badly drawn. 'Stop being eleven.'

Mom shook her head and took my hand between hers. 'We

were afraid you were in danger,' she said. 'Your father and I were in Malta when it became clear that Malcolm Mitchell was on your trail. I thought I could warn you off, but he came to you and that made it dangerous. So we arranged to come to New York, but you were in Atlantic City by then.'

Ken looked at Mom the way he'd been looking at her since we'd become aware of who she was, in the suite in Atlantic City. Like he only partially trusted her. 'How did you hone in on us so fast?' he asked. 'Do we have GPS chips in us somewhere?'

Mom laughed, but Dad looked a little pensive, as if he'd just realized he'd missed an opportunity. 'We weren't tracking you,' Mom said. 'We were tracking Malcolm, which took some doing. And Barry Polk was a great help in that.'

Barry! 'You know where Barry is?' My voice sounded a little hoarse.

My parents exchanged a slightly amused look. 'He's at home with his family, some eight thousand dollars richer,' she said. 'Someone we know spotted him at the Borgata, knew he was a private investigator and a couple of searches made it clear he'd been a classmate of yours, Frannie. We got in contact with him as Dave and Lily Cosgrave, told him you'd helped track down our son's birth parents, and we got him away from Malcolm and into a bus to Manhattan. He lost his phone, though. With the money he won at blackjack he should be able to buy a new one.'

I shook my head in disbelief. 'You know people everywhere,' I said. 'Is Jack Powell really Malcolm's father?'

Dad laughed. 'No! Malcolm's father is, believe it or not, named Mitch Mitchell, and Malcolm has always known that. Jack just says things because he thinks confusion works to his advantage.'

Well, that was nuts. 'Did Malcolm's casino cheating app help Barry win all that money?'

'There is no app,' Dad said. 'Malcolm was playing up to the people he thought were going to invest in *our* work. He had friends at the casino who rigged the game for him as long as he gave back the money at the end of the night.' That was wildly illegal, so luckily I didn't know the friends' names.

I stared at my father. 'You stole my wallet out of my pocket,' I said.

'I needed an excuse to get us into the suite. I think it was worth it.' I couldn't argue with that.

'OK, then, Brad.' Aunt Margie finally broke her silence. 'If you know everything that's been going on, who killed Helen Hawley?'

'I can tell you that,' I said. 'Janet killed Helen.'

Everyone but Ken stared at me.

'Helen was in business, and other things, with Jack,' I went on. 'Janet found out and wanted in and Helen told her to go away. She told me she'd never been to Helen and Marc's house, but we have video footage of her there, checking out the exercise equipment. I'll bet that black object we almost found in Janet's closet is an eight-pound dumbbell she kept as a souvenir, because the other one was found by the cops.'

'She brought her own dumbbell?' Dad said.

'Don't make me make a dumbbell joke,' Ken said. 'She kept souvenirs. Like the VHS tapes she couldn't show to anyone and edited for her own amusement. Janet is just a little retentive, if you ask me. Why would she take video of kids she was harboring for an illegal adoption scheme?'

'We don't know why she did that,' Mom told me, ignoring my brother's infantile sense of humor. 'As for the dumbbell, I can only guess that she thought her own weight would be harder to trace, especially if she hid it when she got home. Nobody suspected her.'

'That's not great evidence, but it's something,' Dad said after a second.

'Jack is rolling over on Janet to get a better deal from the state and the feds,' Ken told him. 'She killed Helen, all right. Jack doesn't want to be an accessory to murder, so he's talking. The troopers told us.'

'Meanwhile, Marc Hawley, after all these years on the lam, is back in New Jersey because . . . Janet wanted him back? Isn't he cleared of Helen's murder now?' I asked.

Dad shook his head. 'From what I understand, Marc was summoned by Janet because she thought you were getting too close, Frannie. She thought Marc, who was supposed to be this mad killer, could intimidate you.'

I rolled my eyes. 'And she'd already met me. I must be slipping.'

'In any event, since Janet knew where Marc was, she could threaten him with exposure, so he made a phone call to try and scare you off,' Mom said, looking happy to be able to assert her own knowledge here. 'It didn't work, of course, because you're you, Frannie. Then she said she could reconcile him with his son Bill, but Bill wouldn't talk to him, and still won't, from what we've been told. So he's cleared of suspicion, but still not in the eyes of his son, who's reeling that his aunt – his mother – is under arrest for the crime. The idea was to stop you, and it didn't. But it probably slowed you down a bit.'

I flopped back in my chair. 'I'm slowed down all right. This whole thing has wiped me out,' I told the gathering. 'I feel like I've been working four cases at once and didn't really solve any of them. I still don't believe Jack is Austin's father, and I don't know who his mother is. I'm a bad investigator.'

OK, so it was an obvious cry for encouragement. And it worked, but from a completely unexpected source. 'You're a very good investigator, Frannie,' Ken said. 'You found Malcolm, you found Jack, you found Janet and they're all behind bars now.'

'My job was to find out who Austin's birth parents are,' I reminded him, quick to stomp on his attempt at being nice to me.

'Give me a couple of hours,' my father said, reaching for his phone.

'No, Dad. The idea is I'm supposed to be able to do it myself.' I was regressing in emotional age by the minute, and I hadn't even asked them why the stupid charging port had to be located under my left armpit. (He told me later it's so the power source would be close to my heart. Did I need to know that?)

My father put his phone back in the pocket of his cargo shorts. He grimaced a bit, possibly being reminded of the disguise he was wearing. From what I'd heard over the years he was a little more dashing than cargo shorts. 'As you wish,' he said. 'You're the gumshoe, Frannie.'

I closed my eyes to relax a bit. 'Sure I am,' I said.

* * *

Later, after Mom and Dad had gone back to their hotel (we offered, but we don't have a spare bedroom and they wouldn't consider displacing one of us) and Aunt Margie had retreated to her apartment, I sat on my bed and looked out the window at the building across the alley. New York is a great place to live.

After a lot of consideration, given that it wasn't *that* late, I picked up my phone and called Carla Cobb.

She did not sound like I'd awakened her, but she did sound puzzled. 'Why are you calling, honey?' she asked. Carla was a woman who called everyone under forty 'honey.'

'You're Austin's birth mother, aren't you?' I said. 'You abandoned him because you couldn't afford to raise him and then you wanted him back. Isn't that right?'

There wasn't so much as an ounce of authenticity in her voice when she said, 'I have no idea what you're talking about, Ms Stein.' All of a sudden I wasn't 'honey' anymore.

'You were working in that area when Austin was put in the Dunkin' Donuts parking lot,' I said. 'I know that because you said you hadn't gotten the job at the airport yet and you were commuting an hour away.'

'That's an awfully big leap. Lots of women were doing that and still are. Besides, it could have been an hour in any direction.'

'Yeah, but you're not denying it. Then you started working at a better job here in New York, that was going to become a career, and you met Spencer Cobb. You two got married and you'd been agonizing over how you'd left your baby, so you started putting out feelers among adoption agencies. And what do you know, Jack Powell and Janet Hawley showed up, and were more than happy to offer you a deal. But you had to say it was Marc and Helen, to keep them out of trouble. That was part of the deal.'

Carla nodded and said nothing.

'You paid to adopt your own baby, didn't you, Carla?' I asked. 'But why didn't you tell Austin?'

There was a rustling on the line, making it seem like Carla was looking away. 'I was ashamed,' she almost whispered. 'I let my baby boy go in a parking lot and I walked away. How could I tell him I was the woman who did that to him after we'd come so far?'

'And I take it the father was not Spencer.' Duh. The years were wrong.

'Oh no, of course not.' That's the polite version of 'Duh.' 'I had heard about Mr Powell through a woman I met at the adoption agency. I had told Spencer I was looking for the baby I'd abandoned, and he thought maybe I could find Austin that way. But nobody would talk until I met this other woman who knew Mr Powell, and he was happy to help, but a little creepy. He said he could find Austin, and he did.' And then claimed he was Austin's birth father, tried to teach a toddler to read a road sign and charged Carla to get her baby back. Yeah, the man was a paragon. 'The father was a boy I knew in high school, and I never saw him again after he found out I was having a baby.'

'Then why all that extra security at the adoption agency? You didn't use Friendly Family; you used Jack Powell. Why did you have to sign all those agreements?' Carla's story was odd, and sad, but probably not unique in Jack Powell's orbit.

'Because Mr Powell told us we could get arrested and they could take Austin away from us if they found out about the money. So we did the paperwork through the agency, like he said, and there was no mention of the money in those papers.' I think Carla might have been weeping, and I felt bad for making her do that. But I had to press on.

'You told me you and Spencer had met with the birth parents before you adopted Austin. You're the birth mother. And you said Spencer knew that. Who did you meet with?'

'We met with Jack and some woman he was working with,' (Janet) 'the one who had fostered Austin, and they brought him to meet us,' she answered after blowing her nose quietly. 'That was so I could see Austin and so Spencer could meet him and know what we were discussing. But it was about how we were going to go through the agency to make it legitimate. I'm sorry I lied to you, but I was afraid the adoption *wasn't* legitimate. Jack gave me a bad feeling. I thought we could get into trouble.'

'And Jack and the woman, who I assume was Janet Hawley, were fostering Austin? Jack was the man who tried to teach him to read a road sign when he was all of two?' That one still astounded me.

'I guess.' Carla's voice was a little stronger but still meek. 'I don't know anything about a road sign.' Maybe Jack thought that was how fathers behaved.

It was all highly unusual, but possibly a rare instance when Jack Powell, pretending he was Austin's birth father, went through a recognized agency and charged the parents behind the agency's back. He insisted on absolute secrecy so no one would ever investigate the adoption. Until I did.

'I'm sorry, Carla,' I said. 'But Austin hired me to find you. I think it would be better if you told him yourself, don't you?' Nothing was going on across the alley. Even the pigeons were heading for another neighborhood tonight.

Carla took a long time to answer, and her voice was shaky when she did. 'I'm gonna have to think about it. You're probably right, but I hope he doesn't hate me when he finds out.'

'Oh, Carla. Have you *met* your son?'

She started to laugh. 'Maybe I'll tell him,' she said.

'I'm giving you three days and then I'm going to tell him,' I told her. We said our goodbyes and I hung up.

I texted Sarah Polk: **Tell your husband he did a lousy job and I'm glad he's back. Let me know when he gets a new phone and be SURE he changes every password.**

She sent back a laughing emoji. I was making people laugh tonight. When I wasn't making them cry.

I finally got some sleep, a real eight hours, and woke up with a new perspective. I showered and dressed, then went out to the kitchen.

There I found an envelope on the kitchen table. On the envelope was written, in cursive, *Darling Daughter.*

And I knew they were gone again.